I'M
BROKEN TOO

A NOVEL

NEEL LATCHMAN

First Edition September 2023

Front cover design, format and interior design

by Neel Latchman.

Editing/ Proofreading by Kaylee Labban.

Special Thank You to these amazing readers

Amber Goodrich, Crystal Howell, Audrey Lee, and

Nicolette "Moons" Joseph.

Very special thanks to the ARC Reader team!

ISBN 979-8-8578-8527-7 (paperback)

Important Note

This material isn't for everyone. *I'm Broken Too* is not safe to read in public. This book is intense, If you don't want to be heartbroken, left with trust issues, or unlock some new kinks, then this is your chance to turn back. But for those who crave the dark stories, revenge, and wipe your tears with the red flags you ignore, I can assure you that you cannot imagine the ride that awaits you when you turn this page. I ask that you read reviews or visit my website at www.neellatchman.com to see the warnings before proceeding. It's important that you know if you feel overwhelmed at any point its ok to stop. Your mental health matters.

This story is based on actual events, if you thought your ex was bad... this will challenge your definition of toxic and manipulative Ex...

Contents

Prologue

Salt Pine Acres, a secluded sanctuary for the immensely wealthy and famous, laid off the grid, shielded from the prying eyes of law enforcement and media. Here, people sought refuge, yearning to live ordinary lives away from the relentless spotlight of fame. However, four years ago, the town fell victim to a brutal massacre perpetrated by a serial killer who came to be known as the Blood Rain Ripper. In the wake of the tragedy, Galan Rain and Dana Scarlet emerged as the lone survivors, forever bound by the horrors they endured.

Now, as Dana's life takes an unexpected turn, the haunting past resurfaces when the notorious killer sets his sights on her once more. When a picture of Dana on a yacht surfaced on social media, exposing her whereabouts, Galan was left deeply concerned for her safety. Determined to protect her, he reconnects with Dana after years of separation, resolute in keeping her shielded from the Blood Rain Ripper's malevolent intentions.

But as Galan strove to safeguard Dana, he found himself entangled with someone from his own past, casting shadows of uncertainty and unpredictability over their fight for survival. Amidst the danger and rekindled connections, Galan must confront not only the present threats but also the ghosts of his past, hoping to secure a future for himself and Dana in the face of the relentless killer.

GALAN RAIN

AGE: 29
SIGN: LIBRA
FUN FACT: "I AM A HOT SLEEPER SO I OFTEN
SLEEP NAKED."

Chapter One

This isn't happening; how did it come to this? This isn't me; this can't be me! No! I'm just a kid. I didn't kill all these people!

"Galan—" As Lillie's soft whisper danced through the air, Galan felt a gentle caress against his cheek. Her touch was tender, an oasis of tranquility amidst the turmoil that had consumed him. With a sense of delicate grace, she tamed his unruly mane, her fingers moving with an almost ethereal elegance, weaving through his locks and gently tucking them behind his ear.

Galan found himself drawn into the mesmerizing dance of her touch, the sensation grounding him in the present moment. The storm of memories that had engulfed him was momentarily calmed as if her fingers held the power to dispel the chaos that had clouded his mind.

Her presence was a soothing balm, pulling him away from the darkness of his past and back into the embrace of the here and now. Feeling weak in the knees and his hands trembling, he let out a breath he didn't realize he was holding.

"Lillie—" Galan shook.

Dana hurried to Galan's side, her heart pounding with concern. With a tender touch, she gently rested her hand upon his quivering shoulder, trying to offer him some comfort amidst the turmoil. The moment her fingertips touched him, she sensed the tremors coursing through his entire body, like waves crashing against the shore. The tension in his arms was palpable, reflecting the inner struggle he was facing. Looking at his furrowed brow, Dana noticed the glistening beads of perspiration.

Galan's breath caught in his throat as he uttered incredulously, "You're alive...?"

"Of course I am!" Lillie replied, her voice carrying a mix of surprise and bewilderment as if the notion of her existence being doubted was unexpected.

"Galan, who is this?" Dana's voice carried concern and ferocity; her piercing gaze was fixed upon Lillie as she posed this question.

"My name is Lillie; Galan and I grew up in the same village as kids," Lillie answered.

Dana's heart raced, thumping loudly against her chest, almost drowning out the surrounding sounds. "You're Paige's little sister," she gasped.

"Oh, you're friends with Morrigan?" Lillie inquired.

"Why are you here?" questioned Galan.

"I'm an event planner; Mr. Scarlet hired me to see this yacht party go smoothly," Lillie replied.

"Mr. Scarlet?" Galan repeated her words.

"When did this happen?" Dana remarked.

"Well, I was hired a couple of weeks ago, but I arrived on the boat today. He told me where I could find you and to give you this package," Lillie explained. She reached into her purse and retrieved an elegant black box with gold accents and silk ribbon tied in a bow with a card handwritten by her father. Lillie handed the box over and backed out of the room. "Sorry if I disturbed you, Ms. Scarlet. And Galan, what a pleasant surprise seeing you again. We should catch up sometime. I was so worried you never made it out of that horrible place," Lillie smiled and closed the door.

Galan sat on the edge of the bed, his emotions visibly swirling within him. He took a deep breath, attempting to gather his thoughts and steady his racing heart. With a nervous gulp, he brushed his hair back out of his face with his fingers. "Dana—" he muttered.

As the box in Dana's hand started to vibrate, both her and Galan's eyes turned towards the rattling sound, curiosity evident on their faces. Dana's heart skipped a beat, wondering what could be causing this unexpected occurrence. Without hesitation, she carefully undid the silk ribbon bow and opened the box, revealing a screen displaying her father's phone number calling. Surprise and intrigue were mixed with a hint of apprehension as Dana glanced at Galan. With a nod of encouragement from Galan, Dana took a deep breath and answered the call, putting it on the loudspeaker so they both could hear. The room filled with anticipation as her father's voice came through the phone.

"Hello?" Dana answered.

"The things a father has to do to get in touch with his child," Mr. Scarlet chuckled.

Galan and Dana breathed a sigh of relief. "Hi, Daddy. Sorry I have been hard to reach these last few years. I just wanted to be alone," Dana explained.

"I understand, Kitten, but things are happening right now, and I just want to know you are safe," Mr. Scarlet replied.

"I'll be fine, Dad; I saw the news about what happened in Salt Pine Acres, too," Dana exclaimed.

"Don't you worry, Kitten; I have a lead on your sister's killer, and she is going to steer me right to him," Mr. Scarlet announced.

"She?" Dana inquired.

Galan quickly turned his attention to Dana.

"She's on the call right now, a survivor of the killer," Mr. Scarlet informed her.

"Hi, Dana! I can't wait to meet you; your dad tells me such wonderful things about his baby girl," Paige remarked. Upon hearing her voice, Galan rose from the bed; Dana immediately froze and stared at him. "Don't you worry a tiny bit; I know exactly how to make that killer come to me," Paige continued, giggling.

"Galan should be with you. Can you hear me, son?" asked Mr. Scarlet.

He knows I'm here? Damnit, Paige!

Galan and Dana exchanged a look of astonishment and shook their heads in unison. "Yes, Sir, I can hear you," Galan answered.

"Wonderful, Morrigan said you would be there. Keep an eye on Dana for me. Also, you and I need to have a little chat. I never got to thank you for saving my little girl. I'll be flying in next week to see her and discuss the details about the Salt Pine Acres situation; join us," Mr. Scarlet insisted.

"Of course, Sir, see you then," Galan replied before ending the call. Galan turned to Dana, still frozen in fear. "We have to get off this boat now!"

"What is Paige doing with my father?" Dana gasped.

"That's what this is about! She baited me onto this boat, sent her sister here to show me that it's easy to get to me, and used that call to show you that she can get to you, too. She wants us to know she is holding all the cards here," Galan deduced.

"But she almost killed me… And she is the one who killed Aria and all those people," Dana remarked shakily.

"And if we attempt to reveal that, she can take everything from us. She knows the picture circulating the news is me; the moment she does that, nobody will believe I didn't kill all those people, least of all your father. Paige will never do something to hurt me; she's obsessed with me, so whatever she's planning here, as long as we do what she says, this thing won't blow up in our faces," Galan claimed. "Destroy that phone, don't trust anything from Paige."

"And then what?" Dana grunted.

"I can also get to her; she made her first mistake sending Lillie here. She knows Lillie is my weakness, but she is also Paige's," stated Galan.

"And what are you going to do? I saw how you looked at her and the relief in your eyes when you saw her. She was your first love, a crush you had over twenty years ago, and seeing you choke up like that—" Dana began before she was interrupted.

Galan's eyes narrowed, and an air of tension enveloped the room as he swiftly moved closer to her. In a chilling gesture, he placed his hand over her mouth, preventing her from making a sound, and drew her closer, grasping her waist tightly. "That's enough…," he groaned softly in her ear.

Galan's gaze softened as he gently removed his hand from her lips, revealing a tender smile. His touch glided down her body. With a sense of urgency, he lifted her up in his arms.

Galan kissed her neck, tracing his tongue down and over her collarbone. Dana wrapped her arms around his neck, moaning softly as he descended her chest. She felt the warm air he exhaled fill her shirt; he closed his eyes and unbuttoned her shirt with his mouth. Galan unhooked the shirt button with his tongue, gently biting and circulating his tongue until it became undone. He pinned her against the wall; Dana wrapped her legs around him as he looked up at her, heaving.

"I came here for you," Galan lowered her, leaned in, and sucked on her neck. "So, now…," he kissed her lips, pulling away while gently biting her lower lip. "You're going to cum for me—" he declared as he looked into her eyes.

Dana's cheeks flushed with a warm blush. Her breaths came in rapid succession, betraying her excitement. With a slight nod, she conveyed her consent and willingness to do as she was told.

"Answer me," Galan whispered.

"Yes," Dana answered softly.

"Yes, Sir," Galan corrected her.

The atmosphere between Dana and Galan grew charged with anticipation as she bit her lips, a subtle expression of her desire. Galan's body responded, tensing with the electricity of the moment. His neck tilted, revealing vulnerability and longing, and he closed his eyes, taking a deep breath to steady himself.

"Yes, Sir," she repeated, her voice filled with warmth and a touch of endearing obedience.

"Good girl," Galan whispered, kissing her neck. Gently putting her on the bed, he walked over to the door and turned the lock.

The party on the yacht raged; the air, filled with music and inaudible chattering, masked the screams coming from Dana's cabin.

❧

Paige's heart pulsed with a sinister blend of excitement and cunning as she stood on the balcony, relishing the warm caress of the Caribbean sun on her skin. The recent meeting with Mr. Scarlet had set her wicked mind ablaze with malevolent thoughts and elaborate schemes. She couldn't wait to set her sinister plan into motion.

Clad in an open, flowing white shirt that seemed to cloak her in a deceptive innocence, Paige reveled in the façade she presented to the world. Underneath her facade of elegance lay her true intentions—black laced lingerie, symbolizing the dark and malevolent secrets she held close.

Her gaze fixated on the yacht sailing gracefully on the glimmering sea. Its beauty and the vibrant atmosphere aboard only added to her delight in using it as a pawn in her schemes.

As she took a sip of her cocktail, the fruity flavors seemed to taunt her victims, mocking their blissful ignorance of the danger that loomed. The enchanting ambiance surrounding her only served to heighten the ominous atmosphere, as if nature itself conspired with her malevolence.

A chilling smile curved on her lips, betraying her true intentions. This moment, standing on her balcony overlooking the sea, felt like the beginning of a diabolical and perilous chapter in her life—a chapter that would leave a trail of chaos and fear in its wake.

Paige's long, curly hair swayed like tendrils of darkness in the gentle breeze, and she closed her eyes, embracing the sense of control she had over the impending darkness. In this moment of reflection, she felt a rush of power and satisfaction, relishing the prospect of a villainous legacy she was about to unleash upon the world.

"Have your fun, Dana. Enjoy him while this lasts. Because sooner or later, you will learn the same thing every girl before you did!" Paige spoke aloud.

Paige sipped her drink and giggled, "Love will lead Master back to me." She turned around, her demeanor devoid of remorse as she strode back inside, her footsteps firm and purposeful. The scene before her was a macabre tableau—a chilling testament to the ruthless efficiency of her malevolence. Three men lay lifeless on the floor, their necks slashed open in a horrifying display of her handiwork.

Chapter Two

As the days flew by, Galan and Dana found themselves back at her place, seeking solace in each other's company. The morning sun had yet to grace the skies with its warm embrace, but Galan stirred from his slumber and cast his gaze upon Dana, peacefully sleeping beside him. Quietly, he slipped out from under the covers, his feet meeting the cold touch of the hardwood floor.

As he rose from the bed, he found himself drawn to the sight outside the large glass window that adorned the room's accent wall, offering a breathtaking view of the sprawling city from he high-rise penthouse. Yet, in the midst of this urban grandeur, Galan was burdened by the weight of his past—a tapestry woven from haunting childhood memories and traumatic flashbacks.

I didn't kill these people! I didn't!

Paige stumbled upon a young Galan standing outside her house. Her eyes widened in shock as she took in the devastating scene before her—inside the once cheerful home, her siblings and parents lay lifeless on the ground, their lives extinguished in a brutal and senseless act of violence.

"What did you do!?" Paige shrieked. In a heart-wrenching scene of anguish and sorrow, Paige couldn't hold back her tears as she desperately shook Galan, trying to bring him back from the depths of his pain. He cried out in agony, his screams echoing the weight of the tragedy they had just witnessed. Paige's heart ached as she pulled him close, wrapping her arms around him in a tight embrace.

She wiped away his tears with tender care, her touch gentle and soothing as she stroked his hair. The world around them seemed to fade away, leaving only the raw emotions they shared. "We have to run away because you killed them. And we need to burn this house down so nobody will ever know what you did!" Paige stated resolutely.

Galan looked up with red, watery eyes. "I just wanted to see Lillie—" he cried.

"Lillie is gone; look at what you did! This is all your fault for loving her!" Paige chastised.

🌱

"Everything ok?" Dana whispered.

Galan snapped out of his thoughts and turned to her. "I'm ok, love," he replied.

"Come back to bed," Dana murmured, her fingers gently caressing the empty spot beside her invitingly.

Galan's hand moved gracefully, gently lifting Dana's palm from the ruffled sheets. A tender warmth spread through his touch as he cradled her hand in his. Bringing her hand to his lips, he planted a soft, affectionate kiss on the back. "I'm going to start my day; I'll have breakfast with you when I get back," he sweetly informed her.

After dressing himself, Galan quietly departed the room, casting one final glance at Dana before exiting. He strolled purposefully towards the elevators, his footsteps a subtle echo in the corridor. As he descended to the lobby, his mind was a symphony of thoughts and emotions.

The moment he stepped out of the building, he broke into a brisk jog, his heart pounding with each step as he immersed himself in the vibrant energy of the city. The bustling streets seemed to mirror his inner restlessness as if echoing the excitement and uncertainty he felt.

The city embraced him with its own rhythm—a captivating dance of lights and shadows, bustling crowds, and honking cars. Galan lost himself in the rhythm of the city, finding solace in its bustling anonymity.

The sun's gentle rays tiptoed into Dana's room, painting it with a soft, golden hue as dawn gracefully unveiled a new day. Having returned from his invigorating morning run, Galan stepped off the elevator. With a soft gait, he undressed while making his way through the apartment, making a beeline for the shower. The sound of running water acted as a gentle alarm, rousing Dana from her slumber.

As the water cascaded down his body, Galan finished his shower and, wrapped in a towel, entered the room. With a simple touch on the wall-mounted dial, the glass window responded, darkening to block the sunlight from shining too brightly on Dana. He then retreated to the hallway, disappearing into the guest room to dress for the day.

A few minutes later, Dana emerged from her peaceful slumber and made her way downstairs, her curiosity piqued to find Galan. The inviting aroma of something delicious cooking in the kitchen lured her in that direction, leading her to discover Galan skillfully preparing breakfast and brewing coffee. Leaning against the open door frame, she found herself momentarily captivated by the sight of him.

With his back turned, Galan smiled, "Good morning, love."

"How are you in this good a mood? The sun is barely up yet," Dana chuckled.

"If the sun woke up next to someone who made him cherish every new day, he would be in a good mood every morning, too," Galan replied.

Dana smiled and said, "Come here."

With the breakfast preparations momentarily set aside, Galan gently moved the pan to the kitchen counter and carefully wiped his hands clean. Closing the distance between them, he approached Dana with an air of tenderness that enveloped the room. As he stood before her, Galan's warm hand found its way to her cheek, his touch sending a shiver of delight down her spine.

Their eyes locked, expressing volumes of unspoken emotions, as Galan leaned in and pressed his lips against hers in a soft, affectionate kiss. Dana's fingers found their way into Galan's hair, gently intertwining with the strands as she drew him closer.

"Your hair is still wet," Dana playfully teased Galan. Her fingers gently reached out and squeezed a handful of his thick, dark hair, feeling the cool droplets of water trickling down from the silver highlights at the tips.

"You're right," Galan's eyes sparkled with mischief as he shook his damp hair. Droplets of water splashed like tiny raindrops around him. With a playful grin, he aimed his hair in Dana's direction, creating a gentle shower of water that sprinkled over her clothes and skin. "Oh no, this just won't do," Galan's mischievous smirk lingered on his lips as he playfully removed his shirt, revealing the toned muscles underneath. With a playful glint in his eyes, he approached Dana, his shirt in hand.

"You're an idiot; you know that?" Dana laughed.

"Am I now?" Galan smiled. "That's not a polite thing to say."

"Deal with it," Dana stuck her tongue out.

"First, I need to dry you off; I wouldn't want you to stay wet and not do anything about it," Galan remarked as he lifted her and walked over to the kitchen island.

"What is it with you and islands," Dana teased.

"This is where I like to eat my snacks," Galan remarked. "Now, let's get you out of this wet shirt." He continued to gently help her remove her wet shirt; Dana lifted her hands above her head. With a tender touch, he lifted the shirt over her head, stopping where her eyes were covered and only her mouth and nose were exposed. Dana's breathing quickened; Galan held her hands together above her head with one hand.

Sitting on the edge of the island counter with her feet wrapped around his waist, Dana asked with a bated breath, "Why did you stop?"

"I think you were right; I might be an idiot. I'm not sure how to get this off. Is it like this?" Galan leaned in and kissed her. "No, that doesn't seem right; maybe like this?" Galan placed his fingers on her lips. Dana slightly opened her mouth, and he slid two fingers in. "No, that doesn't seem right either; I must be such an idiot!" Galan smirked, taking his fingers out of her mouth. He pulled away and brushed his hand on her thigh, moving upwards of her dark pajama bottoms.

"Is it nice to call people names?" Galan whispered.

Dana's heart raced as she felt a lump forming in her throat; she took a deep, uneasy breath before firmly shaking her head. "No."

"No?" Galan replied, moving his hand away from her leg.

"No, Sir," Dana mumbled.

"Good girl," Galan whispered.

Dana bit her lips, and her breathing grew heavier.

"Now, what should I do? Should I keep trying to figure this t-shirt situation out?" Galan wondered.

"Yes... Sir," Dana exhaled.

Dana's apartment phone rang; the building receptionist spoke through the phone's loudspeaker, "Ms. Scarlet, your father is on his way up to see you."

Galan's strong arms swiftly scooped Dana off the kitchen island, effortlessly carrying her over his shoulder as if she weighed nothing at all. With a sense of urgency, he bounded up the stairs, his determined steps echoing through the hallway. Just in the nick of time, the elevator doors slid open, and Galan, with Dana still giggling playfully, managed to slip out of sight before Mr. Scarlet entered the apartment.

In the warmth of her laughter, Galan felt a surge of affection, even amidst the haste. He couldn't help but smile at the sound of her joy, which fueled his resolve to get her to her room as quickly as possible. Dana's laughter was infectious.

Once they reached her room, Galan gently set her down, her giggles subsiding, but a sparkle of happiness still danced in her eyes. With a teasing grin, he said, "I'm really growing to hate visitors. Can't we lock them out?"

"Maybe the ones who don't own the building I live in," answered Dana teasingly.

"Get dressed; I'll see you downstairs," Galan instructed. Leaving Dana's room, Galan made a beeline for the guest room. The urgency of the situation didn't allow him much time for a break. In a matter of seconds, he changed into a fresh, neatly pressed shirt. "Mr. Scarlet?" he called out. Galan found him standing in the kitchen, pouring himself a cup of coffee.

"Galan! I hope you don't mind. I helped myself to some coffee; I couldn't resist. It smells wonderful," Mr. Scarlet mentioned.

"Please, by all means, Sir," Galan approached and extended his hand. "It's nice to meet you, Sir."

"First, pick up your shirt from the floor, and please wipe down the island where my daughter was sitting. Then we can have a conversation. I can still see the imprint on the island, and your hair is a mess; this is not the first impression you want to make! Go get yourself cleaned up and come back to me while I enjoy my coffee," Mr. Scarlet sternly replied.

I always wondered what you were like, the man who raised Aria and Dana. A highhanded douchebag seems to fit the bill.

Galan marched over to him, reached over, and slid the mug of coffee away from him. "I am not someone you can bark orders at, Mr. Scarlet. I am not here to kiss up to you; I'm here to introduce myself in person. You will not waltz in here and look down your nose at me while drinking my coffee. You may own this building, but you don't own me. So, how about I make you the best cup of coffee you ever had, and we can start on a better foot?" Galan remarked.

Mr. Scarlet chuckled and patted Galan on the back, "You've got some balls; I respect that."

Dana entered the room and said, "Hi, Daddy," before kissing him on the cheek.

"Hi, Kitten; how is my little girl?" Mr. Scarlet inquired.

"Nervous and wondering what I missed between you two," Dana glanced at Galan.

"Well, Galan over here was just telling me what I can and cannot do in my building," Mr. Scarlet enlightened her as he looked at Galan.

"Respectfully," Galan playfully added.

"Her ex-boyfriend, Eder, wet himself the first time he met me. But I had my security detail with me, and Dana was just a teenager back then. Now she is a young woman, and I am very proud of her, as I was of her sister; God rest her soul," Mr. Scarlet exclaimed.

"Speaking of that, where is Paige?" asked Galan.

"She will join us later this evening. I wanted to spend the day with my daughter before we handled any business," Mr. Scarlet responded.

"You're not bringing her here, are you?" Dana inquired.

"Of course not, sweetheart; we will have dinner together with her at the hotel she's staying at," Mr. Scarlet informed her.

"Which hotel?" Dana queried.

"Écarlate," Mr. Scarlet answered.

"Is that the one just outside of Salt Pine Acres?" questioned Galan.

"There are over sixteen hundred across the globe, but yes, that's the particular one we are going to. Ms. Paige seemed adamant about being booked there," Mr. Scarlet stated.

That's not good... I told her about Nikki. Is she there for her? Fuck!

"Well, after breakfast, I'll get out of your hair and give you two some quality time together," Galan announced.

"And where will you be all day?" inquired Mr. Scarlet.

"Well, I've been to Écarlate before; I guess I'll get a room and pass the time there till tonight," Galan replied. With a worried expression, Dana exchanged a subtle glance with Galan, gently shaking her head to convey her concern.

"Any trouble getting a room, have the front desk contact me," said Mr. Scarlet.

"Will do; now, how about I fix us some breakfast!" Galan suggested.

"You have to try his food; it's delicious," Dana beamed.

"Maybe some other time; I heard you two expanded Grounded Coffee House. How about I come in for the grand opening of the new head branch, and you can show me how you work," Mr. Scarlet stated.

"I look forward to it," Galan replied as he shook his hand firmly. He leaned over to Dana and kissed her on the cheek, "Have a great day, love; I'll see you tonight."

"Be safe," Dana called out.

"Always," Galan answered with a smile and left the room to gather his things. He dressed in a hoodie and jeans before leaving the penthouse. As he made his way to the elevator, Dana followed him with her eyes, her heart full of affection for him. Galan turned to face her, and with a playful gesture, he blew her a kiss. Dana's lips curved into a soft smile, and she mouthed the word 'Bye' to him as the elevator doors closed, momentarily taking him away from her sight.

Dana is in the safest place for the day, with her father and his security detail. I'll do what I should have done back then. Count your breaths, Paige; these will be your last!

Chapter Three

Later that day, Galan's anticipation grew as he arrived at the hotel. With a sense of excitement, he stepped out of the vehicle and turned his attention toward the majestic mountains. The breathtaking view of Salt Pine Acres stretched before him, captivating his gaze. *This is where everything went wrong; how poetic it's where I make things right again.* With purpose in his stride, Galan crossed the threshold and entered the building. His eyes quickly scanned the surroundings as he navigated through the interior, finally reaching the front desk with confident steps. As Galan gracefully traversed the lobby, the elegantly dressed hotel guests couldn't help but cast glances his way.

"Welcome to Écarlate. How may I assist you today?" asked the receptionist.

"Hi, I would like to book the luxury suite for the day, Galan Rain," Galan replied.

"We do have suites available; I would just need a credit card and I.D.," the receptionist requested.

"Sure," Galan acceded. With swift efficiency, he acquired the requested items and smoothly slid them over to her. "Here you are," he smiled.

"Thank you. Just give me a few minutes, and I will have the room ready for you," the receptionist responded.

"Do you, by chance, know if Nikki is working today?" asked Galan politely.

"Do you know her last name?" the receptionist inquired.

Did I not get her last name… Good job, Galan.

"I'm terrible at names; the last time I stayed here, she brought clothes to my room, if that helps?" Galan informed her.

"I'm not familiar with the store staff, but you can check with them. If she is here today, they will be able to assist you," the receptionist commented.

A warm smile graced her lips as she returned Galan's I.D. card and credit card, accompanied by the room keycard. "Do enjoy your stay at Écarlate. You can contact the front desk if you require anything else."

"Thank you so much. Do have a wonderful day, Miss…?" Galan began.

"Belle," Belle informed him.

"Belle, well, the next time I visit and ask for you, I won't know your last name, too," Galan teased.

Belle's laughter rang through the air as she chuckled, elegantly tucking a lock of hair behind her ear. Galan reciprocated with a friendly wave, expressing his gratitude for her assistance. With a sense of contentment, he proceeded toward the elevators.

After successfully tending to a group attending a wedding, Nikki and her dedicated team began the task of restocking the store's shelves. As they tidied up, Nikki noticed a pair of shoes that needed to be placed on a high shelf just beyond her reach. Bent on remedying this, she started searching for a step ladder nearby.

Unexpectedly, Galan appeared behind her like a helpful guardian angel. Sensing her predicament, he kindly took the shoes from her hand and effortlessly placed them back on the high shelf.

"Oh, thank you so much," Nikki stated. She couldn't contain her excitement as she turned around and saw Galan standing there with a smile that melted her heart. "Galan...!" Nikki whispered his name with sheer joy, her face glowing from ear to ear. She jumped into his arms without hesitation, wrapping them around him in a warm, heartfelt embrace.

As Galan gently put Nikki back down, he smiled, "How have you been, Nikki?"

"I've been great. Wow, it's so nice to see you! Look at you with silver highlights and a scruffy beard," Nikki commented. She attempted to touch his hair, but Galan kindly intercepted her hand and cradled it between his own.

"Somethings changed," Galan observed.

"I know," Nikki raised her left hand and flashed an engagement ring.

Galan's eyes lit up. "You're getting married!" he replied in excitement.

"You seem happy," Nikki teased.

"Why wouldn't I be?" asked Galan.

"I don't know; I guess I was hoping it made you a little jealous," Nikki giggled.

"Well, I took your advice last time I was here," Galan informed her.

"Advice? If memory serves, I rejected you and told you that you could not have me until you could be all mine," Nikki recalled.

"You told me that I didn't want you and that I was only trying to get over the things I was running from," Galan reminded her.

"And?" Nikki replied.

"I stopped running," Galan grinned.

"I always was jealous of that girl who had you wrapped around her finger like that; even the time we spent together, I could see the only thing on your mind was her," Nikki sighed.

"I wanted to say thanks," Galan stated. Nikki was still enveloped in Galan's embrace, feeling secure and comforted by his strong arms. The alluring scent of his cologne lingered in her senses, creating a peaceful and serene moment. He whispered, "Thank you for being more than just a memory."

As Nikki's eyes grew teary, Galan wiped them away. "So, tell me about him!" he requested.

"Who?" Nikki asked as she composed herself.

"The guy who won you over, Miss 'I'm not the type of girl who wants to be owned,'" Galan teased.

Nikki blushed. "Shut up, that was years ago; things change," she beamed.

"Not going to tell me what makes this guy so special?" asked Galan.

"If you must know… It's not a guy," Nikki chuckled.

"My, my," Galan smirked.

"Oh, don't give me that look," Nikki laughed.

"What look?" Galan replied sarcastically.

"Typical guy ego," said Nikki with a smile.

"It's not that; I'm just thrilled that you found someone who made you change for the better," Galan told her.

"Enough about me; what about this girl who has you all in love, huh?" Nikki pried.

"You know what? I need some clothes; can you help me pick something out?" Galan called out as he walked away playfully.

"No! Don't change the subject!" Nikki chased after him.

"Miss, can I have some assistance!?" Galan waved at another staff member.

"Ignore him!" Nikki told the other employee.

"What? I'm trying to get some quality assistance," Galan claimed.

"Stop, or I will kick you out of my store," Nikki joshed.

"Then are you going to help me find something nice to wear?" asked Galan innocently.

"Tell me about this girl, and I will gladly help," Nikki responded with folded arms and a mischievous smile.

Galan flashed a smile and gracefully moved his fingers across his hair, sweeping it away from his face. "It's not the same girl from back then," Galan stated.

"Really? Huh!" Nikki replied.

"It's that girl's... Little sister," Galan confessed.

"Wow, Galan…." Nikki unfolded her arms.

"It's complicated," Galan sighed.

"Simplify it for me," Nikki remarked.

"She was sixteen at the time; I would have never made a move on her back then. I knew how she felt, but I would never do that to a child," Galan professed.

"So, she's twenty now," Nikki said matter of factly.

"That's right," answered Galan.

"So, the moment she turned eighteen, you went after her?" asked Nikki.

"I didn't; I've stayed out of her life these last four years. I wanted her to live her life," Galan replied.

"So, what changed?" Nikki inquired.

"Well, let's just say our past brought us back together," Galan remarked.

Nikki looked at him as he spoke. "You don't know if you love her—" Nikki gasped.

"Where did you come up with that!?" Galan chuckled.

"Galan, I saw the fire in your eyes for that girl the last time I saw you; I don't see that here. I see something else," Nikki claimed.

With a gleam of amusement in his eyes, Galan playfully folded his arms. "Oh yeah? What do you see?" he questioned.

"Fear... Whatever you have with that girl terrifies you," Nikki answered.

"Fear?" Galan repeated.

"Galan, look at me," said Nikki.

As Nikki reached out to get Galan's attention, her hand hovering close to his shoulder, he quickly and gently caught her hand mid-air, preventing her from touching him.

"There you go again... Why won't you let me touch you? This is the second time you have done this since you saw me," Nikki stated.

"Please, Nikki—" Galan whispered.

"Galan, talk to me; let me help you," Nikki offered.

"It was nice seeing you again, Nikki," Galan said. As he released her hand, a mixture of surprise and disappointment briefly flickered across Nikki's face as she watched him walk away.

"Galan!" Nikki called out his name once more, but he seemed determined to put some distance between them, so he continued marching towards the elevators without turning back.

Nikki stood there, watching him go, a knot of emotions tightening in her chest.

Keep it together, Galan; what does she know? You're respecting your boundaries, that's all. You know what it does to you when someone touches you. You're with Dana, and you wouldn't dare hurt her, knowing what she has been through and that she would never do the same to you. Coming to see Nikki was a mistake; that's a bad call on my part, knowing my past with her.

Upon the elevator doors sliding open, Galan stepped inside. As the doors began to close, Nikki managed to slip inside just in time.

"What are you doing?!" questioned Galan.

"I hate seeing you like this; it's not the guy I met last time," Nikki confessed.

"The guy you met last time was running from something; this time, it's not like that," Galan informed her.

"Then talk to me; just give me five minutes of your time," Nikki pleaded.

"What are you trying to prove?" asked Galan.

"That maybe she isn't right for you—" Nikki exclaimed.

"I care about her a lot; it's why I won't let you touch me right now," answered Galan.

"You hugged me," Nikki pointed out.

"A hug and an intimate touch are not the same; family can hug you, but they can't touch you the way a lover can," Galan countered.

"You asked me to be yours, all yours... Was she given that same choice?" Nikki inquired.

As Galan bowed his head, Nikki sensed a tinge of shame in his demeanor.

"Did you ever tell her you loved her?" asked Nikki.

"Not exactly...," Galan murmured, still fixated on the floor, his expression filled with uncertainty.

"But you had sex with her, didn't you!" Nikki stated matter-of-factly.

Galan lifted his gaze from the floor and directed his attention towards the mirrored walls of the elevator, where he caught his own reflection.

"Look at me, please," Nikki pleaded.

Galan refused.

"Please... Sir," Nikki's hand moved delicately towards Galan's chest. He felt a sudden rush of tension as he took a deep breath, and his neck twitched involuntarily. Her palms glided softly from his chest up to his neck, where Nikki's smile grew more pronounced as she leaned in closer. With a gentle touch, she reached up to his chin, one finger at a time, until all her fingers were caressing his face, guiding him to face her with a slow and tender movement.

The look in Galan's eyes changed; the lust behind his gaze grew intense. Nikki pressed against him, feeling his member pressing against her through his jeans.

"Consider this my Bachelorette party, my last hoorah before marriage," Nikki moaned, biting her lips.

No... No... This isn't you. You wouldn't cheat on Dana; you wouldn't do that to anyone. Control yourself, Galan. This is your chance at love. When no one else saw you, Dana did. Nikki rejected you, as well as Aria, Paige, Lillie, and everyone in the middle! Control yourself!

Their lips nearly brushed against each other in the charged moment, but Galan chose to turn slightly to the side and enveloped Nikki in a warm embrace instead. "You're wrong, you know. Maybe I had some doubts, but thank you for reminding me what is important. Congratulations on the engagement," Galan smiled and kissed her cheek.

As the elevator doors parted, Galan stepped out and left Nikki behind, the fleeting connection lingering in the air. He turned around and started walking backward, keeping his eyes fixed on her until the doors slowly began to close, "One more thing, I need a nice suit for tonight. You know my style and with shoes this time. I'll leave the door unlocked. You can leave it in the room." Galan turned away, and with steady strides, he continued his journey as the elevator doors sealed shut behind him, leaving Nikki on the other side.

Galan swiped his card and unlocked the door, stepping inside the room. He traversed the space, making his way toward the balcony, where he stepped out to relish the view. With his phone in hand, Galan dialed Dana's number. After just two rings, she picked up, her voice coming through on the other end.

"Hey, handsome."

"Hey there, beautiful, I just got checked in. I'm about to take a shower and maybe watch a movie to pass the time," said Galan.

"Another shower? Didn't you shower before you left my place?" asked Dana.

"I like the water; being wet feels good, don't you agree?" Galan smirked.

"Shut up, my dad is with me," Dana chuckled.

"You didn't answer the question, though," Galan replied.

"Ask me again when I see you tonight," Dana blushed.

"Ou la la," Galan teased.

"I'm hanging up now," Dana chuckled.

"Hey, before you go, I need to ask you something," Galan stated.

"Sure, what is it?" Dana replied.

"Did you shower?" Galan chuckled.

"I hate you," Dana teased.

"I hate you too, but the 'H' is silent," Galan attempted in a sexy voice.

"I'm hanging up now!" Dana ended the call.

Galan smiled and looked at her name disappear off his screen. *Nikki was right; I did this all wrong. I went above and beyond for Aria, but for Dana, there was no hurdle; she wanted me and got me in the end. She deserves better, and I will be better.*

Chapter Four

Galan found himself standing under the chilling spray of the shower, feeling the cold water mercilessly cascade over his body. With eyes closed, he sought refuge in his thoughts, but this time, it was an unwelcome memory that clawed at his heart, refusing to be ignored.

As the cold water continued to fall, Galan tried to steel himself against the onslaught of emotions that threatened to overwhelm him. He braced himself against the vivid images that flashed before his closed eyes, wishing he could escape the clutches of this distressing recollection.

DANA SCARLET

AGE: 20

SIGN: SCORPIO

FUN FACT: "I DYED MY HAIR BLACK IN MEMORY OF ARIA."

"I just wanted to see Lillie—" Galan cried.

"Lillie is gone, lost to us now; just look at what you've done. This is your fault, Galan, for daring to love her," Paige's voice trembled with a mix of sorrow and anger as she confronted him, her eyes filled with accusation and heartache.

Paige wiped away his tears, gently guiding him inside the house; they stepped with care over the lifeless bodies of her siblings and parents, a heartbreaking scene that weighed heavily on their hearts. As they entered the kitchen, she turned the knobs on the stove's burners, opening the gas release valves. "We have to make this look like an accident; nobody can ever know what you did here tonight," Paige stated.

"Look at what you did, Galan. Now I have to leave, and there will be nobody left who will ever love you. You're a monster, Galan, and nobody will ever love a monster!" Paige declared as she lit a candle in the next room and rushed them both outside into the cold pouring rain. The house exploded into flames, waking the village in the dead of night.

I still remember how it felt; I thought you died in that house that night, Lillie. I still remember trying to run back into the burning house to save you. I remember hearing my own screams when I

approached the flames, and the heat was too intense. I lost everything, and I felt responsible and helpless. Paige left me; she left me to go back to the abusive family I tried escaping. I saw the way they looked at me, those people who gathered in the streets drenched in the rain. They all blamed me for the tragedy that shook the village. It was my fault, but I didn't kill those people; I wouldn't have killed you. But I was out of my mind; I was drunk!

A thirteen-year-old kid got into the liquor cabinet, got drunk, burnt down the house, and killed the family who took him in. Paige did this to me. I was only drunk because she forced me to drink. She made me drink every time she molested me so that no one would believe me if I ever told anyone about what happened. I just wanted to be close to you; I didn't want to lose you back then. I would have done anything to keep you in my life, and I let Paige blackmail me because I couldn't risk losing you. I blame you, Paige. You ruined my old life and destroyed my chance at a new one! But no more. I am not that scared little kid anymore. You leveraged my love for Lillie back then, but I won't allow you to do that to me now.

Galan emerged from the shower, the lingering sense of disquiet slowly dissipating as he turned off the water. Drying himself off, he ventured into the bedroom, where he found the attire he had requested. With purposeful movements, he donned the dark suit. Exiting the hotel room, he made his way downstairs to the lobby. The atmosphere seemed to hum with a mix of anticipation and busyness, guests coming and going, each wrapped up in their own stories.

Alright, let's find out where this bitch is held up.

As Galan neared the front desk, he couldn't help but notice the warm smile that graced Belle's face. "Hi there, ummm...," Galan snapped his fingers, putting on a playful act while trying to play it cool as if he couldn't quite recall her name.

"Very funny, Mr. Rain," Belle chuckled.

"Please, it's Galan," Galan replied, smiling back.

"As long as I am behind this desk, I shall address you as Mr. Rain," Belle voiced.

"I see," Galan responded. With a casual and relaxed demeanor, he leaned on the edge of the desk, interlocking his fingers. The mischievous glint in his eyes remained as he playfully awaited Belle's response. "Suppose you get up and walk around the desk; what would you call me then?"

"I would call you someone who can assist you while I attend to my duties when I am not behind this desk," Belle smiled.

Galan chuckled, "Excellent. Well, now that you mention it, I could use some assistance. A friend is staying at this hotel; we have dinner plans tonight. There should be reservations booked by Mr. Scarlet himself for four."

As soon as the name "Mr. Scarlet" was mentioned, the hotel manager, who happened to be on the floor nearby, perked up and immediately rushed over to the front desk, leaving approaching guests unattended. His eyes widened with a mix of surprise and excitement.

"Hello, welcome to Écarlate; how can I help you, Sir?" the Hotel Manager asked enthusiastically.

Galan turned to him and responded, "Thank you, but everything is fine. There is no need for any further assistance."

"I insist; allow me to tend to your needs personally, Sir. Ms. Belle, can you help the lovely couple behind me get checked in?" the Hotel Manager instructed.

"No, please, there is really no need. I am being well taken care of by Ms. Belle here," Galan politely replied.

"Ms. Belle, do not keep our guests waiting," the Hotel Manager turned to her.

"Of course, Sir," Belle quickly answered.

Galan's bright smile grew dimmer.

"Yes, Sir, as I was saying, do tell me how I can make your stay at Écarlate more accommodating," the Hotel Manager gushed.

"Pardon me," Galan stepped forward, instinctively moving to block Belle's path as she attempted to navigate the desk. "Indeed, I believe you can be a great help to me. Today is not a very good day; see, I am having dinner with Mr. Scarlet tonight, and we are doing so because his daughter and I are quite close. I assume you have met him before, haven't you?" Galan asked the Hotel Manager.

"Y... Yes, Sir, I have met Mr. Scarlet," the Hotel Manager confirmed, now concerned with the change in Galan's tone.

"Beautiful, because in my limited interaction with him, he is quite a no-nonsense type of person. With that being said, I am pretty much on edge because I know I will be grilled tonight at our dinner. After losing his eldest child, I can only imagine it has changed him and made him even more protective of his now only child. Wouldn't you agree that is a fair train of thought?" Galan inquired.

"I suppose that is quite a reasonable assumption," the Hotel Manager sported a worried look.

"Here is how you can assist me, good Sir. I would appreciate it if you personally oversee our dinner tonight. While you do so, in an attempt to take the heat off of me even for a little bit, we can discuss how you left hotel guests unattended and interrupted this young lady who was doing quite an amazing job. We can talk about how you undermined her duties, and in front of another guest, you abused your authority as Hotel Manager for no apparent reason, or is it that you heard mention of Mr. Scarlet's name and came running over here?" Galan stated nonchalantly.

"I don't quite, um... I—" the Hotel Manager fumbled.

"Now you're really in a bind because neither of those options is a good choice, but one is far worse. Because if you heard me mention Mr. Scarlet's name, then those people also heard it. And after you so rudely left them without assistance and rushed over here to assign Ms. Belle to tend to them, do you know what's the first thing they would think?" Galan probed.

"That I came over here because there was mention of his name?" the Hotel Manager gulped.

"You're not just leaving a bad reputation for the hotel but also the Scarlet name. What would happen if word spread and people started talking about guests being abandoned the moment the owner is around? Not to mention I checked in not that long ago, and you didn't bat an eye at me until I came down to the lobby in a nice suit and namedropped Mr. Scarlet's name. How do you think Mr. Scarlet would react to this over dinner in an already tense situation?" questioned Galan.

"I am so sorry; I really did not mean to insult Mr. Scarlet or his guests. I was only trying to offer any assistance I could," the Hotel Manager professed.

"There is no need to apologize; I met the man, and believe me, I know how intense he can be. Don't worry about it, alright?" Galan smiled.

"Please accept my sincerest apologies, Mr…?" the Hotel Manager inquired.

"Rain," Galan firmly grasped the Hotel Manager's hand and shook it upon introducing himself.

"Mr. Rain, thank you for staying with us at Écarlate; if you need anything at all and Ms. Belle over here cannot assist, do not hesitate to come to me, alright?" the Hotel Manager remarked.

"I didn't catch your name," Galan remarked.

"Zam Auclair, a pleasure to meet you," said Zam.

"Likewise. Well, Mr. Auclair, how about you leave Ms. Belle to assist me, and you can give those guests my sincerest apologies for 'hogging' the staff's attention. Send a bottle of your finest champagne to their room, and their dinner will be paid for tonight. My treat as a token of my apology," Galan suggested.

With a friendly smile and a nod, Zam, the hotel manager, hurried back to attend to the other guests, apologizing for any inconvenience caused.

Belle looked at Galan and smiled, "You would take the blame and pay for dinner and champagne so that you can talk to me?" questioned Belle.

"I'm sorry. Remind me of your name again?" Galan teased.

Beaming, Belle rolled her eyes. "How can I be of assistance, Mr. Rain? You were saying something about dinner?" she reminded him.

"Yes, about that dinner, an old acquaintance is also here for said dinner. Could you, by chance, let me know what room she is staying in? If she isn't checked in under Mr. Scarlet's name, her room should be booked under 'Paige,'" Galan explained.

"Ok, hold on just a moment, and I will get that for you," Belle replied.

"Text me the information; here is my card," Galan responded. Delving into his wallet, he retrieved a pristine business card. He slid it smoothly across the table towards Belle, gently within her reach.

"I actually have not had breakfast or my morning coffee, and I would like to get those before I grow irritable," Galan continued.

"No problem, I will have that done in a few minutes; enjoy your breakfast. The café is just on the other side of the bar, down the hall, past the elevator,"

Belle informed him. Pulling the card across the desk, she lifted it up. "Grounded Coffee House, oh my God, I love that place. Do you work there?"

With a confident smile spreading across his face, Galan asserted, "I'm the founder." His words hung in the air as he gracefully moved away and walked toward the Café.

Belle delicately flipped over the business card, uncovering Galan's contact information. Her eyes followed his departing figure, a flicker of curiosity dancing within her gaze as she subtly tucked a loose strand of hair behind her ear.

Chapter Five

After a delectable breakfast at the charming hotel café, Galan couldn't help but sigh contentedly. The aroma of freshly brewed coffee still lingered, adding to the pleasant ambiance around him. Eagerly, he picked up his phone, a glimmer of excitement dancing in his eyes. His heartbeat quickened as he unlocked the screen, knowing that Belle had responded to the information he had requested earlier. He eagerly opened the message with a swift and practiced swipe of his thumb.

This room is on the same floor as mine. Come to think of it, isn't this the same room Malek stayed in? How could she have known Malek was there? She couldn't have, I didn't mention it to her, and Aria isn't alive to give away that information. Quite an odd coincidence.

Nevertheless, Paige has to answer for what she did to me! But I can't make a move inside this hotel... Too many complications. I'll have to drag that miserable she-devil out of here... Or... Maybe not? Maybe I should learn from my past. Those idiot friends very nearly killed me by dosing me with anesthesia.

Galan turned to the lobby and saw the couple from earlier who were at the front desk. *That's it; I can spike her drink and dispose of her without getting my hands dirty! Let's find out which bottle of champagne the couple received.*

After settling the bill with a courteous nod to the hotel staff, Galan swiftly made his way to the lobby. His eagerness to meet the couple was evident in his brisk steps and the warm, welcoming smile that graced his face. As he approached the duo, he raised his hand in a friendly wave to catch their attention, his eyes locked on the gentleman. "Hey, I'm really sorry about earlier. I am under a lot of pressure today, and I didn't really have any consideration for the other guests," Galan apologized politely.

"It's quite alright. Thank you for paying for our dinner tonight; you really didn't have to," the woman responded.

"It's the least I can do; I acted selfishly and out of line. Did the Manager bring you that champagne as well?" asked Galan, his question directed to the man.

"Indeed, he did; thank you again," said the man.

"You know your champagne?" Galan inquired with a smile.

"I'm more of a Dry Reisling enjoyer, but my wife loves champagne," the man replied.

"I'm glad to hear that; I'm not sure what he sent you. I just asked him to send you their finest bottle. I am not much of a drinker, but I have a guest to impress tonight at dinner. Is there anything you can tell me so I don't look like a bumbling fool?" Galan courteously requested.

"Well, it's a Brut Rosé Vintage, but I am not quite that into drinks where I can describe them to you," the woman answered. Chuckling, she continued, "I know my stuff, but I don't know it, too, if that makes sense."

Galan chuckled, "That's quite alright; at least when I order it, I can sound like I know what I am talking about without looking at the menu tonight. Thank you so much, and I hope you have a good stay; I will leave you to it," Galan waved and walked away.

Perfect, a quick trip to the bar can confirm what that bottle looks like, and I can easily find another bottle in the city and spike it with a slow-acting poison. I should check with Dana and find out when they will be joining us.

Galan wasted no time in reaching out to Dana, his fingers typing swiftly on his phone screen. He sent the message with a touch of anticipation, eager to finalize their plans. Moments later, Dana's reply came in, concise and to the point. "Dinner at seven tonight."

It's nine A.M. I have ten hours to put this into motion. I know where Paige is, and she has no clue what's coming to her. This is for all those times you forced me to get drunk and do those things to you. I cannot truly start my new life if the old one is haunting me everywhere I go. This ends today, Paige!

With a hint of curiosity, Galan made his way to the hotel bar, intrigued by the prospect of seeing the Champagne bottle up close. As he strolled along, his eyes caught a glimmer of something special. There it was, displayed in an elegant showcase, the Champagne bottle adorned with exquisite decorations. *Bingo!*

Galan couldn't resist a playful smirk as he turned away from the Champagne display, feeling a renewed sense of excitement for the evening ahead. With a confident stride, he retraced his steps back to the hotel's front desk, eager to see Belle again. As he approached, the soft echo of his footsteps drew

Belle's attention, and she looked up from her work. The sight of Galan approaching caused her heart to flutter slightly, and her eyes sparkled with a blend of curiosity and anticipation. Their gazes met, and a knowing smile graced Galan's lips in response to the subtle smile that played upon Belle's. "Did you enjoy your breakfast Mr. Rain?" she asked.

"It was delicious," Galan confirmed. "Is there a chauffeur service in this hotel? I have some errands to run today."

"Yes, there is. When would you like a driver?" asked Belle.

"Now, please, if possible," Galan replied.

"Right away, Sir," Belle answered.

The surge of adrenaline within Galan intensified, his heart pounding in sync with the electrifying energy coursing through his veins. It was as if the world around him had blurred; he leaned slightly against the front desk, his hand gripping the edge tightly.

Fuck... Calm down, Galan... What are you doing?!

"Your driver's name is Avan; he will bring the car around to the front of the building shortly," Belle notified him.

As the intensity of the moment lingered, Galan mustered a soft but sincere "Thank you" in response to Belle's unspoken allure. Feeling a mix of excitement and urgency, he left the front desk in a hurry, his heart still racing with the electric charge of their brief encounter.

As the sleek black car glided to a graceful stop at the entrance of the luxurious hotel, Galan stood there, his presence commanding and poised. The chauffeur, Avan, emerged from the vehicle, his polished shoes tapping against the pavement as he made his way around to the front of the car. His voice, laced with a respectful tone, broke through the silence, addressing Galan with a touch of formality, "Mr. Rain?"

"That's right," Galan affirmed. Closing the distance between them, Galan moved toward the awaiting car, a sleek embodiment of power and elegance. Avan, ever the consummate professional, seamlessly stepped forward, opening the door of the backseat with practiced grace. The vehicle awaited Galan's entry, its interior exuding an air of opulence and comfort. Galan settled into the plush seat, feeling its embrace as Avan gently closed the door.

Avan hurried around the car, returned to the driver's seat, and turned around. "Where to?" he asked.

"Take me to a place where I can find the finest Champagne," Galan replied.

"Very good, Sir; I know a few places we can go," Avan answered before facing forward.

"Avan," said Galan.

"Yes, Sir?" Avan turned around again.

"Could you stop calling me 'Sir'?" Galan requested.

"I am so sorry if I misgendered you. May I call you Madame?" Avan queried in a panic.

Galan covered his face with his palm, trying to control his laughter, "Calm down, Avan, you can just call me Galan."

"Sir, Galan, ok, I understand," Avan declared.

"Not Sir," Galan repeated.

"Madame Galan, then?" asked Avan. "Mrs. Galan...." Avan looked at Galan as he stared back in disbelief. "Ms. Galan?" Avan panicked.

"Avan, I only like being called Sir when sexual tensions get high. There isn't any of that between us now, is there?" questioned Galan, leaning forward in his seat.

"No, Sir... I mean... There could be? Is that what you want? Because I am ok with that, just—" Avan rambled in a panic.

Galan chuckled and shook his head. "Avan, please stop talking and drive the car," Galan instructed as he patted him on the shoulder and leaned back into his seat, shaking with laughter.

"Sorry, Sir," Avan replied.

"Avan!" Galan yelled in laughter, shaking his head.

"That was my bad. So sorry, we will leave now," Avan claimed, putting the car in gear and driving off. Galan's phone received a message; he looked down and opened it. Belle texted, 'Enjoy an entire day of Avan, smiley face emoji.'

You picked him on purpose to mess with me? Galan smiled.

Chapter Six

*A*van and Galan eagerly departed from the bustling city, their spirits lifted by their successful acquisition of the prized Champagne. As they embarked on their journey, their path led them to a quaint University at the foothills of a majestic mountain called Salt Pine University, or SPU for short. The University sat near the entrance to Salt Pine Acres, an awe-inspiring campus sprawling across an impressive expanse of thirty-five hundred acres, with no buildings for miles until you entered the city. "Here we are," Avan declared as he slowly pulled into the parking lot of a Grounded Coffee House establishment.

"Excellent. Can I treat you to a cup of coffee?" asked Galan.

"Me? No, I don't think coffee would be good for me. If I have coffee, I'm afraid I will get hyper and ruin my calm state of mind," Avan replied.

"This is you calm?" Galan chuckled.

"Yes, Sir... Um, I mean—" Avan panicked.

Galan smirked, "Come on, you'll be the first to be served at the head branch of Grounded." Galan swung the car door open with a graceful flourish, eager to embrace the world outside. As his polished shoes met the solid ground, he was met with turning heads from the students on campus.

"You know, I'm lactose intolerant; when I have dairy, there is never a quiet moment," Avan rambled.

"Avan!" Galan yelled.

"Coming, Sir... Gah, I mean... Not coming like you think, I meant coming like to come to you... Gah! No, that's not it. Ok, let me rephrase—" Avan panicked.

Galan's sudden outburst caught him off guard, and his voice cracked as he called out, "Avan!!!" The sound of his own voice echoing through the University's corridors startled him, and he quickly covered his mouth with his hand, a mixture of surprise and embarrassment crossing his face. He glanced around, realizing that his outburst had attracted the attention of the other students in the vicinity. Their curious gazes made him feel self-conscious, and he offered a sheepish smile to those around him, attempting to downplay the situation.

Avan quickly got out of the car and hurried to the door of Grounded.

You must be smiling, thinking about how miserable of a time I would be having with Avan, aren't you? Those cherry lips are just teasing me... Wait, what am I doing!?

Shaking off any lingering distractions, Galan brushed aside the momentary lapse in judgment and strode purposefully toward the door. With practiced ease, he scanned his thumbprint over the sleek panel, effortlessly overriding the intricate locks that guarded the entrance. The doors yielded to his touch, parting ways with a quiet whoosh.

With a confident pull, Galan swung the door open, revealing a captivating ambiance beyond its threshold. A welcoming atmosphere spilled forth, inviting Avan to step into the embrace of Grounded Coffee House.

"Please, I should hold the door for you," Avan insisted.

"You're my chauffeur, not my assistant. And as of right now, you're my guest," Galan responded.

Avan crossed the threshold and immersed himself in a world of architectural splendor. His eyes widened in awe as he surveyed the expansive interior adorned with soaring ceilings that seemed to touch the sky. The high ceilings imparted a sense of grandeur, filling the space with an air of elegance and possibility.

His gaze wandered, taking in the captivating sight of the modern décor that graced the walls. The sleek elegance of the black walls served as a sophisticated backdrop, contrasting beautifully with the coffee-brown hardwood accents that adorned the space. The furniture, meticulously chosen to complement the surroundings, radiated comfort and style. It was a visual symphony of refined taste and contemporary design.

"Do you like it?" asked Galan.

"It's nice; you own this?" Avan remarked.

"I built Grounded Coffee House years ago, then someone bought it from me, and we worked together to expand it. This being the latest one," Galan answered.

"This is amazing," Avan gazed around the room.

"Let me get some stuff from the back; I'll whip us up something good," Galan informed Avan as he walked behind the bar and through the backroom doors.

Nutmeg in specific amounts can cause hallucinations, but a highly concentrated dose can be fatal.

In the quiet seclusion of the storage room, Galan focused on the task at hand. The shelves were lined with various ingredients, each carefully organized to facilitate his caffeinated concoctions. His eyes scanned the neatly arranged containers until he found what he needed—a bottle of nutmeg concentration.

The recommended dilution is two-tenths of a percent of the final mixture. By the time you realize the taste of the nutmeg, it will be too late.

With the bottle of nutmeg concentrate safely tucked in his pocket, Galan collected the rest of the ingredients he needed from the storage room, ensuring he had everything required to create his masterful brews. He made his way back to the bar, eager to resume the enchanting evening that awaited them.

As Galan approached, he couldn't help but notice Avan perched gracefully on the plush barstool, emanating an air of quiet anticipation. Avan's eyes wandered the room, absorbing the ambiance with a sense of wonderment that was infectious. The surroundings seemed to hold him in a gentle embrace, and the passage of time did nothing to diminish the allure of the moment.

Galan approached the bar with a graceful fluidity, setting down the carefully selected ingredients he had gathered earlier. As he slid his hand under the bar's counter, he retrieved two elegant cups. "Alright, let's see what I can fix you—a lactose intolerant, non-hyper drink," Galan stated.

The sound of the door swinging open drew Galan's attention away from the cups and towards the entrance. His gaze fell upon a small group of vibrant University students, their youthful energy filling the room with a lively spirit. Their laughter and animated chatter enlivened the atmosphere, infusing the space with a sense of fresh vitality.

"Hi? Is this place open?" asked a girl.

"Sorry, it's not officially open; the grand opening is in a couple of days," Galan responded.

"Oh, sorry, we just saw when you guys came in—" the girl trailed off.

"Oh, hey, Sydney," Avan called out as he turned around.

"Avan! Hey," Sydney greeted.

"Oh, you know these people?" questioned Galan.

"Yeah, we all go to school here," replied Avan.

"You go to school and work at Écarlate?" Galan pried.

"Well, yeah. The hotel offers flexible hours and helps us get into places like this University to further our education as long as it furthers our careers there. A bunch of us from Écarlate go to school here," Avan explained.

"That's pretty cool," Galan looked over to the group. "Come on in; Avan said coffee is on him."

"What!" Avan subtly groaned.

"You like her, don't you? Don't worry, I'm not charging you; this is for your benefit," Galan whispered.

"Sydney isn't into me," Avan mumbled.

"That's because you don't shut up and listen; women want someone who can hear them, even when they don't speak. Watch me," said Galan with a smile.

As the group of six settled at the bar, the energy around them continued to buzz with excitement. Avan welcomed them with a warm smile as he made space for Sydney to sit beside him.

"Welcome to the unofficial opening of Grounded Coffee House. I didn't exactly plan for other customers, but I can work with this," Galan proclaimed. He glimpsed the group and smiled. "Alright, let's see, dark circles around your eyes, slightly messy hair, comfortable clothes. I can assume your study sessions have been endless. Pick me ups over guilty pleasure drinks, so espressos across the board except for you two," Galan pointed at Sydney and another girl.

"Oh yeah?" Sydney replied.

"You are in a hoodie that's a little too big, no makeup, but your hair is done nicely. Flawless skin—" Galan continued.

"My skin? What does that have to do with anything?" asked Sydney.

"Stress makes you age and affects your skin," Galan replied.

"I could just take care of my skin well," Sydney responded.

"Maybe, but your lack of makeup and choice of clothing suggests you don't quite care for impressing anyone else. Rather than overexerting yourself, you would go for something calmer, not a coffee for function but rather for taste. Something you treat yourself to, am I wrong?" quipped Galan.

Avan's gaze lingered on Galan, watching as he expertly navigated the intricate dynamics of the group. As he observed Galan's perceptive nature, he couldn't help but feel a sense of admiration for his insight. Galan possessed an innate ability to read people, to discern their true essence beyond mere appearances. Avan recognized the accuracy of Galan's understanding of Sydney's personality. The way Galan had seen through the layers, understanding Sydney's quirks, passions, and thought patterns, left Avan in awe of his friend's perceptiveness.

"That's a nice trick; Avan must have told you a lot about me," Sydney remarked with a smirk.

Galan leaned on the counter, "I see, so you do think about him!"

Avan panicked; his eyes moved back and forth between the two.

"Tell me something, Sydney. Do you wear his hoodie because you look good in it or because you wish he were still with you?" Galan probed.

"Excuse me?" asked Syndey, her smile slowly disappearing.

"I know that cologne; I have one just like it. That hoodie is new, but you bought it oversized and wore his cologne so you can cling to how he made you feel," Galan commented.

As Sydney leaned away from Galan, a sudden sense of unease washed over the group. Avan's face registered genuine shock at the unexpected turn of events. The once lively atmosphere seemed to have shifted, the air now tinged with tension.

"You don't know anything about me," Sydney retorted.

"Then tell me about you over an affogato, that's an espresso poured over ice cream," Galan stated as he maintained eye contact with Sydney, trying to convey his sincerity, but she eventually broke the gaze by turning away. However, Galan didn't let the moment deter him. He exchanged a subtle wink with Avan, silently reassuring him that he had a plan to handle the situation delicately.

With a confident yet casual demeanor, Galan swiftly took off his blazer and rolled up his sleeves, focusing on serving their orders and engaging in light conversation with the group. His effortless charm and friendly demeanor put everyone at ease, creating a more relaxed atmosphere.

Sydney remained quiet, seemingly lost in her thoughts as she twirled her spoon in the affogato. Galan noticed her subdued state, and without drawing attention to it, he subtly signaled Avan, nudging his head toward Sydney.

Avan panicked and shrugged his shoulders; he mouthed, 'I don't know what to say.'

Galan mouthed back the words, 'Now you shut up!?'

"Hey, I'm going to head out back to campus; I'll see you guys in class," Sydney informed the group as she got up from her seat at the bar and walked out the door.

Galan rushed over to Avan, "Now is your chance. Go!"

"To do what? What do I even say to her?" asked Avan, panicking.

"Say anything; she feels vulnerable now after she was so sure it was a trick until she found out someone really did see through her," Galan exclaimed.

"What on earth can I do about that now? She wouldn't want to hear anything I have to say. She thinks I told you those things," Avan pointed out.

"But you didn't, Avan; all you need to do is show her that it's ok to feel that way. She doesn't have to hide that part of herself, especially not with you. Now go before she gets too far away," Galan advised.

Without another moment's hesitation, Avan swiftly rose from his seat, a surge of urgency propelling him forward as he rushed for the door.

"Hey, Sydney!" Avan called out.

Sydney kept walking quickly; Avan ran and caught up to her. "Sydney, wait up," he pleaded.

"What do you want, Avan?" Sydney barked.

"Are you ok?" asked Avan.

"I'm fine," Sydney curtly replied.

"It's ok to feel the way that you do. I want you to know you can be yourself around me," Avan repeated Galan's words.

"And what makes you think I need your sympathy?" questioned Sydney. The intensity of her anger was palpable, leaving Avan momentarily taken aback as she left him standing in the parking lot.

Avan returned to Grounded defeated, his head low and his stride sloppy. The group walked past him on their way out, thanking him for buying them coffee. Avan didn't say a word as he walked up to the bar and sat down quietly. Galan finished cleaning up and donned his blazer.

"Why would you do that?" Avan asked with sorrow in his voice.

"How ugly was it?" Galan remarked with a smile.

"You're smiling? This is horrible! She hates me now, and I made a fool of myself when I went out there. So, why are you smiling? Wait, you knew she would snap at me, but you told me to go anyway!?" Avan retorted.

"I did," Galan responded, his smile ever growing.

"This is fun for you? I really liked her, and you are just toying with my relationship for your amusement!" Avan agonized. "Why do you keep smiling?"

"Because it's exactly what I hoped would happen," Galan replied.

"You purposely set me up to ruin my chances with Sydney?" Avan stated.

"Because, Avan, this is just a setup for step one. Ignore her in favor of someone else. Subconsciously, she will feel insecure and develop a need for the attention she was not given. Now she's in her head wondering, 'Why didn't he look at me, answer me or wave back?' Only this time, you have something extra going for you. She was rude to you when all you were trying to do was be there for her. So the next time you see her, don't be rude but ignore her presence. When the guilt eats away at her, she will come to you to apologize for how she acted out," Galan explained.

"Holy shit, you're a genius," Avan gasped.

"The real genius is what we will do next," said Galan with a smirk.

"What are we going to do?" asked Avan.

"We are going to get you the cologne she is wearing; it's a men's cologne from LVTCH. So, the next time she approaches you with all that guilt and smells that cologne on you, all those unresolved feelings will carry over to you. And that's when you get your shot," Galan enlightened him.

"How do you know to do this?" asked Avan in amazement.

"I've been chasing love my entire life; every time I had my heart broken, I tried to be better so it didn't happen again. Losing love is one of the deepest pains in existence. Come on, let's go get you that cologne and maybe a hoodie so she steals it from you," Galan replied. They hopped into the car, the engine humming to life as they left the University behind and drove back to the city.

Chapter Seven

As the clock struck three, Avan expertly maneuvered the car toward the entrance of Écarlate. He brought the vehicle to a graceful halt, its engine humming with a gentle purr. "Thank you, Avan, it was a pleasure," said Galan.

"No, please, I should be thanking you, Sir… Ah… I mean, Galan," Avan facepalmed.

"Just this once, I'll allow it. Do you remember what I told you?" asked Galan.

"That I should call you 'Sir' if there is sexual tension between us?" Avan responded.

Galan took a deep breath and covered his face. "Not that, Avan, about Sydney," Galan chuckled.

"Walk me through it again; I am still unclear about the plan. I know I seem well put together, but believe it or not, I panic a lot," Avan mumbled.

"You? Never!" said Galan sarcastically.

"It's true," Avan replied.

"Take out your phone and record this. I want you to listen to this and ensure you get it right, ok?" Galan instructed.

"Ok," Avan reached for his phone and started recording.

"You're going to ignore Sydney when next you see her, but not in a rude way. Do it as though you are not overwhelmed by her presence. Act like she doesn't make you panic. The next thing she will do is apologize. She lashed out at you when you were only trying to help, and it will bother her. When she does, and this is crucial, you need to be wearing the hoodie I bought you and the cologne. When she apologizes, let her speak a little before stopping her. Tell her that she doesn't owe you anything. Then get close to her and make contact—tuck her hair behind her ear or lay your hand on her shoulder. The point of this is to get close enough that she smells that cologne on you. And as you walk away, not letting her say her piece, it's going to trigger her the same way the last guy made her feel, and then she would project that onto you. After that, I can't help you. It's up to you to win her over; all I can do is get you in the door," Galan explained.

Avan saved the voice recording. "What if I panic and mess up after that?" Avan remarked.

"All you need is a chance for her to get to know you. I'm sure you would grow on her," Galan smiled.

"Thank you, Galan, for the coffee, and the advice, and the cologne, and the hoodie, and—" Avan rambled.

"You're welcome, Avan," Galan cut him off.

"If you need anything, you can call me day or night. Except at night when I'm asleep and not during the day when I have school or work. You know it's not safe to drive and text, but that's neither here nor there—" Avan babbled.

"There is something you can do for me; just tell Belle I said, 'Nice try,'" Galan's voice resonated with a touch of warmth and gratitude as he uttered the words, cutting Avan short. With a gentle click, he released the lock on the door, and a breath of looming victory greeted him as he stepped out of the car.

I have everything I need; Paige won't make it to tonight. We can finally be free of that wretched woman, and I can finally stop running!

Galan's presence exuded confidence and poise as he strolled through the hotel's opulent lobby. As he neared the elevator doors, the soft glow of elegant chandeliers cast a warm radiance upon his path.

Stepping onto the elevator, Galan calmed his mind. He leaned against the elevator's back wall, arms folded, holding the bags from his errands. The doors closed with a hushed whisper, encapsulating Galan; he stood amidst mirrored panels, the reflections capturing glimpses of his contemplative expression. Galan's anticipation grew as the elevator glided upward, knowing that upon its doors opening again, he would step into a new chapter of his life and be one step closer to achieving his goal of starting a new life. With his phone firmly gripped in his hand, Galan's focus was fixed on the screen, his eyes absorbing the words of Belle's earlier message. The soft glow of the display illuminated his features, casting a faint light on his intense expression. Belle's message revealed Paige's elusive room number. Galan's brows furrowed slightly, a testament to his determination to follow through on his plan. Every word he read felt like a breadcrumb leading him closer to his goal.

There it is, the first room off the elevator; it is definitely the room Malek stayed in. Is there a connection here? Maybe I'm overthinking it; Aria put Malek there, and it's possible her dad did the same to Paige. Perhaps that room is nicer? Regardless of whether it is a coincidence or not, it doesn't affect the plan. Now all I need to do is send up a bottle of that Champagne to the room and show up for a little while.

Galan swiped his room key and entered his room. He shrugged off his blazer, allowing it to slide from his shoulders gracefully. He rolled his sleeves past his elbow and sat with the bottle, carefully removing the cork and keeping the seal intact.

Four drops are the recommended dilution for a bottle that holds only one liter. This entire bottle of nutmeg can easily be mixed in with the Champagne; the concentration would lack any taste and burn like alcohol usually does as she swallows it. And because of the alcohol, it would enter her bloodstream quickly.

Galan poured some of the Champagne and replaced the amount with a high concentration of nutmeg, gently swirling the bottle and mixing the liquid into the Champagne. He carefully placed the seal back on the bottle and walked over to the hotel phone beside his bed.

No... If I call this in, they can trace it back to me. I need a different way to get this bottle in there. I know! Dana can get her father to send a bottle up to the room. I can make the switch the moment they bring it up. There are no cameras in the halls, so it should be easy to do without suspicion. And I have to see her drink it. Paige is crafty; if it gets sent up without any context, she would be suspicious, so I'll need to confront her. All she needs is a sip and its lights out. I will be the last thing she sees before she dies. Consider this a mercy, Paige; I wanted you to die screaming.

Galan dialed Dana, and she soon picked up. "Hey! How is your day going?" asked Dana.

"Not as good as yours, I hope," Galan replied.

"Dad and I are just spending some time together; we aren't doing much," Dana responded.

"Well, that's good; I need your help," said Galan.

"What's wrong?" Dana asked in a worried tone.

"Nothing is wrong; I have a plan to get rid of Paige. I'm taking a page out of Aria's friends' book. They tried to poison me by spiking a drink; unfortunately for them, I don't consume alcohol. I need you to get your dad to send Paige a bottle of Champagne and leave the rest to me," Galan quickly explained.

"Champagne, Galan? What the hell are you going to do with her?" Dana barked.

"Do you trust me, love?" asked Galan.

"You know I do," Dana answered.

"I'm only there as a distraction. Don't worry about Paige, ok? I love you," Galan professed.

No…. You idiot… Why did you say that? Fuck that just slipped out; we have only really been together for a couple of days!

"Ok, I won't; just be safe," Dana responded before she hung up.

🍵 73 🍵

She didn't say it back... Nikki was right. I didn't know if I loved her, but she felt the same way... No, don't jump to conclusions. This is a tense situation; Dana knows my past with Paige, and Paige is the woman who killed her sister and almost killed her. It's fine; let's take down Paige first and then win Dana over the way I should have in the first place!

Galan received a text from Dana, 'On its way now.'

Alright, showtime.

Galan stood up, walked to the mirror in the bathroom, washed his face, and fixed his hair. He stared at himself in the mirror as the screams of the night Paige's house burnt down echoed in his head.

Galan quickly grabbed the bottle and hid it beneath the hand towel he'd dried his face with. He stood in the hallway, waiting for the elevator doors to open, counting as the dial increased the number above the elevator doors. The elevator opened on his floor, and inside was a staff member with a cart, wheeling in the Champagne. Galan walked into the staff member and almost knocked down the bottle of Champagne. He quickly apologized. With the man focused on Galan, he promptly placed the spiked bottle on the cart, moved the towel over the new one, and snatched it off the coach.

Galan stepped onto the elevator and went down two floors to the hotel's shops. He tossed the handtowel into a housekeeping cart and held the bottle of Champagne in his hand as he entered the clothing store. Nikki was nowhere in sight. Galan approached the nearest staff member.

"Excuse me, could you deliver this to Nikki for me, please? Tell her it's from Galan," Galan instructed.

"She's right in the back. Would you like me to get her for you?" asked the young lady.

"She and I are not on the best of terms right now; I wouldn't want to upset her any more than I already have," Galan answered.

"Sure, I can give this to her," the young lady replied.

"Thank you, and tell her congrats on the engagement," Galan finished.

"I will," said the young lady.

Galan quickly went back to the elevator and traveled up to his floor. The doors opened, and Galan exhaled deeply.

Go time!

Galan walked to Paige's door and knocked. The door swung open as if in response to his presence, revealing a figure standing before him. Time momentarily froze as Galan's gaze met the familiar yet unexpected face. A chill traveled down his spine, and his blood ran cold.

"Galan?" said Lillie with a smile.

"Lillie…." Galan whispered.

FUCK!

Chapter Eight

Galan's once-tense posture softened, his shoulders slumping as if a weight had been lifted. His arms gently fell to his sides, the tension dissipating, and his eyes sparked with emotion. His lips parted, a faint tremor betraying his attempt to form words. Galan's mind raced, thoughts colliding and intertwining, each word struggling to find its way past the tangled maze of emotions. Lillie stepped out into the hallway with him, taking his hand gently into hers. "Galan," she whispered in a soft, hushed tone, her words a gentle caress upon his ears, carrying a delicate vulnerability. Galan's breath caught, his heart skipping a beat. With a tender touch, she parted his hands, her fingers gliding along his palms as if tracing the contours of their shared emotion. In a seamless motion, she slipped into his embrace, finding solace within the shelter of his arms. Galan's body remained stubbornly immobile, refusing to obey him. Gasping for air, each breath came in ragged bursts, the surrounding hallway disappearing around him; all he could see was her. Lillie tugged at his shirt. "Come in," she said, looking up at him with her beautiful brown eyes. Entranced by her presence, he followed her lead with a sense of surrender, his actions dictated by an invisible force akin to a puppeteer's strings.

Lillie and Galan stepped out onto the spacious balcony, their footsteps marking the end of the lingering silence that had enveloped them. "Galan, why do you look like you've seen a ghost?" Lillie remarked.

Galan took a deep breath, "Lillie... I thought you were dead. Your house burnt down after...." He turned away, unable to finish his sentence.

"After what?" asked Lillie.

"...After I lost control and killed your family," Galan finished.

"You did what?!" Lillie gasped.

"Nobody knew they were murdered; the fire destroyed everything. I'm sorry if this is how you find out, but I will not lie to you about what happened," Galan confessed.

"Galan, I knew I lost my family in that fire and made peace with that years ago. This doesn't change the pain I healed from," Lillie informed him.

"Why won't you hate me?" Galan inquired.

"Because I do not believe you did that. Not for a moment. I remember every moment of our childhood; I remember that cute kid next door whose family used to beat him raw, kicked him out, and left him to sleep in a rotting cupboard. I remember watching you roam the streets and beg for your next meal as a child, and despite all that, you always managed to smile. That kid would have never done that. I don't know what happened back then, but Galan, that was not your fault. Whatever happened was an accident," Lillie comforted him.

"You don't understand, Paige—" Galan was cut off.

"Paige helped you burn down the house to destroy any evidence of what happened. I know about that, too," Lillie exclaimed.

"What...," Galan fell to his knees.

Lillie slowly got to her knees; as they met on the ground, an unspoken vulnerability washed over Galan, overtaking his emotions like a relentless tide. Tears welled up in his eyes, shimmering with the weight of unspoken words and unsung melodies.

Slowly, like crystalline streams, they traced a path down his cheek, each droplet a testament to the depth of his feelings. "What happened was an accident, but I am alive. This burden has been anchoring you down. Tell me you haven't been dragging this with you all these years," Lillie cupped his face in her palms.

"Please… Stop," Galan whispered, closing his eyes.

"I never stopped thinking about you, Galan. You don't know how it broke my heart to see you after all these years in the arms of another," Lillie professed sadly, her hands tracing a path of warmth and solace, gliding with a feather-light grace down the contours of Galan's neck.

"Lillie—" Galan gasped.

"Do you love her?" asked Lillie.

Do I? Dana didn't say it back. No, this is a trick… This is Paige's doing. No! Stop Galan! Stop, this isn't you. You wouldn't betray Dana like this. It's a setup; this is only meant to tear you from Dana! No! Paige is doing this to you…

Galan backed away and stood up, "No… This isn't me!" He calmed his breathing. "Lillie, I am so happy to see you, I really am. But this can't happen." Galan walked past Lillie and made his way through the room.

"Does she love you?" Lillie repeated loudly.

Galan's outstretched hand hovered just inches away from the door, frozen in hesitation. In that suspended moment, a wave of uncertainty washed over him, causing his fingers to tremble ever so slightly.

"Tell me that she loves you, and I can move on. I promise to leave this city and go back to the life I had. I didn't come here because Paige begged me; I came here because I haven't had a kiss, or my hands held, or a hug in my life and not wished it was yours instead. You once told me that you wanted your first to be your last; I still do, too," Lillie said as she knelt on the balcony.

Galan's eyes grew fierce. He slowly turned and looked at Lillie, "I will not be manipulated, not anymore. As far as I am concerned, you died and burned in that house. And like your sister, you can go to hell!" Enraged, Galan opened the door and slammed it shut after exiting. Lillie was left in tears sobbing on the floor of the balcony.

Galan returned to his room, closed the door, and leaned against it, breathing heavily; tears flowed down his face and dripped on the ground.

Paige, you monster. I can't believe you would stoop so low. The old me would have crumbled, but I am not that person anymore. You will not take any more from me. I almost caved; I still can't believe I did that back there. This has gone too far; we have to do something now before you push me beyond a point I can't come back from.

Galan called Dana; he walked over to the bed and sat down.

Dana answered. "What happened? Did it work?" she asked.

"No, Paige threw me a curveball. I went to finish it, but I found Lillie in the room instead," Galan replied.

"What?!" Dana exclaimed.

"She tried to stir up the feelings I had for her, but I shut it down. Lillie will leave this city soon; I told her she's dead to me, and she could go to hell with her sister," Galan filled her in.

"Where is Paige then?" questioned Dana.

"I don't know, but we know exactly where she would be tonight. D, we need to put an end to this tonight!" Galan declared.

"What are you going to do?" asked Dana.

"She's using your dad to blackmail us; I say we flip the script. At dinner tonight, when she shows, we expose her and let your dad take care of the rest," answered Galan.

"Ok, that sounds like a plan," Dana agreed.

"See you tonight, love," said Galan.

"See you soon, Galan," Dana ended the call.

Galan... There it is again. Am I missing something? Nikki, then Lillie... What do they see that

I can't? Does she not love me? No, Paige is getting into my head; she wants this. I can't let her keep toying with me. I just need a few more hours; the moment she sits at the table tonight, her faith will be sealed.

Galan's mind raced; his childhood memories kept flashing before his eyes, and glimpses of Lillie and Paige looped in his head. Galan kept seeing himself standing in front of that burning building, the heat scorching his skin as he screamed Lillie's name in the pouring rain.

Drown it out; you can't fight your past inside your head and outside in the real world too. Think of her; think of Dana. The day you met her, and she spilled coffee all over you. Remember how you wanted to throw her off the mountain for being a brat. Galan smiled. *Think about how she craved you, how she begged. Despite all your mistakes, Dana chose you, and you did right by her. You waited four years for this; you let her live her life and didn't take advantage of her as Eder did. Dana will be the light that guides you out of the pit Paige left you in.*

Nikki's words echoed in his mind, "Did you ever say you loved her?"

Lillie's followed, "Does she love you? Tell me that she loves you—"

Galan got out of bed, walked into the bathroom, ran the water, and washed his face. He looked up at the mirror and saw his younger self standing in the rain, looking back at him as Paige held him close. Galan lost control and slapped the toiletries off the counter; he let out a furious grunt, stormed out, and walked onto the balcony.

This is my fault. I shouldn't have kept you locked away all those years. I should have killed you when I showed up at your doorstep that day. I couldn't move on; I couldn't let another person in because of the lies and the betrayal. I couldn't handle it, and I turned to you. I should have left you to rot in Salt Pine Acres, but even today, I can't shake the thought of you. Every time it goes downhill, I always come running back. I blame myself; I left something to run back to. Not anymore; I will burn the bridges just to see you drown!

Chapter Nine

The sun descended. Gracefully teasing the horizon line, the sky erupted in majestic golden rays. Galan stood on the balcony watching the sunset. Occasionally, his gaze landed on the mountains where Salt Pine Acres sat atop. Freshly out of the shower, his suit was immaculate, and his mane tamed as he looked out at the vast city, the sunlight delicately fading off his skin as it submerged beneath the horizon. Suddenly, there was a knock at the door before it swung open.

Dana elegantly entered the room; her figure was adorned in an exquisite black dress that accentuated her every curve. Her confident steps echoed on the polished floor, each one amplified by the click of her high heels. The shimmering diamond necklace gracefully embraced her neck, reflecting the soft glow of the room's ambient light.

Taken aback by the stunning transformation, Galan felt his heart skip a beat, its rhythmic cadence momentarily disrupted. A surge of emotions coursed within him as his pulse quickened, his senses captivated by Dana's enchanting allure. In that suspended moment, time seemed to stand still, allowing him to appreciate her beauty. "Dana...." he smiled.

"Hey, you. Aren't you going to tell me how beautiful I look in this dress?" Dana beamed.

This is it; win her over.

Galan gently reached out and tenderly took Dana's delicate hand. With a firm yet tender grip, he guided her toward the balcony. With Dana standing before him, he interlocked their fingers on one hand. "Look up," said Galan.

"Look up?" Dana repeated before doing so.

"Do you see that?" asked Galan.

"All I see is the sky," Dana replied, confused.

"Look further; there is an entire universe out there. There are two hundred sextillion stars; it's not as dirty as it sounds," Galan quickly stated. He and Dana smiled. "A vast universe, mysteries, and possibilities lay among the stars. In an infinite universe, I can, without a shadow of a doubt, truthfully tell you there is nowhere I would rather be than by your side."

Dana's look of confusion vanished. Her eyes moved from the Heavens and fell to Galan's. Galan placed his hand on her neck, stroking her cheek with his thumb. "Dana, I have been searching for love all my life, and I didn't just find it with you; you redefined it for me. Love was about waiting, about setting you free; it was wanting something for you even if I couldn't give it to you then. But I can, and I will surrender to the heavens above to prove my devotion to you," Galan professed as he leaned in and kissed her lips.

Gently pulling back, their lips lingered a hair's breadth from each other, their eyes locked and their breathing unruly. "Say you'll be mine," Galan whispered.

"Yes," Dana gasped.

"Yes, Sir," Galan replied with a smile.

"Yes, Sir," Dana repeated before kissing him back.

Galan pulled away and kissed down her neck. "Good girl," he softly murmured.

Each tender press of his lips against her soft skin sent ripples of pleasure through Dana's body, igniting a primal flame within her. The warmth of his breath mingled with the delicate fragrance that enveloped her, creating an intoxicating symphony of sensations. Galan glided his hands down the sides of her curves until he finally made it to one knee.

Dana's body tensed as the realization of Galan's actions dawned upon her. He gently took her hand and looked up at her, his gray eyes glimmering in the night. "Galan...," she whispered.

"Remember this moment because the next time you see me like this, I will ask you to spend the rest of your life with me," Galan placed both knees on the ground. "Right now, I want to get you out of these shoes and peek at what's under this dress." Galan slipped off her high heels and traced his hand up her leg, lifting her dress. He lifted her leg and placed it over his right shoulder, sliding his body further between her legs. He kissed her inner thigh, slowly moving further and further up. Dana ran her fingers through his thick hair and pulled him closer. Moaning softly, she tilted her head back in pleasure.

A knock at the door broke the tension. Galan stopped and got to his feet; Dana groaned. "Crap, I forgot about that."

"This was you?" Galan smiled.

"I'm sorry I ruined the moment," Dana remarked.

"There will be many more to come; I can forgive losing on this one," Galan smiled and walked to the door.

Galan opened the door; a staff member rolled in a cart with candles, a silver cloche, and a cup of coffee. Galan thanked the young man and closed the door behind him.

Dana strolled into the room with a mischievous smile adorning her lips, exuding an air of playful intrigue. Every step she took seemed to carry an alluring charm as if she held a secret that begged to be discovered.

"What's this?" Galan inquired curiously.

"Well," Dana lifted the silver cloche and revealed a sandwich. "This is a grilled chicken breast, glazed in a smoked honey sauce, with pickles for some sourness that balances the sweet lettuce, tomatoes, and smoked gruyere cheese. Toasted and pressed on both sides; seasoned with—" Dana explained.

"Black truffle salt… This is the sandwich I made for you when we met four years ago," Galan exclaimed, stunned.

Dana picked up the cup of coffee and held it to Galan's nose. "What is this?" asked Dana.

Galan held her hand steady and took a whiff, "A caramel macchiato—"

Dana chuckled and spilled it over Galan's unsuspecting figure. A playful glimmer danced in her eyes as the liquid cascaded down, drenching his shirt and blazer. "Oh fuck, I'm so sorry," Dana smiled.

Galan looked at her, "The first words you ever said to me…."

"Except this time, you don't have on your hydrophobic suit. Hmm, I guess we need to get you out of these clothes, huh," Dana claimed as she undid his blazer button and slid it off his shoulders. Undoing each shirt button, she opened his shirt and gently ran her fingers down his chest. "Guess I didn't ruin the moment, huh?"

Is this… Love?

"Where have you been?" Galan whispered.

"Waiting for you to come back for me," Dana answered before kissing him deeply.

Galan chuckled, "Your dad isn't going to like me coming to meet him underdressed again."

"Don't worry, I had them bring up another suit. We should get you cleaned up; we don't want to be late for dinner," Dana stated.

Galan and Dana hurried to the rooftop restaurant. Stepping off the elevator, they were escorted to their table by a waitress. Galan's fingers gently intertwined with Dana's as they made their way across the rooftop. With every step they took, he held her hand firmly as if anchoring himself to her presence, his eyes fixed on her with an unwavering focus. Despite the allure of the stunning rooftop view and the bustling ambiance of the restaurant, Galan's gaze remained fixated on Dana as they walked over to their table.

Surrounded by a security team, Mr. Scarlet stood upon their arrival, shaking Galan's hand and kissing Dana on the cheek. Galan pulled out Dana's chair for her and sat down beside her.

"You two look lovely," Mr. Scarlet remarked.

"Thanks, Daddy," Dana replied.

"Suit, watch, ring, cufflinks, tie. I'm shocked you didn't come down in a t-shirt and messy hair again," Mr. Scarlet grinned.

"Well, to be fair, we knew we were expecting guests this time. Had a little extra time to look presentable," Galan smirked.

Mr. Scarlet chuckled, "Speaking of guests, Ms. Paige should be with us shortly." Looking behind Galan, he saw the elevator doors open and Paige stepping off. "Nevermind, here she is now."

Galan momentarily closed his eyes; he and Dana looked at each other before turning around to see Paige strutting toward them in a short black laced dress with stockings and high heels. "Sorry I'm late," Paige said as she walked past them and sat beside Mr. Scarlet.

Dana and Galan stared daggers at her, but Paige, unphased by their soured looks, sat with high spirits.

"Shall we get to it?" asked Paige.

"Let's order first; we can discuss that after," Mr. Scarlet suggested.

"I think she's right; let's get this out of the way now," Dana expressed.

"I agree; this can't wait," Galan added.

"You two seem eager to get this underway," Mr. Scarlet observed.

Paige sat back in her chair, keeping calm; she smiled and looked at Galan and Dana.

"Very well, Ms. Paige, your meeting," Mr. Scarlet sighed.

"Four years ago, the Salt Pine Acres Massacre shook the world. Rumors of what society is calling the 'Blood Rain Ripper' surfaced, and the news channels pushed this propaganda on every major network. There was a single photo of a man covered in blood, wearing a suit with a knife in hand. I believe that person to be Galan," Paige began. Dana and Mr. Scarlet sat forward. "Before anyone does something they regret, let me finish.

"Galan is the only reason Dana made it out of Salt Pine Acres alive; whoever took that picture must have had a vendetta against him. I don't think the ripper is Galan; I think it's a woman. A woman he was involved with, and when she found out Galan was in love with another, she came to Salt Pine Acres plotting her revenge," Paige continued.

Zam ran up to the table and whispered in the ear of Mr. Scarlet. "Excuse me, there is something I need to attend to urgently," Mr. Scarlet apologized as he and his security detail followed Zam hurriedly to the elevator.

"What's happening?" Dana wondered.

"I don't know," Galan replied.

"What have you done!?" hissed Dana.

"I'm putting this behind us," Paige responded.

"What?" Galan exclaimed.

"Hurting Master is the last thing I ever want. If this charade continues, he will eventually lose everything," Paige explained.

"What did you do!" Galan growled.

"I put an end to the Salt Pine Acres Massacre," Paige calmly repeated.

"What does that mean?" asked Dana.

"We both know Master is part of that ordeal, but if Dana tells Daddy that I left a knife in her gut, I would never see the light of day again. So, I have a third person who ties into the events of that tragic incident. I will leave here tonight, and you will not see me again. Play along with my story. It's a win-win. Or you can rat me out and tell them the truth: that Master kept me locked away for eight years against my will, and I escaped and killed those people. But then Master's face will be attached to that story faster than you can make it to the elevators," Paige remarked.

"Bullshit! Why would you leave?" Galan prodded.

"Master never gave me a choice," answered Paige.

"Stop calling him Master!" barked Dana.

"If that's true, then why go through all this trouble? Why bring Lillie here? Why go to Dana's father to leverage us?" questioned Galan.

"Because you ran, and Dana was in a hospital for months. I went to him because he had everything I needed to bring you out of hiding. I want to make amends and leave this behind me; I am sure Master can relate to that," Paige relayed to him.

Dana slammed her fist on the table, "Call him Master again, and I swear to God the next bloody massacre to make the news will be yours!"

Galan touched her leg, saying, "Don't let her rile you up."

"This can go one of two ways. You play along, I walk out of here, and you never hear from me again; you have my word. Or, Galan and I both take the fall, and I reveal the truth, not to your Dad but to the world. I won't just destroy his life; I will tear down what you built. Grounded Coffee House will be done for. And while Daddy sweeps it under the rug, it will stain the name Scarlet forever, and I wonder what consequences will come with that? Not to mention the photos and videos I have from Galan's phone—all the voice recordings he made and everything those cameras in Grounded Coffee House recorded," Paige calmly stated.

"You…," Galan groaned.

"Listen to me; I don't want this. I just want my life back. You took me away from everything I held dear, the only family I had left. I want to be with them again. But I can't, knowing what you are capable of. So please, I am begging for mercy. I want my old life back in exchange for your new life. We bury the past and walk away," a tear ran down Paige's cheek as she expressed this.

She's crying?... I've never seen her cry, not even when she lost her family.

Galan stood up and pulled Dana aside.

"Are we going to believe her?" Dana whispered.

"She's serious, D. I don't think she is lying," Galan exclaimed.

"And what if you're wrong about her?" questioned Dana.

"She could have sold me out with those files to your Dad from day one. She was careful about this; she avoided us until this moment. She needed us to listen; we can't do anything to her right now and vice versa," Galan reasoned.

Paige tossed something to Galan; he quickly reacted and caught it. "It's everything I have on you. Have it checked to see if any copies were ever made. It's yours. Mr. Scarlet is coming back soon; what is it going to be? Do we go our separate ways, or shall we sink together?" asked Paige.

"What's the catch?" Dana remarked.

"No catch, but I have one request," said Paige.

"Of course you do," Galan replied.

"I want to say goodbye to Master in private," Paige exclaimed.

"Absolutely not!" Dana immediately responded.

"Deal!" Galan answered.

"What are you doing?" Dana whispered.

"Burning bridges," Galan replied softly.

"Galan, what if she hurts you?" asked Dana.

"She wouldn't touch Master without his permission," Galan stated.

Dana and Galan settled into their seats, their anticipation mingling with a sense of curiosity. As they awaited Mr. Scarlet's return, the atmosphere around them seemed to hold a subtle tension, as if a shift in dynamics was about to unfold. Paige was not brandishing her usual menacing smile. Instead, her eyes carried a genuine sadness, lending an air of vulnerability to her expression. It was as if a veil had been lifted, revealing a depth to Paige they had not seen before.

You're up to something; I can feel it. I don't buy this for a moment, but you're dragging Dana and her father into this. You have no family; I killed everyone else back then. Why would you bring Lillie here if what you truly wanted was to go back to your family and live in peace? You have an ace up your sleeve; whatever you plan to say in private is your endgame. Lillie was your big plan, and that failed. Nothing you throw at me now can save you.

Mr. Scarlet

AGE: 46
SIGN: CAPRICORN
FUN FACT: "I NEVER MARRIED ARIA AND
DANA'S MOTHER. SHE DIED GIVING BIRTH TO
DANA."

Chapter Ten

The table was cloaked in an oppressive silence, each passing moment amplifying the tension between Galan and Dana. Their piercing gazes bore into Paige, who maintained an unwavering composure, poised and patient amidst the storm of their scrutiny. The minutes dragged on, elongating the unease in the room, until finally, Mr. Scarlet reappeared, flanked by his formidable security detail. With an air of tranquil authority, he reclaimed his seat, seemingly undisturbed by the palpable tension lingering in the air.

"You're welcome," said Paige.

A collective gaze descended upon Paige. Every pair of eyes at the table fixated on her, anticipation and curiosity intertwining in a silent demand for her next move.

"What are we missing here?" asked Dana.

"They found your sister's killer," Mr. Scarlet answered.

Galan and Dana's eyes swiftly locked. "Where?" Galan probed.

"She's lying dead on the floor in her room. She ingested a poison of some sort, stopped her heart," Mr. Scarlet replied.

"Wait, what? What do you mean she was poisoned?" Paige panicked.

"A bottle of Champagne was on the floor next to her; it exuded a robust aroma. Not one of our bottles; someone brought it in from the outside. We cross-checked the inventory log, and that bottle was never part of our stock," Mr. Scarlet remarked.

Galan's heart skipped a beat. *No… That bottle went to Paige's room. Oh my God!*

Sensing Galan's momentary tremor, Dana instinctively turned towards him, her concern etched across her face.

"Ms. Paige was right; a love interest in Galan's past was at the hotel. We were ready to apprehend and take her as Ms. Paige had instructed, but she was already on the ground when they entered the room. It seemed as though she was preparing to leave too. Good riddance; there is no justice for a monster who would take a child from a parent," Mr. Scarlet exclaimed. "Staff also said she kept going to Galan's room and was seen standing outside. We speculate she was waiting for Dana; I'm glad this is behind us."

Tears erupted from Paige's eyes, cascading down her face in a torrent of raw emotion. Overwhelmed, she abruptly pushed away from the table, abandoned her seat, and sprinted towards the waiting elevators, her heartache echoing through the empty corridors.

"Ms. Paige?" Mr. Scarlet called.

"Stay here, love," said Galan.

"What's going on?" asked Dana.

"It's Lillie," Galan whispered. "Excuse me," Galan told Mr. Scarlet before going after Paige.

Galan's desperate pursuit fell seconds short as the elevator doors sealed shut, severing his path to Paige. With a surge of determination, he surveyed his surroundings, his eyes alighting upon a nearby stairway entrance. Without hesitation, he sprinted down four flights of stairs to reach the floor where his room awaited, hoping to intercept Paige before the weight of her anguish consumed her entirely.

Paige's desperate attempts to forcefully open the door yielded no results, leaving her disheartened and exhausted. Galan cautiously approached, pausing a few feet away, his heart aching at the sight of her tear-streaked face. Overwhelmed by emotions, Paige crumbled against the unyielding door, slumping down until she found solace on the floor, a shattered figure consumed by sorrow.

"I don't understand what the hell happened to her," Paige sobbed. Tears streamed down her anguished face as she unleashed her pent-up emotions. Frantically, she banged her head against the unyielding door, her despair reverberating through each collision. In a gut-wrenching release, she released a piercing scream, raw and untamed, echoing through the empty corridors, an anguished cry from the depths of her soul.

Galan quickly stooped beside her and put her hand over her mouth, stifling the scream. Paige broke down further into tears, flowing through Galan's fingers.

No… What did I do? I… I killed her.

Galan's consciousness was momentarily engulfed by a haunting flashback, his mind transported to a grim tableau. He stood frozen, staring at the lifeless bodies strewn across the floor of a house, a scene etched with the weight of tragedy and loss. The visceral recollection pierced his thoughts, intertwining with the present turmoil, amplifying his own inner torment.

"Get up; come with me," Galan ordered, taking Paige's hand and pulling her to her feet. He unlocked his room and took Paige inside, walking her onto the balcony.

Paige tried hard to stop her tears; Galan tenderly reached out, his touch a gentle reassurance as he delicately wiped them away. "Stop crying," he whispered. Though briefly soothed by Galan's comforting presence, Paige's inner turmoil proved insurmountable. Despite her attempts to regain composure, the weight of her emotions overwhelmed her once again, and she succumbed to another torrent of tears.

"Kneel——" Galan commanded.

Paige turned to him in tears.

Galan wrapped his hand around her throat; he stepped closer to her, their bodies touching. Paige looked up at him through watery eyes. "I said Kneel… Do it now," Galan softly instructed.

Paige's sorrow ceased; she lowered herself to her knees with quiet obedience, maintaining unwavering eye contact with Galan.

"What happens if you defy me?" asked Galan. His touch lingered on Paige's chin, his finger a gentle anchor that lifted her gaze to meet his own.

"I get punished," Paige replied.

"And how do you not get punished?" questioned Galan.

"I obey Master," Paige responded. Her tears were wiped away once more by Galan. Her eyes conveyed joy and lust, the sorrow fading with each word he spoke.

"Good girl," Galan whispered.

Paige smiled.

"I used to be able to come to you for anything. You were my solace once. Right now, I will put aside everything and be there for you," Galan professed as he knelt before her.

"Permission to speak, Sir?" Paige asked.

"Yes," Galan answered.

"I never wanted this. I know what I did to Master was wrong. I grew up in a house with no freedom. I couldn't leave the house or even speak to another person, much less find someone who loved me. I envied the love Master had for my little sister. The things you did for her... No matter what horrible things I forced you to do, Master did it with so much devotion to her. I wanted that.

"After the house burnt down and I ran away, finally free, Master returned, and I had a chance to have what she had. You had already had your heart broken by someone else, so I killed her because she hurt you. But Master locked me away; you dragged me to Salt Pine Acres and imprisoned me, and I lost that freedom I had longed for all my life.

"But when Master kept coming back to me, heartbreak after heartbreak, all I wanted was to protect you and show you the love you deserved. I acted out when Aria hurt you and lost Master for good then. I know that, and I wanted to earn your forgiveness and return to my old life. I wanted my freedom; I wanted your forgiveness," Paige stuttered, her words drawing to an end as she slowly came to tears.

Galan felt sympathy for her; the sincerity of her words broke through to him.

"I wanted to give you back everything I took from you; I just wanted to be with my family. I know you were in love with Dana, and I am sorry if I caused a riff between you, but she will never be good enough for Master. She won't obey you the way I will. But I knew any chance of a future with Master was lost when I dropped Aria's heart at your feet.

"I sent Lillie to find you; she didn't know you would have been on the yacht or the hotel. She didn't even know I was the one who made it happen. I used Mr. Scarlet's resources to help find her. All I wanted was to be with the family I lost and be free. Lillie was set up to be the fall guy for what happened in Salt Pine Acres. I shared your history with Mr. Scarlet, but I wasn't going to let him take her away. I had enough evidence to tear his empire to pieces and stain his good name. I intended to leverage him into letting

Lillie and I go free once we cleared your name and gave you a chance to have the love you once fought for," Paige explained. She bowed her head, and tears dripped on her thigh one by one.

Galan shook.

No... No... This isn't happening. I ruined the life I always wanted. I told her to burn in hell. She was telling the truth; it wasn't a ploy to drop my guard? No... I was too paranoid about Paige that I missed my chance.

Galan's mind became a kaleidoscope of memories, each fragment a vivid recollection of moments spent with Lillie. The warmth of her smile, the embrace of her hugs—each memory etched deeply within his heart. He was transported back to countless nights spent gazing at the stars, fervently wishing for a future intertwined with hers, their love like a constellation of hopes and dreams. In the midst of Galan's reverie, the haunting memory of the bloody bodies lying in their house and the consuming flames emerged like a dark specter. Yet, amidst the chaos of that recollection, a contrasting image emerged with piercing clarity—Paige shielding him from the scorching heat, her touch wiping away his tears. In that pivotal moment, she became his beacon of solace, a compassionate presence amidst the devastation, offering a glimmer of light amidst the darkness that threatened to consume him.

What have I done?

Galan's heart raced within his chest, its frantic rhythm echoing loudly in his ears. Overwhelmed by a surge of emotions, he instinctively stepped back, distancing himself from the weight of his memories and the intensity of his feelings.

"It doesn't matter what happens to me now; I lost the only family I had left. My life is worthless without love. Whatever Master and Dana decide to do with me is up to them. There is nothing left to fight for now," Paige exclaimed.

Galan hastily bolted out of the room. He hurried through the balcony doorway, unaware of Dana's presence. Dana had hidden; she was pressed against the adjacent wall trying to catch fragments of the conversation taking place, yearning for insight into the unfolding exchange.

Dana emerged from her concealed position, briefly glancing at the door with a mix of hesitation and determination. Without a second thought, she redirected her attention toward the balcony and stepped outside.

Paige looked up from the ground, "Dana…," she mumbled.

"What you said just now about me not being good enough for Galan... You don't know what you're talking about," said Dana angrily.

"That proves my point, Dana. I didn't say that because I hate you or I am jealous. You will never be the girl he needs; you call Master by his name. Master doesn't like that. Maybe he can let it go now, but someday you will not be what he needs, and I am only trying to protect you from the faith those girls before you suffered. He will ruin you, as he did to me. Look at me, Dana; all this is because I loved him and couldn't be what he needed. Please don't hate me; you understand what his love feels like," Paige pleaded.

"I don't believe that for a second; you don't fool me. You're where you are now because you're a monster," Dana stated.

"You think I'm a monster? Just wait because sooner or later, you will see the side of Master that he keeps buried. Being loved by him will only ever end one way. Take it from the person who loved him longer than anyone else," Paige remarked.

"I've heard enough. You gave us a choice; I say we go our separate ways. I don't care where you end up, so long as it's not within one hundred miles of me or Galan. Consider this mercy for my sister; at least your little scheme kept my family and Galan out of that mess," Dana expressed as she walked away.

Dana retraced her steps back to the restaurant, her mind swirling with a mélange of emotions. Meanwhile, Galan, anxiously attempting to reach her, had his eyes darting around, searching for any sign of her. A glimmer of hope sparked within him as he caught sight of Dana stepping out of the elevator. Without hesitation, he swiftly made his way to her.

"Hey, I was looking for you; where did you run off to?" asked Galan.

"To see Paige," answered Dana nonchalantly.

"What?" Galan exclaimed.

"I told her to be on her way and don't ever show her face anywhere near us again," Dana informed him as she quickly paced for the table. Dana sat down and asked for menus.

"Where did you run off to, Kitten?" Mr. Scarlet inquired.

"I went to let Paige know that she needs to be on the first flight out of here," Dana replied.

"Why would you do that?" probed Mr. Scarlet.

"Because she went off on her own and did all this, and they found Aria's killer. What if news gets out about this? Do you know why Grounded Coffee House blew up as much as it did? It's because of that story. If that story comes to a close now, then the hype will go away sooner. As long as people are talking about the Blood Rain Ripper and the Salt Pine Acres Massacre, it saves us millions in advertising. This opens the business up to new merch and themes from which we can profit even more. I want you to keep this quiet and send Paige on her way," Dana explained.

"That's my little girl," Mr. Scarlet smiled joyfully. "I have never felt as much pride as I do right now."

"That's why we built the head branch at the mountain base near Salt Pine Acres?" asked Galan.

"That's right," Dana smirked.

"Aria was right; you are a marketing genius," Galan beamed.

Paige came back to the table; the conversation stood still. "Excuse me, Mr. Scarlet. I just wanted to say thank you for helping me with this. I wanted to see the Ripper be brought to justice, and your resources helped me achieve that. I have no more business here. Can you do me one last favor and fly me out of the city?" Paige requested.

"Fly you where?" asked Mr. Scarlet.

"Somewhere far; I don't want to be within one hundred miles of this place. Maybe back to my hometown where I grew up?" Paige suggested.

"Very well, the jet is on standby at the tarmac. I will have my driver escort you. Are you sure you wouldn't like to stay for dinner? I owe you a great debt," Mr. Scarlet stated.

"You don't owe me anything, Sir. Thank you for the offer, but please, I would like to go now," Paige remarked.

Galan and Dana's eyes fixed upon Paige, their attention attuned to the unmistakable pain resonating in her voice.

"As you wish," Mr. Scarlet conceded.

With a solemn nod, Paige distanced herself from the table, escorted by a member of Mr. Scarlet's security detail. Meanwhile, Dana clasped Galan's hand, her victorious smile aimed at him, but Galan's mind was consumed by the shock of the life he had lost due to his own actions. Amidst Dana's smile, his thoughts plunged into the depths of remorse, grappling with the weight of consequences that had forever altered his existence—thoughts of the life that could have been with his first love.

Chapter Eleven

The air was filled with palpable festive energy as Mr. Scarlet and Dana reveled in the joy of the evening, while Galan, although partaking in the celebration, maintained a guarded silence, keeping his thoughts and emotions concealed about the events that had unfolded.

"The details of what happened today will be covered up. My security were the only ones to know what happened outside of Zam and Paige, neither of which would breathe a word about it. The authorities will handle this with the utmost discretion. I promise you this, Kitten," Mr. Scarlet declared.

"Thank you, Daddy; Galan and I have a lot of work to do for the grand opening of the head branch of Grounded," Dana informed him.

"And you built this from the ground up, correct?" Mr. Scarlet asked Galan.

"That's right, it used to be a butcher's shop. When the owner decided to sell the place, I made them an offer to buy the building, paying month by month until it was mine. I made it into what it was four years ago. Then when Dana bought it from me, her ambitions far exceeded my own. She always did say she could turn it into a multi-billion dollar company," Galan replied.

"Why not have ambitions to carry it further than you did?" Mr. Scarlet remarked.

"Perspective… For me, I went from being a homeless kid to what I am now. The freedom to start over and live a life that overshadowed the one I was leaving behind was enough for me. For Dana, that was commonplace," Galan answered.

"Admirable, I cannot say that I share that journey; neither does my daughter. But we met on common ground, and for that, you earned my respect. Not to mention you are the reason Dana is alive. Losing Aria was hard enough, but I would have gone mad if I had lost my little girl, too," Mr. Scarlet exclaimed.

"I can't imagine what it's like to lose a child like that. I would be broken beyond recognition. How do you do it?" asked Galan.

"I have someone to be strong for; as a parent, it's my duty to pave the way for my children. I would rather lose everything I have and suffer till my last breath than let her see me fall apart," Mr. Scarlet responded.

"Could we have a word in private? I could use some advice," Galan exclaimed.

Dana's gaze shifted purposefully towards Galan, her eyes filled with curiosity.

"Sure, make sure you're not having sex when a girl's father comes over," Mr. Scarlet chuckled.

"Daddy!" Dana's voice trembled slightly, revealing a touch of embarrassment that tinged her words.

With a gentle smile adorning his face, Galan rose gracefully from the table, delicately dabbing his mouth with a napkin, "Yes, well, I'll keep that in mind though I make no promises. Now if you would be so kind as to hear me out, I will be at the bar." Galan's steps carried him purposefully towards the bar, his gaze fixed on Dana as he playfully blew her a kiss.

"Excuse me, Kitten," said Mr. Scarlet.

"Please just go; I can't stand the two of you embarrassing me anymore," Dana chuckled.

Mr. Scarlet approached the bar and stood beside Galan. "What can I do for you, Galan?" he asked.

"Forget about me keeping Dana safe during the Salt Pine incident. That aside, I cared about Dana enough to wait for her and ask you for your blessing before I ask her to spend the rest of her life with me," Galan replied.

"Why do you want me to set aside the fact that you saved Dana?" Mr. Scarlet remarked.

"I want you to measure me for the man I am and not for an unexpected circumstance," Galan responded.

"Then you don't have my blessing," answered Mr. Scarlet promptly. "Galan, let me enlighten you. I deal with people daily, and I know the brown nosers when I see them. Don't try to faint nobility to win my approval; it's an insult to my intelligence. But another thing, you are the one who brought chaos into my children's lives. Aria is dead, and Dana will never have a wedding with her big sister at her side. I will never get to walk both of them down the aisle. Saving one doesn't excuse you from being the reason the other is gone. Though it may not be your intention, you tell me if you were a father and your child wanted to marry someone who was responsible for the death of their family member because they hurt someone so deeply they sought to murder an entire community of people to seek revenge, would you ever entertain that thought?" Mr. Scarlet stated sternly.

"You know, I don't give a fuck about your approval. But I just happen to know that Dana has spent her life trying to get that from you. You give me this made-up scenario to give you an answer that can only go one way? Well, here's the thing, I am not one of those people that are trying to kiss your ass. I don't need anything from you; Dana does. So step out of the fantasy scenario and back to the situation at hand, and you tell me, as a father with a child who lost everything, will you deny her what she wants? Because this sure as hell isn't for me," Galan remarked as he stepped away from the bar and rejoined Dana at the table.

Mr. Scarlet paused at the bar, his gaze lingering thoughtfully for a brief moment before he retraced his steps back to the table, his demeanor emanating a sense of contemplation, "Dinner was lovely. I hope we can do this more often, Kitten."

"You're leaving?" asked Dana.

"Yes, I have work to attend to; I pushed back my schedule to spend the day with you," Mr. Scarlet responded.

"If you leave now, then you won't be here for the grand opening," Dana said sorrowfully.

"I wish I could, Kitten; I'll try my best to be there," Mr. Scarlet assured her.

"I know you're busy, don't worry about it," Dana replied with a sad smile.

As Dana's mood abruptly shifted, Mr. Scarlet's perceptive gaze moved from her to Galan. He exchanged a knowing nod with his security detail, prompting their group to swiftly depart. As Zam interacted with a couple on their honeymoon, Mr. Scarlet's keen ears caught a fleeting mention of Galan's name from the guests, causing a flicker of curiosity to spark within him and a subtle shift in his demeanor as he absorbed this unexpected piece of information.

Mr. Scarlet turned towards Zam, his expression beckoning him with a sense of urgency. Zam responded with equal enthusiasm, swiftly making his way to Mr. Scarlet's side. "Yes, Mr. Scarlet, is everything to your liking?" asked Zam.

"Dinner was fine, Zam; tell me something. What was that young lady saying about Galan?" Mr. Scarlet queried.

"Oh, um, Mr. Rain is paying for their dinner. They were just telling me to give him their thanks," Zam replied.

"And why is he paying for their dinner?" questioned Mr. Scarlet.

Zam's shoulders slumped as he let out a deep exhale, a wave of shame washing over him, his head bowing to acknowledge his mistake. "That would be my fault, Sir. This morning at the front desk, I overheard Mr. Rain mentioning your dinner plans tonight, so I left those guests unattended as they were checking in. Mr. Rain was being attended by one of the newer employees, and I wanted to make sure there were no mistakes in tonight's proceedings upon your arrival," Zam rambled.

"What does that have to with him paying for their dinner?" asked Mr. Scarlet sternly.

"Mr. Rain apologized and took the blame; he told me to tell the guests he was being selfish for hogging the staff and to apologize on his behalf. He sent a bottle of Champagne to them and offered to pay for their dinner tonight so he could protect Écarlate's reputation and by extension yours. I am very sorry about that, Sir; it will not happen again," Zam apologized.

A flicker of surprise crossed Mr. Scarlet's face, his gaze momentarily shifting back to the table where Dana and Galan were seated, their hands intertwined and laughter echoing between them. "Carry on, Zam, also give them a complimentary extra day, breakfast included," he instructed before walking off.

A few minutes later, Dana's phone buzzed with a text message from her father, eliciting an eager spark in her eyes as she hastily unlocked her phone to excitedly read its contents. 'Give Galan my thanks. Quite a rude one he is, but I like him. Tell him I changed my mind.' Dana and Galan huddled together, reading the text message together, their eyes lighting up with joy and anticipation. Unable to contain her excitement, Dana planted a sweet kiss on Galan's lips.

"What is this about?" Dana smiled.

"Come, I'll show you," Galan replied.

Galan and Dana stormed his hotel room in a flurry of unbridled desire. Clutching him tightly, she wrapped her legs around his waist as they locked lips with frenzied abandon. He swept the door closed and pressed her back against it, trailing kisses down her neck while unleashing an inferno of passion. As he placed her on her feet, Galan's heated gaze explored every inch of her exposed body as he skillfully undressed her. He grabbed a handful of her hair and looped it around his wrist, tugging ever so slightly to make her moan. Then his lips trailed down her neck, exploring every inch of her body.

Dana reached up for his neck, and Galan quickly caught her hand. "No, not until I say you can," Galan growled. He let go of her hair and unhooked her bra; he took her to the bed, forcefully pushing her into the plush mattress, holding her arms together above her head. His lips ravaged her body. Dana moaned with each touch of his lips.

Galan took her underwear between his teeth; he slowly slipped them off, his hands gently holding her ankles. With her underwear at the tip of her toes, Galan made a swift flick of his head and tossed them off. He placed Dana's leg over his shoulder, kissing her ankles; he licked his fingers and slid them down the raised leg. Gently leaning on the edge of the bed, his moist fingers rested between her folds.

"Eyes on me," Galan instructed; he slid both fingers into her. Dana bit her lip and moaned. "I am the only one you look at that way, do you understand?" Galan curled his fingers upward and stimulated her G-spot.

"Mhmmm," Dana moaned.

"Tell me you understand," Galan demanded.

"Yes…," Dana gasped.

"Excuse me?" Galan went deeper.

Dana's moan enveloped the room. "Yes, Sir," she moaned.

"Good girl," said Galan as he slowly pulled his fingers out and sucked on them. "Do you remember how you spilled coffee on me today and ruined my shirt?"

"Yes, Sir," Dana replied.

Galan slid a hand under her waist and leaned into her; dropping his body to the side, he lifted Dana off the bed and onto his chest as he lay on his back. "You're going to sit here, and you're not allowed to move until I say so or until you ruin my shirt with your cum," Galan lifted her and seated her over his face.

Galan gorged himself between her legs, the warmth of her was on his lips as he slid his tongue inside. Dana slowly rode his face, moaning his name, her hands on his abs and her head tilted back, her cries of pleasure released toward the ceiling.

Dana screamed and leaned over Galan. The lower half of his face was soaked in her nectar as he lifted her and lay her on the bed. As Galan stood up and unbuttoned his shirt, his lips glistened from her juices. He licked his lips and moaned, "Mmm," wiping the excess with his index finger and licking it off before biting his lips as he held an intense gaze.

"Come and taste yourself on my lips," said Galan softly. Before she could move, Galan pulled her to the edge of the bed, leaned over, and kissed her.

"On your knees, do it now," Galan commanded.

Dana's hands froze as she recalled Galan's request to Paige. The weight of the moment settled upon her, and conflicting emotions surged within her. Doubt and uncertainty clouded her mind, making her question his intentions. The way she looked at him and how he responded to her obedience. Dana's heart pounded in her chest as conflicting emotions swelled within her. She reached for a robe, covered herself, and stepped back.

"Galan, stop," Dana's voice trembled with frustration and vulnerability as she spoke. She turned and walked out of the room, making her way to the balcony.

What did I do wrong?

Galan composed himself and followed Dana out to the balcony.

"D?" Galan softly called out.

"Galan, please, not now," said Dana.

"Did I do something you didn't like?" asked Galan. "Talk to me; tell me so I can stop," he gently pleaded.

Dana turned to him, her eyes glistening with oncoming tears, "I saw you, with Piage, right here. I saw the way you spoke to her and how she listened. Is that what you want from me? You want me to obey Master?" Dana remarked.

She's talking about when I tried to console Paige earlier; she saw that? How much? 'Kneel,' she heard when I asked her to 'kneel.'

"Dana, you are nothing like Paige. Please don't compare yourself to her," Galan pleaded.

"How can I not?" Dana responded.

"Paige was never allowed to touch me. She couldn't call me by my name; she couldn't disobey me," answered Galan.

"See! Disobey, thank you," Dana repeated.

"Love, where is this coming from? What did she say to you?" asked Galan.

"She said I would never be enough for you, and I thought she was wrong, but after seeing you like this—" Dana paused.

"Like what? Because I asked you to kneel and also said that to her?" questioned Galan.

"It's not just that; you don't like it when I don't say 'Sir' after I answer you; just now, when you took my dress off, I tried to reach around your neck and pull you closer, and you didn't let me. You said not until you said I can," Dana explained. "Oh my God, she was right!"

"Dana, please, it's not—" Galan began.

"Why can't we be equals? Over the last few days, you never did any of this stuff. What changed? Why do you have to be like this with me? Why can't we serve each other? Why do you want me to obey you like a good girl...." Dana's eyes fell on him.

"What?" Galan remarked with concern.

"You called her that too... You did it when she did as she was told," Dana gasped, tears streaming down her face.

No, don't tell me you went through all that just so you could get into Dana's head! But here is what you failed to account for...

As Galan reached out his hand, Dana hesitated for a moment, unsure whether to accept his gesture.

But sensing his sincerity and longing for connection, she finally gave in, took his hand, and stepped closer.

"I told you there isn't anywhere I would rather be than at your side. Let me prove that it wasn't just pretty words. I'm going to tell you everything, and if you feel the same and you want to leave, I'll understand. No 'Master,' no 'Sir,' it's just you and me, I promise," Galan stated.

"But what if you need those things one day and you grow tired of me? I don't want you to look at me and see all the things I can't give you. I don't want you to look at me and see Paige," Dana expressed.

Gently, Galan brushed away Dana's tears with his thumb, his touch comforting and soothing. His fingers trailed along her cheek, leaving a gentle caress in their wake, "All I will ever see... Is my future with you. It's what I saw the moment I came back for you."

"You can't know that; we've only been together for a couple of days," Dana sobbed.

"Then why don't I spend the rest of my life proving it to you," Galan answered. His movements were deliberate and purposeful as he lowered himself to one knee before Dana. His eyes never left hers. "I was hoping to do this differently, but I know I would regret it if I didn't ask you this now," Galan said as he took her hand.

"Galan...." Dana gasped.

"I want to choose you today and keep choosing you every day until the end of our lives together. Marry me?" Galan asked.

"Yes…," Dana whispered without hesitation.

Chapter Twelve

Galan and Dana returned home to her place the following morning. In the following days, they worked tirelessly together, overseeing every detail of the preparation for the grand opening of the main branch of Grounded Coffee House. They meticulously curated the menu, trained the staff, and ensured the ambiance reflected their vision. Dana's careful selection of top-performing staff members from various branches worldwide brought a diverse and talented team to the new Grounded Coffee House. She arranged for their relocation to a housing complex nestled a couple of miles up the mountain in the serene surroundings of Salt Pine Acres. This ensured a committed and skilled workforce and fostered a sense of community among the staff, further fueling their dedication to the establishment's success.

As Galan and Dana approached Salt Pine University, they were awestruck by the sight of the massive crowd that had gathered for the grand opening. The buzz of excitement filled the air, and they could feel the energy pulsating through the crowd. Pulling into the private garage of the building, they parked their car and turned to each other.

"Ready?" asked Galan.

"I've been ready for four years now," Dana replied.

Dana and Galan emerged from the car, their attire exuding professionalism and unity. Clad in matching black shirts, pants, and ties, they epitomized the dedication and style of Grounded Coffee House. With pride, they fastened their coffee brown aprons, proudly displaying the logo of their renowned establishment. They stood side by side, ready to embrace the day's challenges and triumphs; their attire symbolizing their shared vision and commitment to delivering an exceptional coffee experience.

Galan and Dana gracefully stepped onto the main floor, their presence commanding attention. The dedicated staff, filled with anticipation and readiness, stood poised at their designated stations, eagerly awaiting the bustling day ahead.

As they placed their thumbs on the biometric scanner, the building's exterior came alive in a mesmerizing display of technology. Brown LED lights illuminated the interior gaps of the walls, transforming the once opaque windows into transparent panes. Delicate coffee bean-shaped patterns adorned the glass, adding an artistic touch to the striking façade. The play of light and shadow created an enchanting ambiance, enticing passersby and beckoning them into the world of Grounded Coffee House.

Galan and Dana exchanged a nod of acknowledgment with the dedicated staff members who stood ready at their respective stations. Their eyes met, brimming with excitement and pride, as they shared a moment of anticipation. With beaming smiles, they turned towards the entrance of Grounded Coffee House, their hands reaching for the door handles and opening them.

Customers flooded inside, their eager footsteps creating a lively buzz in the air. The staff members swiftly sprang into action, skillfully attending to the growing number of orders, delivering trays of steaming beverages and delectable treats to the cozy booths and inviting tables. Galan and Dana, fueled by their passion for coffee, stood side by side behind the bar, their hands expertly maneuvering the espresso machines, blending flavors and crafting artful creations with precision and care. The symphony of clinking cups, friendly chatter, and satisfied sighs filled the space as Grounded Coffee House came alive with the harmonious dance of dedicated staff and delighted customers.

The opening day buzzed with electric energy as time seemed to slip away without respite. The dedicated staff members were pushed to their limits, as the waves of customers seemed endless. Galan and Dana tirelessly rallied the team, encouraging them with words of support and appreciation, keeping morale high amidst the demanding pace. As the day neared its end for the staff, the once teeming crowd gradually dwindled as darkness settled over the city. Although the pace of the day had slightly eased, the coffeehouse remained abuzz with activity.

Minutes before closing, the staff needed time to recuperate. Galan took command, becoming the driving force behind the Coffee House's last stretch. The staff, grateful for the opportunity to rest, watched in admiration as Galan showcased his leadership and dedication. Dana's eyes sparkled with respect as she watched Galan in awe. Despite the long and demanding day, he remained as vibrant and active as he had been from the start. His energy and passion seemed boundless.

With a charismatic charm, Galan engaged in friendly conversations with customers, ensuring everything ran smoothly. However, his attention shifted as he caught sight of someone at the door. A smile spread across his face as he turned to Dana, his eyes filled with adoration. Galan motioned for her to look up, and her heart skipped a beat when she saw her father walking through the entrance.

Dana's eyes lit up with joy, and without hesitation, she hurried out from behind the bar to embrace her father in a tight and heartfelt hug. "You're here!" she exclaimed.

"Of course, Kitten, I wouldn't miss this for the world," Mr. Scarlet smiled.

"Well, welcome to Grounded Coffee House. How can I brighten your day?" asked Dana.

"I'll have an Americano," Mr. Scarlet replied.

Dana swiftly moved behind the bar, her hands moving with practiced ease as she started preparing her father's favorite drink. Meanwhile, Galan approached Mr. Scarlet. "Good to see you, Mr. Scarlet. I'm so glad you made it," Galan stated.

"Please, call me Alexander," Alexander offered.

"How about I call you pops?" asked Galan playfully.

"You know what, stick to Mr. Scarlet," Alexander teased.

"By the way, what made you change your mind?" Galan wondered.

"I misjudged you, and as rude as you were, you were right. I learned not to take things personally, and I couldn't argue with the things you said. You don't even like me, yet you would protect my name. I can only imagine the lengths you would go for my daughter," Alexander explained.

"We don't have to like each other, but as long as we both do what we do for her, you will have my respect. Thanks for giving us your blessing. I cannot tell you how much it means to us," Galan stated. He extended his hand and shook Alexander's.

"Just because you have my blessing doesn't mean the other things I said weren't true. You have a lot to make up for, son," Alexander expressed.

"You're giving me a fair chance to redeem myself. I couldn't ask for anything more. I'll get out of your hair. This is Dana's time," Galan exclaimed as he left the bar and attended to customers.

Galan approached a table of familiar faces: Avan, Belle, and Sydney. "Small world," said Galan with a smile.

"Mr. Rain," Belle addressed him with a smirk.

"Still doing that, huh? I thought you only did that at your desk," Galan teased.

"Avan and I are on the clock. This is actually our lunch break. We have the night shift tonight," Belle informed him.

"Hey!" said Avan with a smile stretching from ear to ear.

"What's up, Avan? You seem rather happy about something," Galan chuckled.

"Is there a reason your coffee is ten times the price of other coffee shops?" questioned Sydney.

"Well, it's the experience, the atmosphere, the expertise that goes into a cup of coffee, and the quality of everything we sell," Galan explained.

"You have to admit the items here were damn delicious," Belle responded. Avan and Sydney wholeheartedly agreed.

"But don't worry, I have a surprise. Next week, Grounded Coffee House will have a coffee fountain. Anyone can come and sit and enjoy a cup for free, as much as they'd like. I know the prices are steep, and it's a university. Not everyone can afford to do this daily, so I want to make it enjoyable for the students as well," Galan remarked.

"Really? Wow, that's amazing," Avan gushed.

"Hey, Avan, come with me for a minute. Let me run something by you," said Galan.

Avan awkwardly exited the booth and followed Galan to the corner by the windows, "What's up, Sir?... Damn it!"

"Keep it cool. So, did my advice work?" asked Galan.

"It did! I totally forgot to tell you!" Avan beamed.

"Avan, how would you tell me? You don't have my number, and we don't see each other," Galan chuckled.

"Well, there is that, but really, how did you know that would work?" asked Avan.

"Don't worry about it, just keep doing whatever you're doing—" Galan sniffed. "Why don't you smell like the cologne I bought you?"

"That's an expensive cologne. I don't want to waste it," Avan replied.

"Avan, the point of getting you that cologne is so that Sydney will think about you when she smells it. Whenever you have to see her, you have to wear it, you hear me?" Galan declared.

"But it smells so nice. I don't want to use it all," Avan whined.

"Avan, you're in a university where ninety percent of the people are rich. If someone else has on that cologne, and she smells it, there is a high chance she won't need you. You need to be on top of your game to win her over first, then worry about the cost of that cologne, okay?" Galan explained.

"I guess you're right. I never thought about it like that," Avan exclaimed.

"If money is the issue, want to make some good money working for me?" asked Galan.

"I already have a job at the hotel, and I'll be in school when I am not there," Avan responded.

"That sucks. It would have been cool to have you on board," Galan claimed.

"Besides, it's getting crazy at the school since the Coffee House was built," Avan told him.

"What do you mean?" Galan pried.

"Rumors have been going around this school since the Salt Pine Acres Massacre. They said the original building burnt down, and a madman killed the entire town. Some blog threads say the killer massacred the town for someone he loved. They say he dressed up in a nice suit, but the girl rejected him for someone else, and in a fit of rage, he killed her and everyone around them," Avan recalled.

"Really? Can you send me that thread?" asked Galan.

"Sure, what's your phone number?" Avan remarked.

"Actually, have Belle forward it to me. She already has it," Galan corrected.

"Why can't I have it?" Avan replied in a sad tone.

Galan chuckled, "Avan, you don't shut up in person. What's going to happen when you can reach me twenty-four seven?"

"Touché," Avan smiled.

"Alright, I'm going to get ready to close for the night. We'll catch up soon," said Galan as he fist-bumped Avan.

Dana leaned over the bar and asked, "Who was that?"

"He works at your dad's hotel. He was my driver the last time I was there," Galan answered.

"I see," Dana responded.

"I'm going to head to the back and pack up. I'll join you soon to close up, alright? You get to tell everyone it's closing time," Galan stated as he blew a kiss and smiled.

Alexander stood up from the bar. "Alright, Kitten, it's time I head back, too. Congratulations again on a successful day. I am so proud of you."

"Thank you, Daddy," Dana expressed as she hugged him.

"Say goodbye to Galan for me, okay?" asked Alexander.

"I will," Dana agreed.

The last customer bid farewell, leaving a quiet, empty cafe. Dana and the diligent staff swiftly began their closing routine, tidying up and securing the premises. In the backroom, they assembled, ready to wrap up the day. Galan, arriving shortly after, joined the group.

"Where did you disappear to?" Dana teased.

"I stepped outside for a bit," Galan remarked.

"To do what?" asked Dana.

"Hide a body," Galan teased.

"Not funny," Dana nudged him playfully.

"I was taking out the trash. The bins are all the way at the end of the parking lot," Galan mentioned. "Come on, it's you're meeting to close."

"Everyone!" Dana commanded. "Today was phenomenal. I picked each of you because I saw your hard work and potential. Today's performance spoke for itself. Not a single customer saw any of you uneasy, overwhelmed, or tired. Smiles all day and amazing service. I haven't seen a team like this since the first Grounded Coffee House. Thanks for an amazing day. Shuttles outside will take you to the housing complex. Have a good night, and let's kick ass tomorrow, too."

"Grounded! Woo!" the staff chanted in sync.

The group eagerly crossed the parking lot to get to their awaiting shuttle. However, their progress was abruptly halted by a piercing scream that reverberated through the deserted expanse. Galan and Dana's hearts raced as they reacted swiftly to the scream, bolting towards the source. With urgency in their steps, they arrived outside, where the rest of the staff had already gathered, forming a tight huddle near the bins. Galan's eyes widened in shock and horror as he witnessed the gruesome scene before him—a girl, stabbed and slashed about her body, lying against the large metal bins. Dana's breath caught in her throat as she finally reached Galan's side, her fingers gripping his arm tightly for support. The sight of the mutilated girl sent a shiver down her spine, and she leaned closer to Galan.

FUCK!

Chapter Thirteen

As the police arrived swiftly, their sirens wailing and lights casting an eerie glow, the campus buildings were bathed in alternating red and blue lights. After the police completed their investigation and took statements from the staff, Galan and Dana included, the tension slowly dissipated. With a collective sigh of relief, everyone was permitted to leave the scene. Galan and Dana sat in silence as he drove them back to her place. The weight of the evening's events hung heavy in the air, leaving them both lost in their own thoughts. The streetlights passed by, casting fleeting shadows on the car, mirroring the darkness that now clouded their minds.

They arrived at Dana's place, stepped off the elevator, and entered her living room. "What was that back there?" asked Dana furiously.

"It's Paige; it has to be," Galan remarked.

"Are you kidding me? Moments before they found the body, you were nowhere to be found, and you're going to tell me that little joke you made about hiding a body by the bins was a coincidence?" Dana hissed.

"Love… Are you kidding me right now?" asked Galan.

"That is too much of a coincidence, Galan!" Dana barked.

"You don't believe that; you would have never gotten in the car with me if you really thought that," Galan replied.

"What did you expect me to do? Say, 'Hey, the person they are calling the Blood Rain Ripper is actually my fiancé, and this is just like what happened to those people in Salt Pine Acres?'" Dana voiced.

"I didn't kill those people in Salt Pine Acres! Garrick, Eder, Bodhi, Meave, Eyla, and Malek had it coming. They locked you in a storage room and tried to drug and kill me. They accused me of being a predator, and they, on many occasions, violently confronted me for no reason. I was pushed at every turn, and I didn't do anything until I found out what they did to you," Galan pointed out.

"How am I supposed to feel about that?!" asked Dana.

"D, please," Galan approached her.

"Stay the fuck back, Galan!" Dana shouted.

"Please don't turn your back on me; I would never hurt you, Dana," Galan's strength faltered as he dropped to his knees, his eyes betraying the fear and pain he held within.

"I don't know what to believe, Galan," Dana whispered.

"I know you're scared, but I swear I didn't do this," Galan promised.

"I took a page from your book; I had hidden cameras installed in and around every one of the Grounded Coffee Houses I built, including this one," Dana informed him. Galan's demeanor changed.

"You did what?" asked Galan in a serious tone.

"If I pull this video and see that you were involved, I will have security in here in seconds to escort you out," Dana remarked.

"Dana, don't," Galan pleaded.

Dana felt an icy chill creep down her spine, causing her to instinctively take a step back. "Galan...." her voice shook.

Galan rose to his feet. "Don't look at that video, please, Dana. If you love me, you won't look," he begged.

"Galan, you need to get away from me right now," Dana responded.

"Give me the phone, D. I'm begging you," said Galan.

"Get out... Now!" Dana firmly demanded.

"Love, you have this all wrong. Please just calm down," Galan stated as he slowly approached her.

"Now!!!" Dana shouted.

"What?" Galan stopped.

As a dozen private security personnel stormed into the room, their presence signaled a heightened level of tension and concern. Galan turned his gaze towards them, his eyes narrowing as he assessed the situation. The sight of the armed men created a stark contrast to the previously serene and safe environment, amplifying the gravity of the events that had unfolded earlier. "On the ground! Now!" said one of the men.

"What's going on here?" asked Galan.

"On the ground!" the man repeated.

"I'm not doing anything until you tell me what this is about," Galan answered calmly.

"Step away from Ms. Scarlet and get on the ground, or we will use force!" the same security personnel replied harshly.

Galan turned to Dana. "Dana, what's going on?" he remarked as he slowly approached her. The security opened fire, hitting Galan twice. Galan fell to the floor, bleeding heavily from his chest. His eyesight faded along with his hearing; everything was now a blurry sight and muffled chatter as the officers rushed to him before he blacked out.

"Ms. Scarlet, are you okay?" asked the security personnel.

Dana, in tears, replied, "Yes, I'm okay. Thank you."

Back at the parking lot, while Galan was being questioned, Dana had texted the building's security personnel, 'On my way home, I may be in danger; wait on the stairwell of my apartment for my call.'

"Ms. Scarlet, we need to get him to a hospital," one of the security personnel informed her.

"Admit him to a private hospital, lock down the floor, and I want all of you guarding him until he is conscious," Dana instructed.

"Yes, Ma'am," the security personnel complied. Dana stood frozen, her heart pounding in her chest as she witnessed the swift and unsettling departure of Galan, his unconscious body being carried away by the security team with only the bloodstained floor left behind.

Dana collapsed onto the couch, overwhelmed by a flood of emotions that engulfed her. Tears streamed down her face as the weight of the situation sank in, and she allowed herself to release the pent-up fear, worry, and sadness that consumed her. Each sob echoed through the empty room. Dana's mind became a tumultuous sea of memories and present realities, the boundaries blurring as the weight of the past and the present converged. The image of Aria's lifeless body flashed before her, intertwining with the fresh scene of Galan being taken away. The pain of loss resurfaced, fueling her anguish as she grappled with the cruel hands fate had dealt her once again. Her vision blurred, and tears cascaded down her cheeks; the lines between past and present blurred as she questioned the unfolding tragedy, desperately searching for answers in the depths of her shattered heart.

Dana's trembling fingers tapped on the screen as she accessed the surveillance footage from earlier. Her gaze was fixed on the camera angle that captured the area near the large metal bins. She scrutinized the playback, her eyes searching for any clue, any glimpse of what transpired. The footage played in slow motion, the seconds feeling like an eternity as she tried to unravel the mystery hidden within those frames. Her heart pounded in her chest, anticipation mingling with fear, as she hoped to find some answers in the images that played before her. Dana's eyes widened as she caught a glimpse of Galan on the surveillance footage, disposing of the trash bags in the bins. She replayed the segment, studying his every move, searching for any subtle details that might have gone unnoticed.

He turned and walked back to Grounded Coffee House. Moments later, she saw Galan return with the girl, stabbing her multiple times and carving her up on the floor against the bins. Dana's heart pounded in her chest as she watched the surveillance footage in horror. The image of Galan, the man she loved, committing such a gruesome act shook her to the core. The realization of the darkness that had been lurking beneath his charming facade filled her with a mixture of disbelief and anguish. She felt a surge of adrenaline, her mind racing to comprehend the implications of what she had just witnessed. Questions and doubts flooded her thoughts, challenging her previous perception of Galan and the reality she thought she knew. Fear and uncertainty gripped her as she grappled with the weight of this shocking revelation.

Dana's world came crashing down in an instant as she watched the horrifying scene unfold before her eyes. She couldn't believe what she was seeing, her mind struggling to comprehend the depth of darkness hidden within Galan. Her gasp turned into a choked sob as shock and disbelief gripped her, leaving her body trembling uncontrollably. She felt the weight of the truth crushing her, and her rapid, shallow breaths echoed in the silence of the room. As Galan stood up, a wave of terror washed over Dana; the sight of his silver-tipped hair and piercing grey eyes sent a chill down her spine. It was as if she was seeing a stranger. Even that far away, Galan's unique physical features were undeniable.

Dana's stomach churned, and she felt the overwhelming urge to vomit. She sprinted to the kitchen, desperately trying to reach the sink just in time to empty the contents of her stomach. The sound of retching echoed through the room as she doubled over, her body heaving with each violent convulsion. Taking deep breaths to calm herself, Dana rinsed her mouth repeatedly, desperate to rid herself of the taste and lingering nausea. With trembling hands, she reached into the fridge, grabbed a chilled bottle of water, uncapped it, and took long, soothing sips. The cool liquid provided momentary relief, helping to quell the racing thoughts and emotions swirling inside her.

Dana's mind raced as she leaned on the kitchen island; flashes of her and Galan on the edge of the island were still fresh in her mind. The memories of their laughter and intimacy now mingled with the horrifying images she had just witnessed. The once comforting space now felt tainted, and she couldn't help but question everything. The island, once a symbol of their love and connection, now served as a painful reminder of the darkness lurking beneath the surface.

Aria warned me about him. I was so stupid. She tried to tell me, but I was too stubborn to listen. They all tried to warn me, and he killed every last one of them! But why is he killing college students? And what was he doing these last four years? Is it linked to this? Should I tell my father? No, not with what Paige did already; if he questions what really happened in Salt Pine Acres, he is going to find out that Galan and I lied to him. There is only one person I can go to right now... Mama B.

MAMA B

AGE: 55
SIGN: LEO
FUN FACT: *UNAVAILABLE* (MY BAD, CAKE IS
MY WEAKNESS.)

Chapter Fourteen

Later that night, a distraught Dana pulled up to a massive mansion sitting on an expansive property. The sight of the well-kept grounds, the imposing iron gates, and the towering walls surrounding the perimeter only added to the sense of unease she felt. She took a deep breath, mustering the courage to step out of the car and approach the foreboding entrance. The weight of the night's events hung heavy in the air as she reached out to ring the doorbell.

A rough voice answered a minute later. "Who is ringing my bell at this late hour?!" Mama B's voice boomed through the intercom.

"Mama," said Dana softly.

"D? Sweetheart, is that you?" Mama B's voice softened as she replied.

Dana, still shaking, replied with a quivering voice, "May I come in?"

"Sweetie, why do you sound so sad? Are you okay? Come in, come in," Mama B responded. The grandeur of the mansion loomed before her, its elegance contrasting with her shattered emotions. Dana's car echoed the vast expanse as she drove down the cobblestone driveway. The gates closing behind her symbolized a temporary respite from the outside world, a refuge where she could find solace and understanding.

Coming out the front door was Mama B, a plump, curvy, mixed-race woman in her silk robe, there to greet Dana. Dana's trembling hands reached for Mama B, her eyes reflecting the depth of her pain. As Mama B locked eyes with Dana, her own expression shifted from warmth to concern, realizing the depth of the terror etched on Dana's face. Without hesitation, Mama B opened her arms, ready to embrace Dana and offer a safe haven amidst the storm that consumed her. "Come here, child," Mama B whispered soothingly, holding Dana tightly in her arms. The warmth of Mama B's embrace enveloped Dana. With a gentle touch, Mama B kissed the top of Dana's head and tenderly brushed Dana's hair. "It's okay, baby. Come inside," Mama B led Dana into the house with a gentle smile, guiding her to the cozy sofa. Mama B joined her, sitting beside her and placing a reassuring hand on her shoulder.

"Child, I've known you for some time. I remember when you first came to me, a feisty little thing. Having you around was always a joy because you were the most fearless of all my kids. What on earth has you this shaken up?" asked Mama B.

"I don't feel safe in my house right now or at my business," Dana replied, her voice quivering with the effort to steady her racing heart.

"And what exactly is making you feel unsafe?" questioned Mama B.

"My fiancé... A guy I fell for when I was a teenager. He came back into my life, and we started a life together. On the day we kicked off the biggest branch of Grounded Coffee House, they found the body of a victim who was stabbed and slashed beyond recognition," Dana began.

"Continue. It's alright, sweetie; you're safe now," Mama B comforted her as she embraced Dana.

Feeling her racing heartbeat gradually slow down, Dana summoned the strength to gather her thoughts and press onward. "It's the same story as the Salt Pine Acres Massacre. My fiancé, Galan, went missing for a couple of minutes just before we ended the day at the Coffee House. When I asked him where he went, he said he was hiding a body. I thought he was joking because afterward, he said he was taking out the trash. The bins were a little far, that's why it took so long. But then, moments after, when everyone departed for their homes, they spotted a body in the bins. While the police were questioning everyone and Galan was occupied, I told the security personnel at the penthouse to wait for my call. I didn't know what to think, so I waited until I was home because I didn't want the police involved. He was begging and seemed innocent, and I thought maybe I was paranoid. But then I mentioned I had cameras hidden around the Coffee House, and his demeanor changed. He stopped begging and demanded I hand over my phone and not look at that video," Dana explained.

"And then what happened?" coaxed Mama B.

"Then I gave the signal. The security personnel were only supposed to apprehend him, but when Galan refused to comply and turned to me, they opened fire. He's lying in a hospital bed right now, getting medical attention. I came straight here because I didn't know what else to do. I can't call Daddy, and I have no one else to turn to," Dana informed her.

"I see. You can stay here as long as you wish, baby," said Mama B, gently kissing Dana on the cheek.

"Thank you, Mama," Dana replied.

"Now, this Galan, do you truly believe he would do this?" questioned Mama B.

"I don't know what to think, but I saw it. The video caught him dragging the girl to the bin and killing her," Dana responded, her hand trembling slightly as she handed her phone to Mama B. They both watched the video in silent anticipation. The weight of the moment hung in the air as Mama B's eyes absorbed the contents of the screen.

Finally, breaking the silence, Mama B turned to Dana. "They never caught the killer four years ago. He killed almost the entire town, and even with a picture circulating, his face was covered in blood, and the heavy downpour obstructed any clear view of who he was. Why would someone that elusive just kill a person in the middle of a University on the day of your grand opening, no less?" Mama B pondered.

"Saying it out loud does sound stupid, especially because Galan works there too. We own Grounded Coffee House together. I bought it from him when we moved to Salt Pine Acres. Why would he kill that girl?" Dana wondered.

"Consider this, they never found the bodies of Garrick Wilder and Eder Barlow. It's unlikely that Galan is the Blood Rain Ripper. I wish he was. Then I could finally get some closure for Bodhi. My son was taken from me, murdered, and left in the street in pieces. There was no way I could display his body at a funeral," Mama B exclaimed.

"What do I do?" Dana remarked.

"Live your life, sweetie. If Galan comes for you, he has to go through me," Mama B smiled.

"I just don't understand why he would do this," Dana sadly stated.

"Do you want an answer?" asked Mama B.

"I love him, Mama. I fell for him hard, and he always tried to do right by me. He's charming and romantic, and when he asked me to spend my life with him, I believed every word he said. I don't want to believe he did this, but I can't deny what I saw. And I don't care about love; I saw the red flags and ran without a second thought," Dana answered. The butler finally came downstairs and hurried to Dana and Mama B on the chair.

"Goodnight, Madame. Sorry to keep you waiting," said the butler.

"Can you make us some tea, please? We would also like a slice of cake," Mama B instructed.

"Yes, Madame. Coming right up," answered the butler, his crisp voice cutting through the air as he swiftly made his way to the kitchen.

"Cake? I'm not really hungry, Mama," Dana informed her.

"You will eat what I put on your plate, missy. No complaints. You're all skin and bone; you need some meat on you," Mama B gently pinched her cheeks. "As for your problem, if Galan was a threat to you, he could have killed you back then. From what I understand, a young man saved you and got you to a hospital four years ago. I'm going to guess Galan was that person," Mama B surmised.

"Yes," Dana answered.

"He won't hurt you. I don't think you have anything to fear from him, though that may not be the case now because you did get him shot. But bullet wounds take a couple of weeks to heal, so while he is in the hospital, you can go get your closure there. See if he would come clean about it," Mama B suggested.

"Thank you, Mama," Dana hugged her.

"You're welcome, baby, and don't worry. If it doesn't go well at the hospital, people die there every day," Mama B winked.

The butler reappeared, his hands steady as he lowered the tray in front of Dana and Mama B. With a gentle grace, he presented each of them with a plate adorned with a delectable slice of cheesecake and a steaming cup of tea.

The next morning, Dana awoke to the soft glow of the rising sun and peered out of the window from her guest room. A sense of curiosity and anticipation filled her as she admired the tranquil surroundings. Just as she was lost in the beauty of the moment, a gentle knock echoed through the door, and the butler's voice called out to her, alerting Dana that Mama B requested her presence in the foyer. Dana descended the steps, faltering as her eyes scanned the foyer. Time seemed to freeze as her gaze locked onto Galan, suspended in chains, a haunting sight that sent shivers down her spine. Shock and disbelief washed over her, threatening to swallow her composure.

Chapter Fifteen

Dana's eyes widened with horror as she beheld the sight of Galan, his body suspended by his wrists. Her heart raced, and without another moment's hesitation, she swiftly descended the steps, her urgency fueling her every step. As she reached Mama B, her eyes met with a scene of heightened security, bodyguards scattered throughout the room.

"Mama, what is this?" asked Dana in a panic.

"This is closure. After you went to bed, I sent for Mr. Rain. I figured I would save you the trouble of going to the hospital, so I brought him to you. They removed the bullets and patched him up, but he is still loopy from the blood loss. Get your answers, and I will take care of the rest," Mama B instructed.

"Dana...?" Galan's words, though strained, forced their way past his lips. "Love?"

Dana's gaze briefly met Mama B's, seeking reassurance and strength before she turned her attention toward Galan. With measured steps, she approached him.

"Galan," Dana answered softly, her voice filled with empathy as she took cautious steps toward him.

"D... You're ok?" Galan's tears flowed freely, his emotions spilling over as he released the weight he was carrying. "I was so scared they'd killed you."

"Scared who would kill me?" asked Dana, her brows furrowing in confusion. The tears streaming down Galan's face puzzled her, leaving her searching for answers within the depths of her own uncertainty.

"The men at the penthouse. I thought I lost you forever," Galan, fighting through his emotional turmoil, forced his words out.

Mama B's focused gaze never wavered as she listened to Galan's words, her eyes narrowing with intensity as she weighed the implications of his revelations. The weight of her experience and wisdom guided her thoughts as she processed the information with a discerning mind. Mama B understood that Galan's words held profound meaning, potentially unraveling a web of hidden truths and unforeseen consequences.

"I'm fine. They weren't there for me. I called them for you," Dana informed him.

"For me? Why?" asked Galan.

"You know why," Dana stated.

"Because of that girl?" asked Galan, his voice choked with emotion, tears flowing freely down his face.

"So you admit it," said Dana.

"I'm sorry. Believe me, I didn't know it would happen. I saw her, and I panicked. Please, D... Don't leave me," Galan begged.

"You slaughtered a girl and left her body a hundred feet from our Coffee House!" Dana hissed.

"I didn't kill anyone; I swear I didn't. Please—" Galan broke down in tears, unable to speak.

"I saw you. You took out the trash, and then—" Dana choked on her words.

"And then I ran into her, but I ended it quickly," Galan confirmed, breaking down further. "It was just one kiss, but if I could take it back, I would do anything to repent for my sins. Please, love...."

"Wait... What kiss?" asked Dana, confused.

Galan's struggle took its toll, and his body succumbed to unconsciousness once more, leaving Dana standing there, her breath shaking. As she stepped back, a sense of helplessness washed over her; Mama B approached, her hand finding its place on Dana's trembling shoulder.

"Baby, something doesn't add up," Mama B stated.

"You saw the video. What am I missing here?" Dana wondered.

"That's definitely the person in the video—the hair, the build, those grey eyes. But he didn't even care that he was shot. All he was concerned about was you. Go over that footage again. I want you to keep your eyes on Galan from the moment he left the building to the time he got back inside," Mama B advised as she turned to the bodyguards. "Get him to the guest room, have him cleaned up, and get me a medical team, now!"

"Yes, Madame!" answered the men as they quickly did as she instructed.

"You have to go to work. Business stops for no one. I will keep your fiancé here. Go home and gather yourself for as long as you need to. Find out what you missed, and I will call you when Galan is on his feet. Ok, sweetheart?" Mama B expressed.

"Yes, Mama," Dana complied.

"Now go have breakfast and get ready for work. I will leave you with one of my bodyguards. He will take you to and from wherever you need to go," Mama B informed her.

"I don't usually eat before I—" Dana exclaimed.

"You will sit down and have the pancakes I made for you, yes?!" Mama B replied.

"Yes, Mama," Dana agreed.

"Now hurry before they get cold, sweetie. I'll be in the garden if you need me before you leave," Mama B kissed her atop her head. Dana entered the kitchen, sat down, and finished her breakfast.

Dana left Galan's car at Mama B's. Her newly assigned bodyguard drove her back to her place to shower and get dressed for work. Dana's gaze fixated on the haunting bloodstain on the floor, each glance invoking a surge of unease in the pit of her stomach. Despite her efforts to push past it, the remainder of the traumatic events that had unfolded weighed heavily on her.

Getting back into the car, Dana was driven to Grounded Coffee House to begin her day of work. As she stepped inside, the bustling atmosphere of the café greeted her, filled with the energy of students and customers. However, an underlying sense of emptiness permeated the space, amplified by Galan's absence. Despite the hustle and bustle around her, Dana couldn't shake the feeling of something missing, a void that echoed throughout the café. Determined to carry on, she mustered her strength and immersed herself in her tasks.

Chatter infected Grounded Coffee House like wildfire, spreading the news of the murder that had occurred the previous night. Each passing conversation carried a different version of the events, leaving Dana overwhelmed by the contrasting accounts. Amongst the murmurs, she couldn't help but catch snippets about Galan's absence, further fueling her unease. Lost in her thoughts, Dana found herself staring blankly at the bar, her mind absorbing the information, trying to make sense of the swirling chaos around her. It was a moment of introspection as she grappled with the fragments of truth and speculation, searching for her own path through the web of rumors and uncertainty.

"Excuse me," a student broke her concentration. A young man of Japanese descent with long straight hair, wearing a leather jacket over a grey hoodie and a kunai pendant necklace, said, "May I have a GHC mocha latte?"

"Yes, coming right up," Dana replied.

"Are you ok?" the student asked as he leaned closer to her. "You look like you haven't slept a wink in days."

"Our coffee is that strong," Dana teased.

The student chuckled. Dana's focus shifted back to her task at hand, skillfully preparing the student's drink. With a gentle smile, she handed him the freshly made coffee, their hands briefly touching during the exchange. Though the weight of recent events remained, this small interaction served as a reminder of the connections she shared with the customers, even amidst the chaos that surrounded them. Dana found solace in the simple act of providing a warm cup of coffee, hoping to bring a moment of comfort to those who crossed her path. "Here you go, one GHC mocha latte. Don't worry; I made this one really weak for you so you can get some sleep tonight," Dana chuckled.

"Thank you. If I have to wake up and listen to my roommate talk to his girlfriend all night, I will kill myself," said the student.

"If you do kill yourself, could you do it away from the Coffee House? I have enough problems here," Dana teased.

"Definitely. Wouldn't want to add to all this drama. People all over campus are talking about the body they found," the student stated.

"So I've heard," Dana replied.

"Hey, don't worry about it. Maybe you should use that in a slogan. Our coffee is so strong, even the dead are drawn to us," the student joked.

"I'll keep that in mind," Dana laughed.

"Well, I need to get back to class. Don't drink any more strong coffees, alright? Ja ne," said the student.

"Pardon? What was that last part?" asked Dana.

"Ja ne?" the student repeated.

"Yes, that, the only word not in English," Dana teased.

"Well, the next time I see you, I'll use it again and again until you figure it out," the student told her.

"I don't even know your name," Dana responded.

"Shinoda Genji," he introduced himself, taking a sip of his latte as he backed away. With a nod, he turned and gracefully left Grounded Coffee House.

Dana's attempt to share her name was cut short as Genji hurriedly left the coffee house. Despite the missed opportunity, she smiled, appreciating the brief connection they had shared. The day flew by in a whirlwind of activity, serving customers and attending to the bustling café. As nightfall descended, Grounded Coffee House closed its doors after another successful day.

As the shuttle filled with departing employees, Dana made her way to a waiting car that would take her back to her place. Upon entering her apartment, the sight of the bloodstained floor immediately stirred her unease. The haunting reminder clawed at her mind, refusing to be ignored. With a heavy sigh, Dana knew she couldn't escape the weight of what had transpired.

What kiss was he talking about? Was he in his right mind? He did lose a lot of blood.

Casting the phone's screen onto her television, Dana spent the night on the sofa, engrossed in rewatching hours of footage, meticulously tracking Galan's every move. With an unwavering focus, she observed Galan's journey, scrutinizing every step he took. The footage revealed a moment when he approached the large bins and later reappeared, dragging a girl along with him. She reviewed the footage dozens of times, trying to find something she may have missed.

I just don't get it. What did he mean? He stepped out of the frame for only a few seconds before returning to the bins. What happened in those few seconds?

With a determined focus, Dana swiftly scrolled through the different camera angles, searching for a vantage point that would capture Galan's actions more clearly. The screen displayed a new perspective, revealing the crucial seconds when Galan had gone off-screen in the previous camera angle. In this new footage, she witnessed Galan dragging the girl, their struggle unfolding before her eyes. The gravity of the situation intensified as Dana recognized the urgency to uncover the full extent of Galan's actions and bring justice to those affected. Each camera angle provided a puzzle piece, and she was determined to fit them all together and shed light on the truth hidden within the shadows.

In a momentary lapse of intention, Dana accidentally skipped back and forth through the camera angles, eventually landing on a different feed. To her surprise, the screen revealed Galan entering the café through the back door. Her heart skipped a beat as the realization sank in—Galan's presence in the café raised new questions and heightened her sense of urgency.

Wait! What the fuck is this?

Dana quickly went back a few frames, determined to confirm her suspicions. It became unequivocally clear as she scrutinized the footage— it was indeed Galan. She meticulously noted the timestamp, preserving the damning evidence. She scrolled forward through the other camera feeds to the bins, where he was also seen stabbing a woman at the same time.

Two of them... He can't be in both places at the same time. Oh my God... He didn't kill that girl...

Dana swiftly returned to the camera angle, capturing Galan entering the café through the back door, and rewound the footage a couple minutes. Her eyes widened as she observed him engaging in conversation with a woman who appeared to be around her own age. A wave of unease washed over her as Galan uttered the name "Aria."

Chapter Sixteen

*D*ana sat in front of a screen, replaying the footage repeatedly, her eyes fixated on the footage. The audio played, confirming her suspicions; her ears did not deceive her. Galan's voice clearly uttered the name "Aria."

Paige told me that Galan tried desperately to find love. When girls broke his heart, he would go after girls who carried the same name just to fill that void... I can't deal with this right now. What's more important is that Galan didn't kill that woman. Someone else did!

Dana called Mama B. "Hello, sweetie," she answered.

"Mama, it wasn't Galan," Dana immediately stated.

"I figured as much. What did you find?" asked Mama B.

"Someone is trying to frame him. They wore the same clothes, the hair, the eyes. I think whoever it was knew we would see it unfold on camera, and they planned that murder," Dana replied.

"Are you sure?" questioned Mama B.

"Yes, I am sure. I have two cameras that show Galan was in two places at once," Dana proclaimed.

"Why Galan?" Mama B wondered.

"I wish I knew, but Galan doesn't have any enemies. He has no one else. The only person from his past left and is in the Caribbean at the moment. Dad personally saw to that," Dana remarked.

"And this friend, are you sure it couldn't be them?" asked Mama B.

"Positive. If they wanted Galan to take the fall for those murders, they could have," Dana responded.

"What does that mean, they could have?" Mama B probed.

"She was another survivor of the Massacres, and she doesn't like Galan or me very much, but she worked closely with Dad to find the person responsible for those murders. If she wanted to point the finger at Galan, Daddy would have listened," Dana informed her.

I'M BROKEN TOO

"Keep that bodyguard close to you whenever you leave your house. I'll let you know when Galan is awake," said Mama B.

"How is he doing?" asked Dana.

"Not too good, I'm afraid, but don't you worry, okay," Mama B assured her.

Standing in a dimly lit room, Mama B cast a shadow over the bruised and battered figure of Galan, who was bound to a chair with his hands tied behind his back. Bloodstains marred the scene, bearing witness to the violence inflicted upon him. With a hardened expression, Mama B abruptly ended the call on her phone and slipped it back into her pocket. The gagged Galan, unable to speak or defend himself, remained at her mercy, his predicament painting a grim picture of the dangerous situation he found himself in.

"I don't need to stall anymore, young man," Mama B's hand closed around Galan's throat, tightening her grip and eliciting a pained groan from him. The pressure she exerted conveyed her authority and dominance over him, a chilling display of her power. However, just as abruptly as she had seized him, she released her hold, allowing him a moment to recover. Galan's groan of pain echoed through the room. "I got my confirmation. My baby girl is too consumed by her love for you that she can't see it. But a mother burdened by the loss of a child carries no such burden. I ought to carve you into pieces and scatter you on the streets like you did Bodhi, but I would lose my baby girl in the process. Dana, along with Maeve, Eyla, and Eder, became part of my family and even that hothead Garrick. My kids are free to live their lives as they see fit, but what I will not allow is murderers to weasel their way into their lives.

"Dana would forgive me if something happened to you, but I would never forgive myself if something happened to her. So you will die in one piece, dressed in a nice suit to cover the bruising and scars from your time with me," Mama B called out for a doctor, her voice filled with firmness. In response to her command, a doctor swiftly entered the room; he retrieved a needle from his coat, preparing to administer anesthesia to Galan. "You know I taught little Maeve this trick. I once told her if she was a great surgeon, she could make it look like an accident."

Mama B gestured to the doctor, indicating her desire for him to proceed with the injection. As the doctor moved closer to Galan, needle in hand, Galan's body tensed, his struggle evident as he fought against his restraints. Desperation filled his eyes, and he attempted to let out a scream, only to be muffled by the gag in his mouth. The combination of his physical resistance and the suppressed sound of his distress added an even more harrowing element to the already tense and unsettling atmosphere in the room. "They would have had you on this stuff when you got surgery. An autopsy would discover the cause of death was an overdose because you had so much blood loss. My baby girl will mourn you and be free, and I will have avenged my kids. The one thing a mother's rage will never forgive is the loss of her child. Now I have to break the news to my sweet girl that her fiancé died in his sleep," Mama B exclaimed. Despite Galan's valiant efforts to break free, his struggle gradually weakened. The binds that held him securely to the chair seemed to become even more constricting as his energy waned. Slowly but surely, his body succumbed to the anesthesia. With a heavy thud, Galan's weakened form slumped in the chair, and the room went quiet once his struggle came to a halt.

"Clean him up, treat his wounds, and leave him on the bed. By the time Dana sees him tomorrow after work, he will already be feeding the maggots," instructed Mama B. Following her directives, the doctors swiftly untied Galan from the chair, carefully maneuvering his lifeless body. With a somber efficiency, they transported him to the guest room. The room became a silent sanctuary for Galan's motionless form.

Meanwhile, Mama B left the room, seemingly unfazed by the events that had transpired. Pouring herself a glass of red wine, she returned to her room and continued a movie she had paused.

❦

As the sun cast its gentle glow into Dana's room, she awakened to the promise of a new day. Determined and resolute, she prepared herself for the day ahead, taking care with each step of her morning routine. Dana was accompanied by her loyal bodyguard as they embarked on their journey to Salt Pine University. Silent and composed, Dana carried with her an air of introspection, her thoughts veiled behind a stoic demeanor. As she entered her workplace, she took a moment to gather herself, ensuring that her emotions remained hidden beneath a veneer of professionalism. With a practiced ease, she made her way towards the main floor.

With a focused mindset, Dana greeted the staff members with warmth and professionalism as she made her way through the Coffee House and walked over to the front door, scanning her fingerprint and opening the doors.

As Dana approached the bar, a bright smile adorned her face upon recognizing Avan, Belle, and Sydney. Seeing the familiar faces, she took over as their Barista. "Avan, right?" asked Dana.

"Oh my God, you know my name! The customer service is amazing here. I never gave my name here before. This is so exciting," Avan rambled.

"I overheard it previously. Galan is my fiancé. You spoke to him on the opening day," Dana informed him.

"Fiancé?" asked Belle.

"Yup," Dana responded. She discreetly lifted her hand with a subtle yet deliberate movement, allowing her ring to catch the light and gleam with a silent proclamation.

"Oh my... Galan must have told you about our sexual tension when I called him 'Sir.' I am so sorry," Avan remarked. "I didn't know he was engaged. I would have tried harder to not call him 'Sir,' but my allure must have been too powerful."

Struggling to contain their amusement, Belle and Sydney exchanged playful glances, their lips twitching with restrained laughter. Despite their best efforts to stifle their mirth, a few suppressed chuckles escaped, adding a lighthearted atmosphere. "Sure, Avan. He was falling head over heels for your allure," Belle agreed.

As a subtle waft of Avan's cologne reached her senses, Dana couldn't help but be intrigued. The pleasant and alluring fragrance tickled her olfactory senses, piquing her curiosity. With a playful yet inquisitive tone, she leaned closer and asked, "Is that from LVTCH?"

"Oh no... It's too powerful! I didn't want it to work on his fiancé, too!" Avan exclaimed frantically.

"Too? Who was it supposed to work on?" asked Sydney.

"Umm, Galan said that if I wore that perfume, it would help me get you," Avan replied truthfully.

This guy really needs to stop talking. What did Galan tell him?

"Oh my God, that's why he did that whole 'read my life' thing with you. Did you have someone else plan how to get together with me?!" Sydney raised her voice.

"No, no, I think Avan misunderstood. Galan does that to everyone. It's part of his charm here at Grounded Coffee House. He did the same with me. By looking at you, he knew how to break down who you were and how to get to you and then gave you your item of choice without you asking. Trust me, he did it to me and my sister before. It's trippy, but I think Galan meant that the cologne will get you any girl. LVTCH was founded by my late sister. Galan and I are part-owners, so he pushes her products a lot," Dana explained.

"Trust me, Syd, the more you hang around Avan, the more you realize he rambles on about things he shouldn't when he really doesn't mean to," Belle stated.

"Exactly. I'm sure there was no sexual tension between him and my fiancé," Dana chuckled.

"I'm pretty sure you're wrong. You weren't in the car with us. The way he kept yelling my name, it was magical. I really think there was a spark between us," Avan declared.

Dana leaned over the table toward Avan. "If there was a spark, and you are trying to poach my fiancé, Avan, you're going to be the next one who dies on campus," Dana smiled.

Belle and Sydney erupted into contagious laughter, their amusement unfurling at Avan's endearing loss of composure in response to Dana's playful threat.

"Now, what will you lovelies be having?" asked Dana.

"Three GHC mocha lattes, please. Almond milk and topped with cinnamon," Belle answered.

"Coming right up," Dana replied. As she turned and prepared their drinks at the machines, Sydney turned to them and told Belle and Avan about another girl found dead on campus. Dana stopped and came back to the bar. "Did you just say there was another?"

"In the dorms, they found a girl stabbed over a hundred times, and her heart carved out of her chest," Sydney informed her.

"What the hell?" Dana gasped.

"These bloggers are taking it too far," Belle remarked.

"What do you mean, bloggers?" questioned Dana.

"Well, it started on Eder Barlow's social media when he went missing. Then the comments were being flagged and taken down, so people started a blog," Belle clarified. While she explained, Dana returned to making their drinks while listening attentively. "Everyone came up with conspiracy theories about it. They said he was dating a girl at the time, a billionaire's daughter. And for the most part, it was just angry fangirls spewing nonsense. But then, when the Salt Pines Massacre occurred and the Blood Rain Ripper story came to light, many people flocked to the blog, each with their own theories.

"One theory, in particular, gained a massive following, saying that the Ripper killed the town for a woman who didn't love him back. The guy who started the thread claimed his brother left their home and flew to Salt Pine Acres to ask a girl to marry him. The guy never saw his brother again, and after the whole thing, they received a large sum of money with a note saying that he married the girl and needed to stay out of the public eye for the sake of their relationship. Not only has he not seen his brother, he hasn't seen the girl he supposedly married either.

"It became somewhat of a cult following, and people started killing those who broke their hearts. There have been dozens of cases in the surrounding areas, not just here at SPU," Belle explained.

"A copycat killer?" asked Dana.

"Killers. That's why this place is so popular. They said he burnt down the original Grounded Coffee House because she bought it to impress Eder Barlow, which ended in a bloody love triangle. And when Eder's fan base got a hold of this, it went viral, and this killing spree started happening everywhere. Fragile men started murdering the women who couldn't love broken men," Sydney corrected.

With a gentle touch, Dana placed their carefully crafted drinks in front of Avan, Belle, and Sydney. The warm aroma of freshly brewed coffee filled the air, a comforting gesture amidst the weight of the conversation. "Geez, the things people would believe," Dana exclaimed.

"You'd be surprised. One of the theories was that the original owner of Grounded burnt it down and killed those people because he couldn't let go," Avan added.

"Really?" Dana remarked.

"It's why this place got so much attention on the opening day. Everyone wanted to see the Serial Killer Barista, even if it was just rumored. This story originated here, and the locals eat this up. Before you officially opened, Galan came here with Avan. The students who knew the rumors wanted to see who he was," Sydney stated.

"Wait, is that why the six of you came in that day?" questioned Avan.

"I don't know their names, at least not all of them. I was with a friend I call Moons. We live on campus together. The others were really her friends, but we all get along," Sydney explained.

"Anyway, we should head back to class. Tonight, we have a shift at the hotel," Belle suggested.

"Bye-bye, tell Galan I said hi," Avan called out.

"Oh right, tell Galan I emailed him the blog's website. He hasn't responded since," said Belle. Avan, Belle, and Sydney got up and left together.

This may not be an entirely bad thing after all. If these murders keep up, then it's free marketing for Grounded. I need to tell Galan what's going on. I'll see you soon.

BELLE LUBAHN

AGE: 21

SIGN: CANCER

FUN FACT: "NO ONE SAYS MY SURNAME CORRECTLY SO I NEVER TELL PEOPLE WHAT IT IS."

Chapter Seventeen

Dana stood outside Grounded Coffee House, the familiar click of the door lock signaling the end of another day. She waved goodbye to the departing shuttle of employees, a gesture filled with gratitude and appreciation for their hard work. With a tired yet determined stride, she made her way to her bodyguard, who'd parked nearby. Opening the door, she settled into the back seat. "Take me to Mama B's, please," she said.

Dana's unease intensified as the silence in the car grew increasingly unsettling. She turned to the driver, her voice filled with a mix of confusion and concern, repeating her words in an attempt to break he silence. Leaning slightly to the left, her gaze shifted over the driver's shoulder, and her eyes widened in horror. A chilling sight met her eyes—a trickle of blood had stained the side of the car window. Overwhelmed with fear and shock, Dana's scream pierced the air as she hastily exited the car.

Caught in a moment of uncertainty, Dana's mind raced as she surveyed the desolate car park, searching for a place of refuge. In a split-second decision, she realized that seeking shelter within the familiar walls of the café might provide a sense of security. With a surge of adrenaline, she sprinted towards the back door, her heart pounding in her chest.

As Dana rounded the corner, her hurried steps abruptly halted, causing her to stumble. Her attempt to regain her balance was met with a chilling sight— a mysterious figure concealed within the shadows was positioned just behind the café's back door. The figure's presence sent a shiver down Dana's spine, heightened by the enigmatic aura surrounding him. The dim light revealed fleeting glimpses of striking gray eyes and silver-tipped hair, yet the person's face remained concealed beneath the shadowy veil of their hoodie. A sense of trepidation filled the air, leaving Dana on edge, unsure of the stranger's intentions and wary of the imminent encounter that awaited her.

Dana's heart skipped a beat, her breath catching in her throat as the figure's intentions became chillingly clear. The glint of the blood-stained knife in their hand sent a surge of adrenaline coursing through her veins, heightening her senses.

The weight of the words "Justice for Eder" hung in the air as the hooded assailant marched closer.

Dana's heart raced as her desperate pleas for help echoed through the empty streets. The hooded man's menacing presence loomed closer, his footsteps closing in on her with alarming speed. Panic fueled her legs as she sprinted, her lungs burning with exertion. With every ounce of strength she could muster, Dana pushed herself onward, hoping against hope that someone would come to her aid. Her voice cracked with fear as she continued to scream, her cries becoming a haunting symphony of desperation and terror in the desolate surroundings.

Dana was finally close enough to reach the ear of a few students who were strolling on campus. "Help!" she yelled one more time. Two male students came rushing to her aid, while a third ran to get help.

Dana saw the students approaching her and ran toward them for help. The men dropped their bags and sprinted ahead. Dana ran past the two men when she felt a sudden jolt as she was tripped by one of the students rushing to her aid. Pain shot through her body as she landed hard on her hands and knees, the fall causing her to fracture her wrist. She turned to see one of the men standing there with a smirk on his face. The men stopped and smiled at each other.

"Oops, looks like she fell for you," said one of the guys.

"No, no, how could she fall for a guy like me?" the other laughed.

Dana mustered all her strength and got back to her feet. Despite her weakened voice, she attempted to scream for help, hoping that someone nearby would hear her plea, but her voice betrayed her. She scanned her surroundings, desperately searching for any sign of assistance. With her fractured wrist throbbing in pain, tears welled up in her eyes as she realized the severity of her situation.

"Justice for Eder, bitch!" the students shouted as the hooded man finally caught up.

Dana's adrenaline surged as she sprinted through the maze of campus buildings, her heart pounding in her chest. The fear and pain fueled her determination to escape her pursuers. She darted around corners, seeking refuge in the labyrinthine pathways, hoping to lose them in the confusion.

"Spread out, don't let her get away," instructed the hooded man.

Dana's heart sank as she frantically searched for open doors or any sign of help, but the campus seemed deserted. The eerie silence only amplified her fear, and the weight of the situation bore down on her. She continued to run, her voice growing hoarse from the repeated cries for assistance. The empty pathways and closed doors intensified her feelings of isolation and vulnerability.

She noticed two girls running toward a dormitory building. She quickly rushed to the door and placed her hand on it. As she pulled the door open, one of the guys kicked it shut, and the other grabbed Dana's hand, yanking it off the door handle.

The three men quickly dragged Dana into an alley and held her against the wall. "Pretty girls like you always break good men's hearts, so now we're going to even the playing field," one of the men stated.

Suddenly, the three men were knocked to the ground, courtesy of Genji's swift and powerful kick. Genji looked up at Dana with a determined gaze and yelled, "Run!"

Dana's heart raced as she burst out of the alley, her eyes immediately drawn to the sight of campus security and the flashing red and blue lights. She waved her arms frantically, desperately seeking their attention. The security officers quickly noticed her distress and rushed towards her, their expressions reflecting a sense of urgency. With adrenaline pumping through her veins, Dana relayed the horrifying situation, informing them that Genji was being mercilessly attacked by a group of college students.

The piercing sirens and flashing lights jolted the men, causing them to abandon their attack and flee the scene. However, their ruthless assault had already taken its toll on Genji, leaving him severely battered and stabbed.

After the doctor examined her hand and treated Dana, she sat in the hallway until another doctor finally emerged from Genji's room. Dana anxiously approached him. The doctor informed her that Genji had suffered some injuries but would recover. Relief washed over Dana as she thanked the doctor and entered the room. There, she found Genji sitting on the bed shirtless with a bandage around his stomach and his face bruised, with a busted lip.

"Where is my brother?!" a man shouted in the halls. In came a tall, tattooed Japanese man with multiple piercings on his ears and one on the bridge of his nose. His right eyebrow was slashed twice, and his hair was messy. He rushed into the room, bumping Dana out of the way. His cologne smelled of sweet spices and tobacco.

"Hey, what's your problem?" Dana barked.

"Shut the fuck up," he groaned at Dana. Turning to Genji, he said, "Outoto, what happened to you?"

"Some guys were trying to hurt this girl. I helped her get away, but they jumped me," Genji replied.

"Baka! You could have gotten killed for this slut!" stated Genji's brother.

"Kaito, it's not like that—" Genji began.

"Yamero... Come and show me who did this," Kaito instructed.

"Kaito, I don't think we should—" Genji pleaded.

"Now, Genji!" Kaito demanded.

"Hey, I don't think he should be moving right now—" Dana interjected.

Kaito turned and grabbed Dana by the throat, slamming her against the drywall. "This is your fault for getting my little brother in this mess. Maybe I should start with yo—" Kaito hissed.

A gun was suddenly pressed against his head. Kaito slowly turned to find Mama B approaching with her army of bodyguards. "Young man, take your grubby hands off my child's neck, or you will be the one who stops breathing."

Kaito tightened his grip and stared back at Mama B. "Lady, you don't scare me with these guns. I've seen worse situations. Try me, and I will take her to the afterlife with me."

"You have no value for your life, but do you value his?" Mama B waved her hand, and all guns aimed at Genji.

Kaito immediately released his grip and, holding his stare, stepped closer to Mama B. "Easy. Before I line these halls with all of you, know who you're threatening. Touch my brother, and I will descend a different kind of hell on this earth," retorted Kaito stoically.

"Mama, stop. His brother got hurt protecting me. It's just a misunderstanding," Dana claimed as she turned to Genji. "Thank you for saving my life, Shinoda Genji."

"Shinoda?" Mama B whispered.

"I'm sorry your brother got hurt because of me. Let me pay for his medical bills," Dana offered.

"We don't need your money. Just stay away from my brother. Genji, let's go," Kaito called out, keeping his eyes on Mama B.

"Mama, let them pass," Dana pleaded.

After a few seconds, Mama B waved her fingers, the tension in the room dissipated, and the men reluctantly lowered their guns. Kaito wasted no time and quickly moved to help Genji off the bed and guided him toward the door. Genji turned to Dana and said, "Ja ne," smiling as they squeezed through dozens of bodyguards.

"Are you okay, baby?" Mama B held Dana in her arms.

"I didn't get hurt, thanks to Genji. Thanks for picking me up," Dana answered.

"You're coming back to my house, okay?" Mama B stated.

"Yes, Mama. I really need to see Galan. I'll explain everything when he's awake," Dana told her.

"Of course, baby. Now come, let's get you home safely and fix you something to eat. You're shaking," Mama B suggested.

Chapter Eighteen

Mama B and Dana returned to the mansion, accompanied by a convoy of vehicles that served as their escorts. Their attention was immediately captured by a captivating sight outside the window. A fierce, burning orange glow embraced their skin, casting an ethereal aura on their faces.

The convoy of cars screeched to a sudden halt, jolting Dana and Mama B into action. Sensing the seriousness of the situation, they swiftly exited the vehicle and rushed toward the source of the chaos, their hearts pounding with apprehension. Their eyes widened in disbelief as they beheld the once-majestic mansion engulfed in flames, its structure consumed by the destructive inferno. The crackling heat and billowing smoke filled the air; their minds raced, grappling with the enormity of the situation as they stood there.

Amidst the chaos and devastation, Mama B remained resolute, her calm demeanor a pillar of strength. With a steady gaze, she observed her beloved home consumed by the raging inferno, her heart heavy with sorrow yet her spirit unwavering. Meanwhile, Dana's emotions overcame her, and in a moment of desperation, she cried out Galan's name, her voice echoing through the turmoil. Reacting instinctively, she made a frantic dash toward the mansion's gate. Mama B swiftly reached out, firmly grasping Dana's hand, drawing her close, "Baby, no, he's gone, he's gone," she said calmingly.

"Let me go, Mama!" Dana's desperation and anguish manifested in her words as she fought against Mama B's firm grip.

"Galan died last night," Mama B whispered. Dana's struggle gradually subsided. "I'm sorry, baby, I couldn't tell you; I wanted you to be with me when I broke the news."

"What do you mean he died?" Dana's voice quivered as she spoke, her body still trembling.

"The doctors treated him, but he was in too much pain with the bullet wounds. They administered anesthesia to stop the pain while treating him, but his body was too far gone; he had lost too much blood and didn't make it. I'm sorry, sweetheart," Mama B explained.

"No. You're lying; tell me you're lying to me. Galan can't be gone," Dana shrieked.

"Baby...," comforted Mama B.

"If he's gone, it's because of me. I acted rashly, and he got shot because of me. I came to you and dragged him from the hospital, then accused him and pushed him when he was already fragile! It's all my fault!" Dana burst into tears.

Mama B held her tighter, "Hush baby, don't say that. This isn't your fault."

The head of security came to Mama B, "Madame, you need to see this."

With Dana in tow, Mama B cautiously made her way toward the front gate, their hearts heavy with trepidation. Their shock deepened as their eyes fell upon a devastating scene before them. The once pristine driveway, now stained with tragedy, was strewn with lifeless bodies, and blood meandered through the grooves of the cobblestone.

"Get my child to her house safely, the rest of you; find out who did this," Mama B instructed.

"Yes, Madame," the head of security personally escorted Dana to a vehicle.

"Mama, please don't leave me alone right now," Dana whined, tears streaming down her face.

"I wish I could keep you by my side, but being around me makes you a target. I have enemies who often come after me, but none have been this ruthless. This is an open declaration of war on my family; my baby girl shouldn't be anywhere near this. Find yourself a driver and some security, and close up shop before nightfall until we can handle this," advised Mama B. She reached for the gun on her waist and gave it to Dana, "Stay protected at all times."

"What will you do, Mama?" asked Dana.

"This is a minor inconvenience, sweetie. My empire extends far beyond a single mansion. Who do you think taught your Daddy to become who he is?" Mama B chuckled.

"Come here," Mama B exclaimed. Dana rushed to her, and Mama B hugged her tightly, planting a kiss on her cheek. "Don't worry, baby. Mama will always be there for you. Now, you have a lot on your plate. Get some sleep. Tomorrow's troubles can wait for now," she said.

"I will," Dana agreed as she left Mama B's side and entered the awaiting SUV. The head of security took her back to her abode.

As Dana returned to the penthouse, the weight of recent events weighed heavily upon her. With a heavy heart, she settled onto her bed, the emptiness beside her a stark reminder of Galan's absence. As she gazed into the void, her eyes welled up with tears, the floodgates of her emotions opening once more.

In an effort to find solace and perhaps a glimmer of hope, Dana reached for her phone. She scrolled through the saved videos until she found footage from the opening day of Grounded Coffee House. Her trembling finger pressed play.

She fixated on Galan's infectious smile and boundless energy, evident in every frame of the video. Even amidst the hustle and bustle of the café, he never missed a chance to steal glances at her, his eyes lighting up with adoration. She was touched by his unwavering affection, realizing that his love for her extended beyond the moments when she was aware of his gaze.

What have I done… It hurts so much; I don't want to do this. I don't…

Overwhelmed by the weight of her emotions, Dana made the decision to switch off her phone, the screen fading to black. The silence that followed was deafening, amplifying the profound emptiness that surrounded her in the house.

In the morning light, Dana emerged from her slumber and readied herself for the day. With a sense of purpose, she descended to the lobby, where a building driver awaited to transport her to work. Quietly contemplating the road ahead, she embarked on her journey, resolved to face the challenges that lay before her.

Amidst the chaos and personal loss, Dana summoned her inner strength and wore a mask of resilience, determined to keep up appearances. As the day commenced, Avan and Sydney, familiar faces and cherished patrons of the Coffee House, entered the establishment, approaching the bar with warm smiles. They greeted Dana with a friendly wave, unaware of the pain she concealed behind her brave facade.

Dana smiled and approached them. "Hello, my lovelies; how are we today?" she asked.

"Not too good; everyone on campus is starting to grow a bit uneasy, and many students are leaving the dorms. There was another attack last night," Sydney stated.

"I want to leave too, but this is happening at every college. Even with all their security measures, the extra security, the metal detectors, the random checks, it's not stopping it," Avan added.

"I read another theory: all of the victims of the schools, they all have something in common—they aren't locals. The girl they found on the first night, the girl from the dorm, and last night's attack, were all people who came here from the outside," Sydney announced.

"I'm not from around here; I came to work at the hotel a couple months ago. And I only took that job because they have a program that gets us into SPU, which is nearly impossible to get into," Avan panicked.

"I grew up here; I'm not leaving," Sydney declared.

"Guys, where is Belle?" asked Dana.

"I didn't see her today; she must be working at the hotel," Avan replied.

"The hotel? Wait, aren't you a driver at the hotel?" questioned Dana.

"Yes, I am," answered Avan.

"How would you like to be my chauffeur?" Dana inquired.

"I already told Galan I can't; when I am not working there, I am in class," Avan responded.

"I'll triple what you make at the hotel, and you get to keep your job there," Dana offered.

"You need a driver? Hire me!" Sydney suggested.

"How about I hire both of you? While Avan works at the hotel, you can drive me; that way, you both have time for school," Dana proposed.

"Look, I'm a local; those killers aren't coming after me; Avan is a big target who panics for everything," Sydney informed her.

"Heyyy, I do not panic; I am very poised in a tense situation," Avan declared.

As Sydney playfully feigned a strike towards Avan, his high-pitched outburst echoed through Grounded Coffee House, startling the patrons and staff, briefly interrupting the usual ambiance of the bustling café.

"Don't do things like that; it turns me on!" Avan shrieked. In a moment of realization, Avan's face flushed with embarrassment as he became aware of his unintentionally loud outburst, prompting him to quickly cover his mouth in shame. Meanwhile, Dana and Sydney struggled to stifle their laughter, exchanging amused glances as they found humor in the situation.

"The job is yours, Sydney," Dana decided.

"When do I start?" asked Sydney.

"Today," said Dana.

"Beautiful," Sydney replied.

"What do you guys study here at SPU, by the way?" Dana wondered.

"We're film students. SPU is a major stepping stone to Hollywood; their film program is the most well-funded anywhere in the world," Sydney remarked.

"That's right, getting into that film program is not easy. It's why Belle and I took the opportunity to work at the hotel. Solely because they are a major benefactor of SPU, and their employees can get into SPU ahead of the waitlist," Avan explained.

"Lucky, some of us had to work really hard to get into SPU, you know," Sydney teased.

"Well, don't forget little old me when you guys go off to Hollywood," Dana chuckled. "So, what will you be having?" asked Dana.

"The regular GHC mocha, the way we like it," Sydney responded.

"I'll be right back; I'm going to call Belle and find out what time we are meeting up later for drinks," said Avan.

"Drinks, huh?" Sydney exclaimed.

"It's our ritual; we go out for a beer every month; you guys wanna come?" asked Avan. "I mean, not come... Damn... I don't mean come; I mean come like... With me. Not come with me, I mean with me and Belle—" Avan rambled.

"Sure, I wouldn't mind a beer," Sydney replied. "What about you? Um... What was your name again?"

"Dana, Dana... Rain," Dana answered.

They don't seem to know who I am; better to keep it that way. I don't want them connecting the dots with what happened in Salt Pine Acres, especially with that whole 'Justice for Eder' thing. What is that anyway? I wonder if they know. Drinks might be a good way to find out. I wish Galan was here; he would know what to do.

"Dana?" Sydney called out. "Hey, you spaced out on us; you ok?"

"Yeah, sorry, it's just been a lot of restless nights," Dana replied.

"So… Drinks?" Sydney repeated.

"Drinks sounds nice," Dana looked at Avan and leaned over the bar. "I can't wait to tell people Avan made me come." Dana's voice took on a playful and flirtatious tone as she addressed Avan, her eyes sparkling with mischief and amusement.

"Ohhhh my…." Avan dropped his phone, stunned by her playful teasing. Dana turned and started making their drinks. Avan picked his phone off the floor and tried to compose himself before he walked off to a corner and called Belle.

As Dana and a fellow staff member ventured outside to carry out the trash, the bustling parking lot was filled with students going about their day. Engaged in their task, they swiftly disposed of the bags. However, as Dana turned around, she was caught off guard by the sudden presence of Genji, standing unexpectedly close to her. The surprise caused her to jump, her heart racing. "Geez!" Dana gasped.

"Did I scare you?" asked Genji.

"No, I almost jumped out of my skin because I was sad," Dana smirked.

"Well, I didn't mean to make you sad; I wanted to see if you were ok," Genji remarked.

"Me? You're the one who was assaulted and stabbed," Dana stated.

"I wasn't the one who was screaming, 'Help, help, oh help me,'" Genji mocked her while playfully acting out her actions.

"Shut up!" Dana responded, embarrassed.

"But seriously, how are you doing? I was worried about you," Genji exclaimed earnestly.

"You were?" asked Dana.

"Of course, you really scared me," said Genji as he reached out and tucked her hair behind her ear.

"But why would you do that for me?" questioned Dana.

"Have I not made myself clear?" Genji stepped closer.

"No...," Dana whispered.

"If you died, who would make the coffee?" Genji whispered back. "And why are we whispering?"

"Weren't you going to kill yourself? Maybe you should do that tonight," Dana muttered.

Genji's intense gaze scanned Dana from head to toe, creating tension as he purposefully closed the distance between them, their bodies almost touching.

The proximity and the weight of his stare stirred a mixture of anticipation and uncertainty within Dana, leaving her momentarily breathless as she awaited his next move. "I can think of something else I want to do tonight."

"Genji!" Kaito approached, carrying two cups of coffee and interrupting the charged atmosphere between Dana and Genji. Genji's attention shifted as he turned to face his brother, accepting the cup from him. The brief interruption brought a momentary pause to the tension, allowing Dana to catch her breath and collect her thoughts.

Kaito's fierce gaze bore down on Dana, his eyes conveying a sharp intensity that seemed to cut through the air like a knife as he walked away; the weight of his gaze lingered, leaving Dana with a sense of unsettled curiosity. "I'll be in the car, don't waste too much of your time here," Kaito called out as he walked away.

"I should head back to work now; nice seeing you again, Shinoda Genji. I'm happy you're doing ok," said Dana.

"I'll see you around?" asked Genji.

"Sure," Dana replied as she walked away.

With the coffee cup in hand, Genji made his way toward the car, where his brother was perched on the hood, patiently waiting. A group of girls surrounded Kaito, attempting to engage him in conversation, their presence and interest evident. As Genji approached, he navigated through the buzzing crowd, ready to join his brother and the lively atmosphere surrounding him. As Genji walked away amidst the bustling crowd, he turned his attention to Dana, his voice carrying a hint of farewell as he shouted, "Ja ne!"

Dana turned and smiled. *Wait, he still doesn't know my name.* "I'm Dana, by the way," she called out.

"I'm well aware!" Genji replied, smiling.

"Shut up and get in the car, baka!" Kaito exclaimed.

As Genji and Kaito settled into their car and drove away, Dana's gaze locked with Genji's for one final moment. Their eyes met, a silent exchange of emotions and unspoken connections before the car disappeared from view.

Avan D'Giovani

AGE: 21

SIGN: LIBRA

FUN FACT: "I THINK GALAN IS IN LOVE WITH ME. I UNDERESTIMATED THE POWER OF MY ALURE. I GUESS BEING THE STRONG SILENT TYPE IS A CURSE."

Chapter Nineteen

Dana concluded the operations of Grounded Coffee House at six, finding a measure of reassurance in the remaining daylight amidst the relentless turmoil. While the shuttle prepared to depart from the parking lot, Sydney and Avan leisurely approached, extending warm greetings to Dana with cheerful gestures.

"Hey, Boss Lady," said Sydney.

"Hey guys, I just need to arm the security, and we can leave," Dana informed them.

"Where is the car?" asked Sydney.

"It's on its way," Dana replied.

Within a matter of moments, a sleek vehicle from Écarlate glided to a halt nearby.

"Wait... Isn't that a car from the hotel lot?" questioned Avan.

"That's right," Dana confirmed.

"How?!" Avan gasped.

"My mom knows the owner," Dana chuckled.

"B-but... But I...." Avan stammered.

"You missed your chance," Sydney chuckled as she high-fived Dana.

"By the way, where is Galan?" Avan remarked.

"Oh, don't worry; he didn't want to be near you because of all that sexual tension," Dana smirked.

"I knew it...." Avan whispered.

"Get in; we will swing by the hotel and get Belle," Dana instructed.

"Belle hasn't answered all day; it must have been a busy day," Avan stated.

The trio climbed into the plush rear seats, and the vehicle smoothly transported them back to Écarlate. Upon arriving, the driver parked the car at the entrance and courteously handed the keys to Dana, who accepted them with gratitude. Meanwhile, Avan and Sydney eagerly entered the establishment, searching for Belle.

As the others ventured inside, Dana opted to stay in the car, her gaze fixated on a collection of cherished photographs capturing her and Galan.

Bittersweet memories flooded her mind, evoking a cascade of emotions as she reminisced about their all-too-brief time together.

I can't keep doing this. I have been avoiding coming to terms with Aria's death, and Galan was the only one who distracted me from the pain. Now he's gone, and I can't do this; the two people I could have gone to are dead... Both because of me. Paige killed Aria because I bought Galan's café and he died because of me. It's all my fault, Eder, Galan... Aria...

Dana's eyes brimmed with tears, but she swiftly brushed them away, determined to regain her composure. Shortly thereafter, Avan and Sydney returned without Belle and joined Dana inside the car.

"Where's Belle?" asked Dana.

"She didn't come to work today," Avan stated worriedly.

"Is she usually hard to reach?" questioned Dana.

"Not for me. We started here together and became close friends; she wouldn't avoid me," Avan explained.

"I don't like this," said Sydney.

"You think something happened to Belle?" Dana wondered.

"Oh God, something happened to Belle!!" Avan panicked.

"Avan, no, calm down. It's just a question," Dana stated.

"Belle isn't a local," Sydney remarked as she looked at Avan and Dana.

"Let's not jump to conclusions," Dana said calmly.

"Maybe we should cancel drinks tonight," Sydney suggested.

"Maybe she's at the bar waiting for us," Avan replied with a hint of hope.

"That's the spirit. Positive thoughts," Dana smiled.

"Alright then, let's go," Sydney responded, hopping into the driver's seat.

Afterward, they embarked on a drive towards a sophisticated club on the city's outskirts. Exiting the car, the trio made their way into the establishment. As they stepped inside, their eyes scanned the premises, and joy spread across their faces when they spotted Belle seated alone at a cozy booth.

Avan's eyes sparkled with excitement, and he hurriedly approached Belle, his face beaming with delight. He smoothly slid into the booth beside her, enveloping Belle in a warm, affectionate hug. "Oh my God, Dana thought you were dead!" Avan exclaimed.

Belle chuckled, "What?"

"Ignore him; he's just being Avan," said Sydney.

Dana and Sydney joined her at the booth. "I hope you don't mind if we crash your ritual; Avan invited us because he thought you died," Dana teased.

"I think I've heard about enough deaths; let's drink!" Sydney remarked.

"Amen to that," Dana agreed.

The bartender arrived at the table, placing four cold beers before them. Without hesitation, they took a swift sip, reveling in the refreshing taste. However, to the astonishment of Sydney, Belle, and Avan, Dana swiftly finished her beer in one gulp, leaving them wide-eyed and speechless.

"Easy, girl…," Sydney chuckled.

"Bartender! Keep 'em coming," Dana called out.

"Owning a Coffee House must be harder than I thought," Belle commented.

"Is everything ok, Dana?" Avan inquired.

"You know that attack that happened on campus last night? It was me," Dana informed them.

"No, they attacked a guy," Sydney corrected.

"They were coming after me. They chased me from Grounded to the main campus. I got dragged into an alley, and they were going to kill me when a guy fought and gave me a chance to escape. Campus security and police were already on the scene, but as fast as they responded, it was too late. They had badly beaten and stabbed the guy who saved me," Dana clarified.

"Oh my God…," Avan gasped.

"Dana, are you sure you're ok?" questioned Belle.

"No… I'm struggling to cope right now," Dana answered as the bartender placed another beer before her. "Thank you," she said softly.

"Dana, it's ok. Take some time and get yourself together. You don't look any older than us, but you're running a business and dealing with these things all at once. You need to unwind. This can't be good for you," Sydney exclaimed.

"If I stop, I'll go crazy. Something would haunt me, and I would lose it. Doing all this is just better than facing my demons," Dana claimed.

Unfazed by the attention and fueled by her determination, Dana swiftly lifted the newly placed beer and chugged it down once more. Locking eyes with the bartender, she signaled for yet another round.

"And what about Galan?" asked Avan.

Despite her best efforts, Dana struggled to contain her emotions, her attempts to hold back tears evident to Sydney and the rest of the group. They could clearly see that their previous actions had touched a sensitive nerve within her.

"Galan left me… For good," Dana softly replied.

"I'm so sorry," Belle responded.

"We're here for you; you don't have to do this alone," Sydney added.

"Anytime you need us, we will be there. Except when you know we have school and work. Sometimes we would need a vacation so you can't bother us then. And then, of course, we would have our own problems, and we need sleep and all that but any other time, we will be there for you," Avan rambled.

"Thanks, Avan; I'm sure she feels so much support right now," Belle chuckled.

Dana managed to summon a fleeting smile, allowing a brief respite from the emotional weight that burdened her. As the night unfolded, she continued to consume beer after beer, finding solace in the company of Sydney, Avan, and Belle, who joined her in her endeavor, attempting to provide a welcome distraction from her inner turmoil.

As the night wore on and the music grew louder, the energetic atmosphere enticed them to hit the dance floor. Dana was caught up in the rhythm but eventually excused herself from the group to make her way to the restroom. However, as she navigated her way back, she stumbled unexpectedly, colliding with Kaito.

"I'm so sorry," Dana murmured. As she regained her balance and pushed herself away from Kaito's chest, her hands unintentionally brushed against his toned abs through his shirt. A wave of familiarity washed over her, and she was captivated by a distinct and enticing scent surrounding him. Curiosity piqued, so she gazed up at him, her eyes searching for recognition in his face.

Dana's gaze locked onto Kaito's chiseled jawline, drawing her attention before her eyes met his intense, piercing gaze. With a calculated, deliberate motion, he lifted his drink to his lips and took a sip, never breaking eye contact. Breaking the silence, Kaito's voice cut through the air as he spoke her name, seeking confirmation. "Dana, right?" he inquired, his tone carrying a blend of familiarity and intrigue.

"No, your name is Kaito," Dana's words slurred as she answered.

"Right—" Kaito said as he put down his drink. "I think you've had too much to drink; maybe you should sit down."

"I don't take orders from you… What, you thought I would just obey, Sir?!?" Dana replied, her voice slightly trembling as she mustered a response.

"Sit," Kaito firmly commanded.

"Yes, Sir…," Dana replied, quickly sitting in a booth beside him.

I'M BROKEN TOO

Kaito sat beside Dana, the proximity between them heightening the tension in the air. Sensing the need for some liquid courage, Dana turned towards the bartender, catching their attention and requesting another round of beers to ease the atmosphere. "I think you've had enough," Kaito stated.

"You're not the boss of me," Dana responded.

As the bartender promptly delivered another beer, Kaito abruptly rose from his seat and positioned himself between Dana and the bartender. "Can't you see she's had enough? Yet you bring beer after beer for her. You can drink that yourself; go get her a bottle of water and come back," Kaito instructed as Dana looked on.

Kaito sat back down, "You are in no condition to be out here. Point out the people you came with, and I'll get them to take you home."

Dana surveyed the club, her gaze scanning the surroundings until she spotted the individuals she wanted to point out. Sensing her intention, Kaito followed her line of sight and turned his attention to the people she had identified. "Those are the people you came with? They are in no better condition than you are. Come, I'll take you home, and I'll make sure your friends get home safe, too," Kaito declared.

"I'm not going anywhere," Dana slurred, her body swaying slightly as she spoke, her words carrying a hint of drunkenness.

"I said, come," Kaito rose to his feet, extending his hand towards her.

"I can take myself home," Dana insisted as she attempted to stand up from the booth. However, her first step proved unsteady, causing her to stumble. Kaito reached out and caught her in his arms.

"Baka... Come on, let's get you home," said Kaito.

Recognizing Dana's need for assistance, Kaito swiftly lifted her into his arms, cradling her with care. He carried her towards his car, gently placing her in the front seat. Taking a moment to ensure her safety, he securely fastened her seatbelt before starting the engine and driving off.

As Dana gradually regained consciousness, her eyes adjusted to the familiar surroundings of a room at Écarlate. Sitting up in the bed, she surveyed her surroundings, her head still reeling from the effects of intoxication. In search of answers, she scanned the room, hoping to find clues or someone who could provide clarity amidst her foggy state of mind. *What am I doing here?*

Soon after, Kaito entered the room, gently carrying Sydney, Belle, and Avan and carefully placing them on the second bed. He then approached Dana, holding out a bottle of water to help alleviate her thirst.

"Drink," Kaito ordered.

Dana looked up, her eyes meeting Kaito's as she accepted his bottle of water. Grateful for the gesture, she took a small sip, allowing the cool liquid to quench her parched throat, "What are we doing here?" asked Dana.

"You're here because you're irresponsible and stupid," Kaito replied.

"Excuse me?" Dana remarked.

"You went out with a group of people who are no better at navigating themselves through the night than you were," Kaito stated.

"I said I didn't need your help," Dana fumed.

Kaito sat next to her on the bed, "You didn't want my help. There is a difference."

"Yet you went out of your way for a group of strangers," said Dana.

"Not for them—" said Kaito.

"What… Me? Why would you do anything for me?" questioned Dana.

"Because you're hurting and can't deal, and I didn't want to see you ruin your life," Kaito explained.

"I don't need your pity, and I am not hurting," Dana muttered.

"I lost my parents when I was five; the day my little brother was born, my mom passed away during childbirth. My father killed himself shortly after that.

The only thing I have in this world is my little brother, and if anything happened to that idiot, I wouldn't be able to cope too. He's the reason I keep myself together; you just need to find that thing that keeps you together," Kaito expressed. "Now, I am going to go back and try to enjoy what's left of this night."

As Kaito started to rise from the bed, Dana's hand shot out and grasped his, tugging him back towards her, "Maybe... You could enjoy it right here?" asked Dana. In a moment of vulnerability and longing, Dana leaned closer to Kaito, her words lingering in the air. Without further hesitation, she closed the gap between them, pressing her lips against his; her hands found their way to his neck, guiding him into the kiss. Dana straddled him and wrapped her arms around him as they kissed.

Chapter Twenty

Kaito and Dana entered the bathroom, their gazes filled with unbridled passion. Without hesitation, Dana slammed Kaito against the wall, a rush of desire pulsating between them. With an intense urgency, she seized his shirt, forcefully ripping it open, revealing the chiseled contours of his chest. Simultaneously shedding her own top, Dana discarded any inhibitions as she became lost in the moment.

Her hands moved to Kaito's belt, swiftly undoing its confines. The sound of the buckle relinquishing its hold echoed through the room. Zippers glided downwards as Dana unzipped his

KAITO SHINODA

AGE: 27
SIGN: PISCES
FUN FACT: *UNAVAILABLE* (HE CALLED ME
BAKA, HAD ME BLUSHING AND SHIT UNTIL I
LOOKED IT UP.)

pants, exposing a tantalizing glimpse of what lay beneath.

Dana lowered his pants just enough and took him into her mouth with unquenched hunger, her lips enveloping him with a fervor matched only by her yearning. As Kaito's head leaned back, he surrendered to the sensations coursing through his body as she sucked his cock. His jeans were grasped firmly by Dana's hands, keeping her steady.

"Look at me!" Kaito's voice escaped as a throaty moan, a fervent plea that stirred the depths of Dana's being.

As Dana engulfed him completely, her desire unyielding, she gazed up at Kaito with eyes full of devotion. Slowly, she began to withdraw, savoring every moment, releasing him from the depths of her intoxicating embrace.

A hushed whisper reverberated with appreciation as Kaito uttered, "Good girl."

Dana's movements halted abruptly. Galan's voice echoed hauntingly in her mind. For a brief moment, conflicting emotions threatened to consume her. In that fleeting pause, as her mind wrestled with the echoes of the past, Dana chose to focus on the present moment. With renewed ardor, Dana let go of the intrusive thoughts.

A smile graced Dana's lips as she willingly sank to her knees before Kaito, a spark of devotion dancing in her eyes. Sensing her willingness to continue, Kaito gently leaned off the wall, his lust evident in his every movement. With a tender touch, he lifted her chin.

"You're not done," Kaito's voice resonated with a hint of command. His fingers brushed the strands of hair away from her face, gathering them into a seductive ponytail.

"Open," Kaito commanded.

"Yes, Sir," Dana submitted, biting her lip before once again enveloping him with her mouth.

Dana burned with uninhibited lust as she skillfully moved back and forth on his throbbing cock. Her lips tightly wrapped around his shaft, and her jaw was almost unhinged to take in his girth. With a relentless fervor, he accelerated his rhythm, delving even deeper into the depths of her throat.

Dana's nails dug into his lower back as she drew him closer. His grip tightened, his body tensed, and a deep, guttural moan escaped his lips as he released his salty essence into her throat, mingling with the intoxicating sight of his desire spilling out around her lips as he gently pulled out of her mouth.

"Look at me while you swallow," Kaito whispered, his voice laced with a commanding yet intimate tone. He requested her unwavering gaze as she complied, a distinct audible gulp resonating through the air as she submitted to him. With a deliberate gesture, she wiped the remnants off her lips, savoring the taste, before sensually licking it off her fingertips, embracing the lingering essence of their shared pleasure.

Kaito lifted her effortlessly from the floor, positioning her enticingly over the countertop in front of the massive bathroom mirror. The cool touch of the granite met her skin, sending shivers of anticipation down her spine as he bent her over and removed her pants, leaving them pooled around her ankles. A sharp, arousing slap landed on her cheeks before he guided himself inside her. The change in his breathing echoed his arousal as he glided into the warmth of her inviting slit.

With each deep and forceful thrust, her moans of pleasure grew louder. Kaito wrapped his fingers around her neck, his grip firm yet controlled; he leaned close to her ear, and he whispered, his voice deep with an intoxicating blend of desire and command, "Look at me while I fuck you!"

Her eyes locked on his as they gazed at each other's reflection. Nearing his climax, Kaito relinquished his grip on her throat, his hand now tightening firmly behind her neck. With an assertive force, he pushed her down onto the countertop.

With each intensified stroke, Kaito's movements became more commanding as he pinned her down. The resonating sound of their skin colliding filled the room, harmonizing with the crescendo of Dana's impassioned screams, a symphony of pleasure that echoed through the walls.

As Kaito's thrusts grew more powerful, the countertop quivered beneath their passion. The surrounding bottles danced and toppled, their contents spilling off the countertop.

As Kaito's thrusts reached their climax, Dana felt an overwhelming sensation of being completely filled by him. The warmth of his release spilled out from her; his member slapped against his leg as he withdrew.

With her legs trembling uncontrollably from the intense pleasure, Kaito refused to grant her a moment of respite. Swiftly, he maneuvered her, turning her over and guiding her to sit at the edge of the counter while his cum dripped down the edge of the countertop from her pussy.

A memory of Galan flashed before Dana's eyes, recalling their shared moment on the kitchen island as Kaito's tongue piercing traced her neck.

Dana blocked out the memories and kissed Kaito. Holding him tighter, she wrapped her legs around him. They ended up in the shower; the glass walls grew foggy as their naked bodies pressed against them, their moans filling the room together with the steam of the shower. Kaito's back was riddled with scratches, and his neck and chest were loaded with love bites as they fucked under the shower.

The two ravaged each other in what felt eternal; Kaito pinned her against the tile wall as the water cascaded between them. He fucked her hard as though he was trying to put her through the wall and into the next room.

Without stopping, he leaned to her ear, his heated breath on her neck. "Cum for me," he said. Dana's nails dug deeper into his back, hearing his words. "Cum," he repeated as his rhythm quickened.

"Cumming…." Dana moaned.

"Good girl…," Kaito groaned.

"Yes!" Dana muttered hoarsely.

"Good girl—" Kaito whispered.

The lines of reality blurred as her visions of Galan turned into the present with Kaito.

Dana moaned as she climaxed, Kaito finishing together with her. He slowly kneeled to the floor, still holding Dana in his arms. She kissed him as he lowered to his knees. He let go of her, and she slid to the bathroom floor, gasping for air, unable to steady her breathing. Her legs trembled uncontrollably, cum trickling down her legs. She was utterly captivated by Kaito's presence, unable to divert her gaze as he knelt by her side. Each inhale he took seemed to fill his chest, his sculpted physique accentuated by rivulets of water dancing down his chiseled abdomen.

Kaito's hand extended towards her lips with delicate intention, his thumb gliding tenderly along her quivering lower lip as he spoke in a soft voice. "You're mine now. I don't care whose ring is on that finger. You belong to me," said Kaito as he got out of the shower, swiftly dressed, and departed, leaving her sprawled on the floor, attempting to regain her composure.

Chapter Twenty-one

Dana struggled to regain her balance, her weakened body trembling as she fought to rise from the floor. Her unsteady steps transformed into swaying limps as she hastily reached for a nearby towel, its fabric absorbing the lingering moisture from her shower. With conviction, she darted out into the room, her wet hair clinging to her skin, only to discover Avan, Sydney, and Belle still sound asleep on the bed. Yet, a noticeable absence loomed as Kaito remained nowhere to be found within the confines of the room.

With a surge of hope, Dana sprinted towards the door, her heart pounding in her chest. Desperately yearning for a glimpse of Kaito, she gripped the doorknob tightly. Swinging the door open, she found herself face to face with Galan, his hand hovering in mid-air, about to knock. Galan froze, but not before catching Dana's voice as she called out Kaito's name.

Dana's breath caught in her throat as a flood of emotions overwhelmed her. Her voice faltered as she attempted to form words, but her body betrayed her, rendering her speechless. Sensing her distress, Galan stepped forward, crossed the threshold into the room, and enveloped her in a warm embrace. Breaking the silence, Galan whispered softly, "I missed you so much."

"Galan…," Dana gasped.

"Are you ok? I've been trying to call you!" Galan remarked.

"You're alive!?" Dana remarked, shocked to see him.

"I'll explain everything; I'm just so glad to hear from you. I was afraid you never wanted to see me again," Galan expressed.

"I didn't call you...." Dana stated. Her flustered state intensified, and her cheeks grew warmer as she finally managed to find her voice.

"Then someone texted from your phone. They said you were heavily intoxicated and that they checked you into a room here because you were out cold and couldn't show them to your place," Galan informed her.

Dana: *Kaito*...

"I can leave if you want. I know you're hurt, and I want to give you that space to think about things—" Galan continued.

Dana: *I still have his cum dripping from me.*

"Yes, please leave," Dana quickly agreed.

Galan came to a sudden halt, his expression transforming from a smile to one of shock. His eyes widened as Dana's words resonated within him, "O... Ok, I understand. I really am sorry, love; I know what I did was wrong. I had a moment of weakness and caved to the temptation. I will give you all the time you need; please just give me a chance to explain everything in the future. And if you don't want to marry me anymore, I understand," Galan exclaimed.

"Goodbye, Galan," Dana's voice quivered with sorrow. In an abrupt and unexpected gesture, she swiftly closed the door, cutting off any response from Galan. Leaning against the door for support, Dana felt her heart breaking as tears streamed down her face, impossible to suppress them any longer. Overwhelmed by a wave of emotions, she covered her trembling mouth, attempting to stifle her cries, her sobs becoming silent gasps for air. Slowly, she slid down the door, sinking to the floor, consumed by the weight of her anguish.

Galan remained rooted outside the closed door, his own tears falling relentlessly to the floor below. The shock of Dana's sudden departure lingered on his face, a mix of disbelief and heartache etched across his features. He couldn't comprehend how things had unraveled so swiftly. Feeling the weight of his emotions overwhelming him, Galan leaned against the door, sliding down to the ground, tears streaming down his face in parallel to Dana's. With both on opposite sides of the door, they sat back to back, the door serving as a painful barrier that separated them in their shared sorrow.

With trembling hands and tears blurring his vision, Galan retrieved his phone and navigated to his contacts. Each entry named "Aria" became the target of his sorrowful determination. Deleting them one by one, he sought to erase any reminders of the past, of the moments they had shared. Tears fell onto the screen as he wiped away the traces of their connection from his phone.

Continuing his emotional purge, Galan scrolled through his messages, searching for any remnants of their conversations. The final message was dated the day he had visited Dana on her yacht. With each thread, memories flooded back, reopening wounds that were still raw. With a mixture of anguish and resolve, he deleted every trace, every word exchanged, until only a void remained, a void that mirrored the emptiness in his heart.

Galan: *I did this… All on my own. No one to blame… But myself. I should have done better.*

Galan took a deep breath, wiping away the lingering tears on his cheeks, and exited the hotel. With a heavy heart, he stepped into his car and embarked on the drive back to his apartment, the engine's rumble providing a somber soundtrack to his thoughts. As he navigated the familiar streets, he couldn't help but notice the town's revitalized appearance. Salt Pine Acres stood proudly, restored to its former glory, except for one notable absence—a vacant lot that marked the spot where Grounded Coffee House once thrived.

Galan's grip on the steering wheel tightened as he passed the vacant lot, memories flooding back of the countless conversations, shared laughter, and stolen glances within those walls. Galan's gaze lingered on the shattered remains of the building, mirroring the state of his own spirit.

Driving into the garage of the condo complex, Galan sought solace within the confines of his penthouse suite. As he ascended to the top floor inside the glass elevator, his surroundings seemed to blur, his mind lost in a whirlwind of memories and unanswered questions.

The moment Galan stepped out of the elevator, a jarring scene awaited him in his living room. Blood bags lined the floor, accompanied by gauze stained with the evidence of medical procedures. Invoices from doctors and hospitals were scattered about. He trudged through the living room, each step a burden, as he made his way toward his own room. However, his gaze couldn't help but be drawn down the hall to a locked door—a familiar sight that stirred his racing heartbeat.

Galan scanned his fingerprint and entered the empty room, his footsteps echoing in the stillness.

Dana stood in the bathroom, her eyes fixed on the disarray surrounding her and the remnants of the passionate encounter she and Kaito had shared. As she surveyed the scene, flashes of their intimate moments played vividly in her mind, intermingling with Galan's own tormenting thoughts.

Both Dana and Galan found themselves haunted by the same overwhelming question, their minds trapped in the relentless grip of what had transpired between them.

What have I done…

In the following two weeks, Galan made relentless attempts to reach out to Dana, his desperate calls numbering in the hundreds, only to witness each one being rejected without a response. Amid his efforts to reconnect, Galan sought solace in the ice pond atop the jogging trail, finding moments of respite within its freezing embrace. Regular doctor visits allowed his wounds to be diligently treated, and Galan's body gradually began to heal, restoring him to his former self. The scars on his chest closed over time, aided by medical care, until they became nearly imperceptible, a testament to his physical recovery.

Returning from his morning run, Galan sought a moment of relaxation as he switched on the TV, sipping his coffee. News of an impending storm and public advisory tips were being announced. As he flipped channels, his tranquility was swiftly shattered by the grim reports that dominated every major news network—news of ongoing killings spreading across the world. The name "Blood Rain Ripper" echoed relentlessly. Galan turned to his laptop and delved into his emails, searching for the link to the blog he had requested from Belle. With resolve in his eyes, he tirelessly browsed through every article, immersing himself in the content day and night. Scrolling through thousands of posts, his attention was suddenly captured by one particular article that stood out from the rest, causing his heart to skip a beat.

As Galan meticulously filtered through the chilling feed of school killings, his focus eventually settled on the entries related to SPU. With a mix of dread and morbid curiosity, he scrolled through the harrowing records of every recorded murder, each entry documenting the tragic fate of the victims. Pictures and videos depicting their untimely ends were showcased. Galan's eyes scanned through them with an unsettling carelessness until his gaze froze upon a video that brought his world crashing down.

In that haunting footage, Galan saw himself, a nightmarish embodiment of the person he feared he had become, committing the heinous act against the woman they had found on that fateful first night. Shock and disbelief coursed through his veins as he struggled to comprehend the gravity of what he had just witnessed, his mind grappling with the horrifying truth that he was somehow involved in these senseless killings.

What the fuck is this?

Every detail, from the hair and build to the haunting gray eyes, mirrored his own appearance. But the shock only deepened as Galan continued to scroll through the disturbing videos. Another clip played, this time revealing a familiar voice that sent shivers down his spine. Dana's voice, pleading for help, was captured by a terrified student in her dorm room. The sight of Dana, running through the campus in desperate search of assistance, struck Galan's heart with an indescribable heaviness, unraveling his emotions in a torrent of anguish and concern.

I'M BROKEN TOO

As Galan's trembling fingers hovered over the screen, he mustered the courage to pause the video, freezing the haunting image of the assailant chasing Dana. There, in a freeze-frame, he confronted the chilling truth—the person pursuing her bore an undeniable resemblance to himself.

She thought it was me... That's what she meant when she said those men came for me. She thought I had killed that girl and attacked her. I need to tell her it wasn't me.

❧

Dana poured her energy into the café, channeling her determination amidst the grim backdrop of escalating killings. With an unexpected surge in customers, drawn by the macabre fascination surrounding the Salt Pine Acres Massacre, Dana decided to embrace the dark theme. She crafted unique, themed drinks that captured the essence of the tragedy while also offering merchandise that commemorated the events.

As the business thrived, Avan, Sydney, and Belle joined Dana at the bar for their daily GHC mocha.

Genji's arrival at the coffee house drew the attention of everyone present, including Avan, Sydney, Belle, and Dana. His brother, Kaito, followed closely behind him, the two of them taking seats at the bar alongside Avan and the girls. As Dana turned with the drinks in hand, her gaze met Kaito's subtle smile, causing her cheeks to flush with a deep blush. Their exchange spoke volumes, conveying a shared connection that couldn't be hidden. Dana's smile grew, a mix of joy and shyness playing on her lips as she tried to conceal her excitement. However, her friends, Sydney and the others, quickly picked up on the blossoming interaction, their curious eyes turning towards Kaito, awaiting further revelations.

"Oh, hello, Mr. Jawline," Sydney exclaimed.

"I have a jawline, too," Avan rolled his eyes and mumbled. "It's just not that great."

As the others continued to observe, Kaito paid no attention to their presence, his focus solely on Dana. His gaze remained fixed on her.

"Hey, Dana, two coffees to go, please," Genji called out.

"Coming right up," Dana replied.

Avan turned to Belle, "Hey, isn't that the guy who got attacked before?"

Belle and Sydney looked over. "Oh my God, it is him!" they replied in unison.

"You know, you're terrible at keeping secrets. We can hear you over there," Genji remarked.

"Why didn't you leave? Nearly half the school left the dorms, and only the locals stayed on campus," Sydney stated.

"Why don't you mind your business over there," Kaito retorted.

"Well, excuse me," said Sydney in disbelief.

"Hey, behave while you're in my café, got that?" Dana exclaimed.

"Or else?" asked Kaito.

"I'll throw you out myself," Dana answered as she approached the bar.

"I would like to see you try," Kaito chuckled.

"Get him, Avan!" Dana called out.

"Get him what? A coffee?" Avan panicked.

"Why do we keep you around again?" asked Dana as she teased him.

"If one of the killers comes, he can slow them down while we get out of there," Belle answered.

"That is so hurtful," Avan responded.

"Aww," said Sydney as the girls laughed.

"But, really, guys, didn't they find two of the guys dead on campus that same night? It was never reported, but rumors are going around that they were killed," Belle announced.

"Serves them right for killing innocent people like that because nobody loves them! I say good riddance," Dana commented as she handed Kaito and Genji their carefully crafted coffees. Her eyes met Kaito's once again, a subtle yet meaningful connection passing between them in that fleeting moment.

"Since then, the killings slowed down, not just in SPU," Avan stated.

"Yea, the rumors say the real Ripper killed them. They're saying the girl who inspired the Salt Pine Acres Massacre is here, so they're cautious about who they attack. And with most of the outside students gone, they don't want to take chances," Sydney added.

"Who comes up with this stuff?" questioned Dana.

"It's all anonymous, no user names, no profiles, it's just content," said Belle.

So, it's just marketing, essentially? I used this to my advantage for my business. I bet we can re-engineer these rumors to that blog's disadvantage.

"What if we could stop the killings?" asked Dana.

"How?" Sydney remarked.

"You guys said the killings slowed down when they found the killers dead right? All of this revolves around the Ripper, so what if "The Ripper" ordered them to stop," Dana suggested.

"Well, don't stop there. What do you have in mind?" Sydney inquired.

Dana huddled closer to them. "What if we give them a reason to believe it was the real Ripper. Build off the rumor that is going around?" she stated.

"I'm with you so far, Boss," Sydney replied.

Dana continued, "I have a lot of edible fake blood that I'd ordered for the new drinks. What if we staged a murder, like a massive murder scene, and among them was the girl who the Ripper was in love with. But we can really sell it, justice for Eder; that's the thing they say before their kill, right? This viral element of the killings came from Eder Barlows fans, right? So what if we can bring his fans and the Ripper's fans all in one place. Then flip the script and scare them to stop!"

"This all sounds great, but can we unite those two followings?" questioned Belle.

"Eder Barlow, I met him once. I have a picture of us from the time I met him. We use that, plus our fake murder scene, to get the attention of both factions, then we have "The Ripper" threaten everyone on the thread. Hundreds of customers come in here, and I can get them to participate. We show the scene and make it look like the Ripper is hunting anyone who participated in that blog. Fear will force them to stop and shut down the site. If a couple murders here reduced the killings, just imagine what the massacre as big as Salt Pine Acres' would do!" Dana explained.

"Dana, you might be on to something," Sydney expressed.

"I like it," Avan stated.

"Count me in," Belle added.

"Are we making this happen?" asked Dana.

"Oh yeah, we're doing this," Sydney remarked.

"Ahem," said Kaito. "You're still lousy at secrets, Baka."

"Count me in; I'm one of the survivors. It'll help sell the story," Genji declared.

"You would do that?" questioned Dana.

"Of course," Genji replied with a smile.

"How long would this take?" Belle wondered.

"I have the blood, and I have the patrons. All we need is someone to pose as the Ripper," Dana answered.

"Maybe I can help," Galan's unexpected presence at the bar caused Dana's heart to race with a mix of emotions. She turned her attention towards him, her eyes meeting his, as a wave of anticipation washed over her.

Avan turned to him, "Galan! How have you been?"

"I've never been worse in my life, but things might get better soon," Galan replied as he turned toward Dana.

"Galan—" Dana murmured.

"This is work-related. Can I see you in the back?" asked Galan.

"Sure," Dana agreed.

As Galan and Dana made their exit, a subtle tension filled the air; Genji and Kaito noticed this, their gazes lingering on Galan.

"So, um, I kinda have this thing where my allure makes people fall for me. I just want to make sure there is no sexual tension building between us," Avan said while directing his words to Kaito.

"I should have stayed in Japan...." Kaito mumbled as he sipped his coffee and shook his head in disbelief.

Sydney and Belle patted Avan on the head.

Galan and Dana found their way to the privacy of her office at the back of the coffee house. Once inside, Galan turned to face her, "Dana, I wasn't the one who killed the girl that night out by the bins; it was—"

"It was a copycat. I know, Galan," Dana finished his words.

"You knew?" asked Galan.

"Not at the time. At the time, I was very scared and did what I did because it was what I thought was the best thing to do. I'm sorry you got shot, but we never got to have this conversation. How are you still alive? I was on my way to see you the moment I found out it wasn't you, and we found Mama B's house on fire, bodies scattered all over her property. And she assured me you were in there because you had died," Dana exclaimed.

"I can explain, but you're not going to like it," Galan stated.

"Try me!" said Dana.

"Mama B was sure I was dead because she was the one who killed me, or at least thought she did," Galan informed her.

"Bullshit," Dana replied.

"She beat me till I was near death, and then she injected me with an overdose of anesthesia to kill me. The autopsy would have shown me dying from an overdose and blood loss. Because of that, the autopsy would have made it seem like a normal dosage was too much for my body to handle," Galan explained.

"I don't believe that for a second. Why would Mama let me come see you if she beat you so badly and left your dead body for me to find, huh? Wouldn't I see the bruises? You were shot, not assaulted," Dana remarked.

"She kept it where you wouldn't see, mostly my back and torso, places that would be covered with clothes. When you found me dead, you wouldn't have checked for bruises. Why would you? And she knew that," Galan stated.

"You were alive all this time... I mourned you for days. I was a wreck, and you couldn't tell me you were ok? Someone sent you a message from my phone, and you responded to that, but it never occurred to you to pick up the phone and call me?" asked Dana.

"I did! I tried calling. Hundreds of times. Dana, you're the first person I called. I couldn't come back to your place; I saw the way you looked at me, the way you were hurt. I couldn't do that to you. I wanted to let you know where I was, and you could let me know when you were ready to talk about it," Galan declared.

"You mean the girl you called Aria? The girl you ran to when my sister died so you could find someone else with the same name and fulfill some sick sense of relationship with the person who didn't love you back?!" questioned Dana.

"How do you know that's why I did it?" asked Galan.

"Because Paige told me you did that years ago before she left a knife in my gut. Is that what you have been doing for four years? All this about giving me time to live my life and waiting for me when really you were chasing the name of a girl who didn't love you, and you left the only girl who wanted you!" Dana retorted.

"Dana...." said Galan sadly.

"I loved you, Galan! I did when nobody else gave that to you; I did! And you chose her... No, you chose her name over me. How am I supposed to feel about that? How should I feel knowing that you may only want me because I was the next best thing to Aria?" Dana remarked.

"Dana, you were just a kid when we met. A good man would never go after a child. Do you know who does things like that? Paige! She did that to me, and it fucked me up. I could never have done that to you. I care about you too much to even consider it, even if it was for my benefit," Galan expressed. "I will never be the monster she is."

"Maybe you're not like her, but you never wanted me. You want someone who obeys your every word, who calls you 'Sir' and does as you say. You have been trying to replace someone, and this goes deeper than Aria. You've been trying to replace Paige, haven't you? I saw how you were with her, and then you tried to turn me into that same person!" Dana voiced.

"I was… But I let all of that go when I asked you to marry me. Dana, I love you and have been trying to do right by you ever since. Please believe me when I say none of this was me. I wasn't lying about Mama B. I'm not hiding the Aria replacement thing, and I don't want to change you. I just want you," Galan professed.

"If you're telling the truth about Mama B trying to kill you, then you must be the one who destroyed her home!" Dana stated.

"No, that wasn't me. I swear," Galan avowed.

"Galan, I know you're good with words, but I don't buy it. If what you're saying is true and she did try to kill you, then burning down her house and leaving dozens of bodies behind like that could only point to you. It's the same thing you did to Aria...," Dana pointed out.

"Alright, then, let me prove it. If you don't believe me, then I'll get the proof from her," Galan stated.

Chapter
Twenty-two

Galan, resolute in his determination to prove his innocence, carefully contemplated a plan that could vindicate him. Meanwhile, Dana stood restlessly, her mind consumed with thoughts of exiting the room. Suddenly, an ingenious idea sprang into Galan's mind, sparking an exhilarating wave of excitement. "I've got it!" he exclaimed.

"What?" asked Dana.

"Let me use your phone," Galan said.

"Absolutely not," Dana promptly replied.

"Mama B would answer your calls, plus she would be caught off guard the moment she hears my voice," Galan explained.

"And what is that supposed to prove?" questioned Dana.

"I just need you to hear how she reacts to me," Galan stated.

"No, find another way; you're not dragging me into this," Dana stated resolutely.

"Dana, what are you talking about? Why am I being treated like the bad guy here?" Galan remarked.

"I don't know, Galan... Maybe because you were dead, and then you showed up at my hotel room out of the blue, and now you're saying a woman who is like a mother to me and my sister tried to kill you," Dana commented.

Galan stood in shock, bewildered by the abrupt shift in Dana's emotions toward him. As he tried to make sense of the situation, his gaze fell upon her hand, and to his astonishment, he realized that her wedding ring was nowhere to be found. "Your ring...." he mumbled.

"Don't do that," Dana uttered.

"Do what, Dana? What is going on?" asked Galan.

"I just need some time, Galan; I need some space right now," Dana answered.

"Dana, talk to me, please; tell me what's going on. Is it that you don't love me anymore?" Galan probed.

"Why are you here, Galan?" questioned Dana.

"I came because I saw a video of you screaming for help while someone that looked like me chased you through SPU," Galan replied.

"I know that wasn't you, Galan," Dana responded.

"Then why am I being treated this way?" asked Galan.

"Because you died! You died, and you left me without anyone, Galan! You have no idea how deep my pain was, how much I cried every night wishing you were still next to me when all along you were alive, and you could have told me that you were," Dana fumed.

"I tried calling you; I told you that," Galan repeated.

"Bullshit! You called so much, but it didn't leave a single missed call on my phone, but you get a text from me, and suddenly your phone words fine?" questioned Dana.

With a sense of urgency, Galan swiftly retrieved his phone from his pocket and dialed Dana's number. The phone rang persistently, each ring amplifying his anxiety; the call was abruptly rejected. "See...." Galan showed her. He opened the call logs; Dana scrolled for minutes, only seeing her name appearing on each call. "D, I swear I was being honest about everything. I love you and will do whatever it takes to win your heart back. Please just give me a chance to do so. Name it," Galan pleaded.

Dana thought for a moment, "Ok, then help me pull this Ripper plan off. I'll think about it after, I promise."

"Thank you, love; I promise I will do better," Galan professed.

"I'll meet you back on the main floor; I just need a moment, alright?" said Dana.

"Of course," Galan conceded as he left the room with a smile.

Dana's hands trembled visibly as she reached for her phone, the anxiety palpable in her movements. With a shaky breath, she unlocked the screen, revealing her wallpaper—a poignant picture capturing a tender moment between her and Kaito.

What am I doing? I swore I would have stopped the day I saw Galan again. I don't know if I can go back, and if Galan finds out that I was involved with someone, who knows what he will do. Kaito was just a distraction; I need to end things soon before this gets ugly. I love Galan; the last thing I want to do is hurt him. I'm doing the same thing Aria did to Malek; I am not my sister...

As Dana prepared to return to the main floor, she made a conscious decision to change her wallpaper, symbolically distancing herself from the emotional attachment depicted in the previous image.

Feeling a mix of curiosity and concern, Galan found himself seated at the bar alongside the rest of the group. Just then, Sydney's voice rang out, calling out to Dana, "What's the plan here, Boss? Are we doing this or what?"

Dana approached the bar. "Damn right, we're doing this. We've got a survivor, willing participants, and the resources we need. And now we have a Ripper," Dana informed them as she looked at Galan.

Galan smiled, "Alright, little Miss Marketing Genius, walk us through the plan."

As the days unfolded, Dana diligently put her plan into motion, driven by her unwavering determination to put an end to the Ripper killings. With each passing day, she meticulously executed the steps necessary to bring her strategy to fruition.

Dana: *We need to get customers to join in. We can tell them it's a marketing campaign, taking full advantage of the viral story of the Salt Pines Acres Massacre. And everyone will sign a contract prohibiting them from discussing what we are doing.*

A steady stream of customers, numbering in the dozens, formed a queue, eagerly awaiting their turn to sign the contracts being distributed by a group comprising Avan, Sydney, Belle, Galan, Kaito, and Genji.

I'M BROKEN TOO

The second thing is the make-up. Blood isn't going to be enough; we need real-looking wounds. Avan, Sydney, and Belle, that's your job. You guys are the film students; surely you can get special effects make-up done, costumes, that sort of thing. We're also going to need actors, screams, and people running; find us some so we can set the stage for the big finale.

Avan, Sydney, and Belle strategically dispersed themselves across the campus, purposefully seeking out aspiring acting students and skilled make-up artists to collaborate on their mission of bringing the murder scenes to life.

Money is no object here; millions can be sunk into marketing, but with this, we have a free press. Everyone involved will be compensated for their time, and Grounded Coffee House will cater food and drinks on the day. Galan and I will handle things on that end.

Dana and Galan took on the task of liaising with various caterers, ensuring that the culinary aspect of the event was well taken care of. With a keen eye for quality and meticulous attention to detail, they met with multiple catering services, carefully selecting the ones that met their standards. Alongside finalizing the arrangements, they prepared cashiers' checks and set aside envelopes filled with payment for all the participants involved on the event day, from the caterers themselves to the supporting staff and performers.

Genji, you're the one who adds to the authenticity of this whole thing. You have police records and footage of the attack on campus. You will be the one who confirms this whole stunt with undeniable proof.

Avan, Belle, and Sydney collaborated to set up a modest yet impactful set where Genji could deliver his testimony regarding the killings. They enlisted the assistance of a talented acting student, who provided guidance and coached Genji in his performance, ensuring that his portrayal would be authentic and compelling. Improvising a script that captured the essence of Genji's experiences, they worked together to refine the dialogue, aiming to convey the gravity and urgency of the situation.

Once the video was recorded, the team meticulously curated additional evidence, establishing Genji's credibility as a genuine survivor of the attacks. With unwavering resolution, they compiled corroborating materials, such as photographs, eyewitness accounts, and any other pertinent information that could support Genji's story.

And last but not least, The Ripper. We're going to recreate the ensemble of the picture that has been circulating since the original incident. A blood-

covered assailant, wearing a crisp, unstained suit. We're going to need to get you a haircut and dye those silver tips away. The weather report says a major storm is looming; it's set to make landfall six days from today. This means SPU will be closed until the storm passes. This entire area will be empty; students and staff will vacate the premises to seek shelter, and the rest will be safely locked in their dorms, so we have the cover of the storm to get this done.

Galan returned to the solace of his apartment, seeking a moment of introspection. As he stepped into his walk-in closet, his gaze fixed upon the suit he had worn on that fateful night of the incident. He took the suit to a tailor to make some final adjustments. The meticulous attention to detail extended to his appearance as well. The make-up department worked closely with him, carefully cutting his unruly mane and skillfully dyeing the silver strands to match his desired aesthetic. Galan's transformation was complete, projecting a powerful presence befitting his character.

As the group gathered inside Grounded Coffee House, their eyes were drawn to the ominous sight outside. The sky loomed overhead, engulfed by dark clouds that cast an eerie atmosphere. The rumbling thunder reverberated through the air, shaking the very foundations of the surroundings. Amidst the chaos, lightning streaked across the sky, illuminating the land with its electric brilliance.

The only thing that's left is the girl who brings both Eder Barlow's and the Ripper's followers in one place. That's where I come in. The girl at the center of the Salt Pine Acres Massacre.

Dana joined them on the main floor. "Ready to put this to rest once and for all?" she asked. As the six others turned their attention toward Dana, a unanimous agreement was conveyed through their resolute nods. At that moment, a shared understanding and determination seemed to fill the air. Dana, with a mischievous smile adorning her face, embraced the anticipation and excitement that permeated the room.

SYDNEY YEARWOOD

AGE: 22

SIGN: GEMINI

FUN FACT: "ANIME GOT ME INTERESTED IN FILM."

Chapter Twenty-Three

As the crowd inside Grounded Coffee House swelled to capacity, more than a hundred customers eagerly assembled, adorning themselves with blood and special effects make-up, fully immersing themselves in the atmosphere of the event. Meanwhile, Galan found solace outside, his gaze fixed upon the turbulent clouds swirling in the heavy winds. Dana, with a purposeful stride, stepped outside the bustling Grounded Coffee House in search of Galan. "Hey," Dana softly called out, her voice carrying through the door as she peeked outside. With a deliberate pace, she ventured out, taking measured steps towards Galan. Galan turned to face her, his gaze momentarily captured by her presence before his attention was soon drawn back to the turbulent storm clouds above.

"What are you doing out here?" asked Dana.

"Just staying out of your way while you get everyone ready," Galan replied.

"You're part of this too, you know," Dana pointed out.

Galan's smile lingered momentarily as he maintained his gaze on the swirling clouds above. Standing beside him, Dana followed his eye-line, her eyes also fixed on the captivating yet foreboding sky.

The gravity of their situation hung in the air, and Dana's words broke the silence, "We need to talk," she said.

"Sure," Galan agreed.

"I've been really dismissive of you lately—ever since the night I got you shot, actually. And you're right; you haven't done anything, and yet I treat you like you did. I shut you out and kept you out of arms reach. And the truth is that I'm afraid you would never love me," Dana began.

"Because I tried to replace your sister with another girl named Aria...." Galan interjected.

"Yes, it's partly that," Dana confirmed.

"That would kill a part of me, too, if the roles were reversed. I know it's messed up," Galan responded.

"I just don't know how to deal with this, Galan," Dana informed him.

"Well, you heard about that from Paige; it's my fault because you should have heard it from me," Galan stated.

"We have some time now...." Dana exclaimed.

Galan kept his gaze upward, "You know Lillie was my first crush, then Paige came into the picture, and everything went south. I started dating when I got older but was never good enough for those girls. I was too fat, too awkward, too poor; essentially, I was never good enough in any aspect. Time went on, and I got desperate for love. I loved 'LOVE,' and I wanted it; I already had nothing, and my idea of love is all that kept me going. I had a family that didn't want me, friends that didn't care, and a line of relationships that ended because someone else was better. I just wanted it to be me.

"The harder I tried, the further I seemed to get from it, and I could never shake my first because she was the only one who truly loved me back. She was everything I imagined and more, and I thought I'd lost that forever. When I was thirteen years old, I got drunk one night—Paige had forced me to drink some strong liquor, but I couldn't handle it too well. The next thing I knew, I was standing over dead bodies. The family that took me in when my parents didn't want me was lying dead and bloody on the floor when

Paige found me. She then burnt the house down with all of them inside, destroying any evidence. So, because of me, she was forced to leave her home; I took everything from her," Galan explained.

"I heard about the things Paige did to you; this isn't your fault. If she didn't do those things, you would have never ended up in this," Dana comforted.

"If I hadn't loved Lillie, I wouldn't have ended up in a situation like that...." Galan proclaimed.

"Galan...," said Dana sadly.

"I want to blame her, I do, and for many years I did. But I have to accept that all those people who didn't want me were because of me, not her. I blamed her, and I went back to her. That's when she killed eight people," Galan continued.

"She what?!" Dana gasped.

"Every girl who came after that moment was killed by Paige because they couldn't love me. I didn't know at first, but I had to do something the moment I found out. So, I locked Paige away. I ran and came to Salt Pine Acres and worked as a building maintenance personnel for a butcher's shop while the owner was sick and couldn't stay open. I locked her away for years in that place until Grounded was a success, and I bought a unit at the condo complex. I gave her a room, made sure she stayed locked inside, fed her every day, and ensured she was cut off from the world.

"I didn't kill her because no matter how hurt I was, she always consoled me; she always lent an ear and helped me work through my pain. I fell for her, and she became submissive to me. 'Sir' and 'Master' came from her; when she seduced me as a child, she called me 'Sir' to give the impression that I was older, and 'Master' when she became submissive to me. Finally, I was being validated and felt what I presumed to be love. Whenever I hear that word, it makes my blood burn with lust; I feel a tingle down my spine, and it makes my neck curl to my shoulder.

"I got off on the praise, and anyone who showed me that level of submission won my heart. But even as fucked up as I am, I knew I couldn't love a monster who would do something like that to a child. I tried replacing her, her sister, and the ones that came before, to no avail. I was too broken to love. So I shut myself out and buckled down; I pushed my efforts to make Grounded what it was and used it to leave her behind and start a new life. That's when I met your sister and fell in love again, despite every effort not to. I hadn't felt like that since—" Galan explained.

"Since Lillie," Dana finished.

"Yeah...." Galan confirmed. As he turned to face the floor, a solitary tear escaped his eye, cascading down to the ground. The tear, a poignant symbol of his inner turmoil, glistened briefly before resting on the surface below. Observing and attuned to Galan's emotions, Dana noticed the solitary droplet as it landed. A pang of empathy washed over her as she witnessed the tear, recognizing the depth of Galan's emotions and the weight he carried. She approached him gently, her presence a comforting anchor amidst the storm within. "I had spent so long emotionally unavailable that I almost forgot how it felt to be in love with someone. And I would have done anything to have a second chance. But, as faith would have it, I met you when you were too young, so I couldn't back then. And I will not apologize for turning you down because it's what I wished someone would have done for me. Instead, I was a six-year-old who couldn't stop thinking about sex and was forced to drink alcohol so that I could keep seeing the girl I had a crush on. I couldn't hold hands with friends because my mind would race; it's why I don't allow anyone to touch me without permission," Galan continued.

"You've never done that to me," Dana pointed out.

"No, I refused to be the monster Paige was; I held my beliefs strongly. Even if I felt that way, I never allowed myself to be overrun by those urges. And when I did, I treated you like Paige's and Lillie's replacement. When I saw the pain in your eyes, I let it all go; I swore I would be better for you because you mean more to me than I can ever prove," Galan confessed.

"Galan...." Dana's eyes grew teary.

"You saw me with one girl named Aria; the truth is, there were many. So much so I lost count; she was just the last one. I tried so hard to recreate the love I had for Aria, but when Paige threatened you, I found you again after all those years. It felt amazing not having to fight those urges, but no feeling was greater than letting go of my burdens to prove my love for you was beyond my past and my shortcomings. I understand how you feel, trying to win someone from a shadow you feel like you can't compete with. It took me over twenty years to do it; I can wait twenty more while I prove it to you and another twenty and another twenty until my dying breath. I love you, Dana, and I want you to be happy," Galan declared, turning for a moment with a smile.

I don't deserve him; I can never be honest with him.

"By the way, I know you're in love with Kaito," Galan stated.

As Galan spoke those words, Dana's heart sank, descending to the depths of her stomach. A heavy feeling settled within her, causing her blood to run cold.

"I heard you calling his name out that night when you opened the door at the hotel. I saw the way you pushed me away, and it's ok. Don't destroy what you have with him for me; I will not let you sacrifice your happiness for mine. That's the real reason I can't be inside. It breaks my heart thinking about you with someone else, but today I am here for you; I will give my all to see your vision through," Galan avowed.

"You knew… And you didn't say anything—" said Dana in a hushed tone.

"I don't want you to think you have to choose. You asked for time and space, and I can give that to you. The last thing I want to do is hurt you, and making you choose means you lose one of us, and I wasn't ready to let you get hurt by that choice," Galan expressed.

"Why tell me then?" asked Dana.

"I saw the guilt in your eyes; I don't want you to feel guilty about who you love. I spent my whole life searching for it, and nothing would make me happier than knowing you found it, whether it is me or not," Galan stated.

Dana walked up to him and hugged Galan tightly. "I'm so sorry I hurt you," Dana sincerely apologized.

"Awww, big old softie," Galan chuckled. Dana laughed through her tears and punched Galan. "Go on inside; it's almost time," Galan informed her.

"When today is over, we need to finish this talk, ok?" said Dana.

Galan's smile remained resilient in the face of Dana's emotional outburst. Turning his gaze back to the skies, he seemed to find solace and perspective amidst the turbulent atmosphere. His smile held a sense of acceptance and understanding as he recognized the depth of emotions that had stirred within Dana. Meanwhile, Dana, determined to regain her composure, pushed open the doors leading back into the café. As the doors swung open, the sounds of chatter and activity from within flooded their surroundings, grounding them in the present moment.

Chapter Twenty-four

Dana entered the café, her presence commanding attention from every corner of the room. As her confident strides brought her closer to the center, a hush fell over the crowd, curiosity glimmering in their eyes. With a voice resonating with authority, Dana announced, "It's almost time to get started. Everyone knows their roles; get positioned. Café bodies stay here, campus bodies, you can get started in finding spots and panicking bystanders, you can go crazy." Just as the anticipation reached its peak, a bone-chilling scream shattered the tranquility of the café, instantly gripping the attention of every patron. Heads swiveled in unison, and eyes widened in horror as a woman emerged from within, tightly clutching another figure in her trembling arms. The room became chaotic as the ghastly sight of a gaping neck wound and the crimson cascade of blood sent shockwaves through the air.

Amidst the rising panic, Dana's instincts kicked in, propelling her forward with an urgency that matched the pounding of her heart. Pushing through the bewildered onlookers, she reached the distressed duo and swiftly assessed the dire situation, her mind racing to decipher the unfolding tragedy.

"Dana!!!" Avan screamed.

As Dana's gaze ascended towards the upper level, the source of the voice became apparent— Avan's urgent cries reverberated through the café, intensifying the sense of dread. Without a moment's hesitation, Belle propelled herself through the frantic crowd, her determination guiding her steps toward the staircase. Following closely behind, Dana's agile strides matched Belle's pace, their shared concern propelling them forward.

Ascending the stairs, their hearts pounded in their chests. When they reached the top step, they gasped in disbelief. The scene that unfolded before their eyes was nothing short of a nightmare. Avan stood there, cradling Sydney in his trembling arms, his anguished face etched with a mixture of shock and grief. The evidence of violence was stark—Sydney's lifeless body bore the harrowing wounds of a knife plunged into her chest, with her throat and face brutally slashed.

"Oh my, God!" Dana gasped.

"What happened?!" Belle inquired.

"She asked me to meet her in the upstairs restroom... I found her on the floor with another person covered in blood," Avan replied while crying.

"Another body?" asked Dana before she ran into the restroom and found a guy stabbed to death on the floor.

As the ambiance of Grounded Coffee House flickered with warm, dimmed lighting, a sudden darkness engulfed the entire space, leaving patrons and staff momentarily bewildered. Galan, who happened to be standing outside the establishment, witnessed the unfolding of this unexpected turn of events. His sharp gaze caught the precise moment when the building lost power, and the once vibrant café was shrouded in darkness.

"Justice for Eder!" a disembodied voice crackled through the café's PA system, cutting through the tension-laden atmosphere. Its sudden presence added an eerie layer to the already chaotic scene, further heightening everyone's apprehension. Startled by the announcement, Kaito and Genji quickly reacted, their senses heightened as they sprinted up the stairs, their footsteps echoing through the cafe. Avan, visibly trembling, cradled Sydney's lifeless form in his arms, his despair palpable. Overcome with sorrow, Belle wept silently beside him, their grief intertwining in shared agony. The devastating tableau halted Kaito and Genji in their tracks, leaving them momentarily speechless, their eyes locked on the scene that unfolded. As the weight of the moment settled, Dana emerged from the restroom, her presence drawing Kaito's attention.

"What is this?" asked Kaito.

Dana shook her head, her eyes filled with uncertainty. She parted her lips, mouthing the words with a sense of urgency; her silent message carried on the faint whisper of her breath, "I don't know."

Galan's desperation grew as he attempted to open the door, only to find it stubbornly unyielding. His finger pressed firmly against the biometric scanner, hoping for a response, but it remained unresponsive, further deepening the sense of entrapment that enveloped the café.

Suddenly, the roar of an engine behind Galan shattered the tense silence. Turning swiftly, his eyes widened in recognition and disbelief. The driver's seat of the employee shuttle held the figure from the unsettling video, the one who had eerily mimicked his appearance. Galan locked eyes with this doppelgänger, a mix of confusion, anger, and fear swirling within him.

In an instant, the shuttle's engine revved, its vibrations echoing through the air, and the blinding illumination of high beams pierced Galan's vision. Acting on pure instinct, he threw himself aside, narrowly escaping the path of the oncoming shuttle. The deafening crash of the vehicle plowing through the large glass door filled the café, sending shards of glass flying and chaos erupting within its walls. The crowd of patrons became helpless victims, trampled under the merciless wheels of the shuttle, while others were violently pinned against the opposite wall, their lives cut short by the force of impact.

Piercing screams reverberated through Grounded Coffee House, mingling with the panicked footsteps of those desperately fleeing for their lives. Dana, Kaito, Genji, Avan, and Belle, their faces etched with horror, reached the banister of the upper level. As they looked down upon the devastating scene below, a mixture of disbelief and grief washed over them. The aftermath of the shuttle's rampage painted a grim picture—dozens of people lay injured and crushed, a few unfortunate souls losing their lives upon impact. The haunting message "Justice for Eder" adorned the side of the employee shuttle, glaring in red.

Kaito grabbed Genji and Dana, "Come on, we're leaving now!"

"I can't just leave everyone here; this is my doing!" Dana stated.

"Suit yourself," Kaito replied as he jumped over the banisters and onto the shuttle. Genji turned to Dana. "Genji!" Kaito yelled.

"Come with us," Genji pleaded.

"Genji! If she wants to fucking die here, let her, baka! Now move your ass!" Kaito ordered. He swiftly disembarked from the shuttle, cautiously approaching its interior. As he peered inside, he discovered the driver had exited the vehicle.

With a sense of urgency, Genji swiftly followed his brother's lead, both of them dashing out through the chaotic doorway. The swarm of terrified patrons flooded the outside, scrambling towards their cars, their desperate cries filling the air. Regaining his composure, Galan rose from the floor, his gaze fixed on the unfolding pandemonium surrounding him.

As individuals rushed to their vehicles, a chilling realization spread through the crowd—their tires had been maliciously slashed. Despite the damage, panic overrode rationality, and people persisted in their attempts to escape, the scraping sound of rims against the asphalt punctuating the air as they frantically drove away.

With horror etched on their faces, onlookers watched as a car suddenly erupted into flames in the parking lot, sending shockwaves of terror through the area. Kaito and Genji, caught just outside the blast radius, were momentarily knocked back by the force of the explosion. Before they could fully process the terrifying event, another vehicle further away burst into flames, its fiery demise accentuating the sense of chaos and danger that enveloped the scene.

Dana, Avan, Belle, and the others hastily descended the staircase, a surge of adrenaline propelling them toward the exit. Burdened by the burden of carrying Sydney, Avan struggled with each step, his strength waning. Sensing his vulnerability, the doppelgänger emerged from behind the shuttle, a sinister intent gleaming in his eyes. As swift as a predator, he lunged forward, driving his knife into Avan's shoulder.

Avan's agonizing scream pierced the air, petrifying Dana and Belle as they watched the horrifying scene unfold. In a desperate act of self-preservation, Avan mustered every ounce of strength he had left, pushing the assailant away and freeing himself from the knife's grip embedded in his shoulder.

"Run!" Avan's urgent voice rang out, his adrenaline-fueled determination pushing Dana and Belle forward as they raced toward safety. Galan, his eyes filled with concern, spotted Dana amidst the chaos and hastened towards her, ensuring she was safely guided towards the exit.

Galan's attention then turned back to the interior of the café, his gaze fixated on his doppelgänger who had risen from the floor, concealing his identity behind a mask that only revealed his piercing eyes. As Galan's eyes locked with those familiar eyes, fragments of the past flashed before him like a haunting slideshow.

Memories flooded his mind, transporting him back to the time he was caught sneaking around Aria's house, the weight of those encounters resurfacing with a pang of unease. His mind raced, connecting the dots as he realized the similarity between his past encounters and the unfolding chaos within Grounded Coffee House.

In a vivid recollection, Galan's memories intertwined with the present. The image of the car wreckage crashing through the café, leaving his staff pinned against the wall, resurfaced with a jolt. The realization struck him like a lightning bolt, deepening the mystery surrounding the events and intensifying his desire to uncover the truth behind this sinister replication of his own identity.

What is this? Someone is recreating the scenes at Salt Pine Acres. Who the hell is this guy?

I'M BROKEN TOO

As the doppelgänger made his way to the shuttle's rear, curiosity and a growing sense of dread tightened Galan's grip on reality. With a forceful pull, the imposter swung open the door, and a fine mist emerged from within, accompanied by an almost imperceptible, haunting whistle that permeated the air. At that moment, Galan's senses sharpened, detecting the distinct scent of gas that filled his nostrils.

A surge of memories flooded Galan's mind, his thoughts instantly transported back to the devastating incident that had obliterated Aria's house. The pieces of the puzzle began to connect, forming a chilling realization.

"Everybody get away from the café!!!" Galan shouted as he swiftly turned on his heel and sprinted, his heart pounding with a mix of adrenaline and urgency. Reaching a safe distance, he reunited with Dana, Avan, and Belle, their faces reflecting both relief and concern. Their attention was refocused on the shattered building.

However, their eyes were drawn to the movement atop the roof, capturing their curiosity and fascination. Galan's gaze fixated on the imposter, his doppelgänger, who had taken a seat with a megaphone and a tablet in hand. The enigmatic figure seemed to command attention as they prepared to address the surrounding chaos.

As the doppelgänger raised the megaphone to his lips, the group watched, captivated by the unfolding scene. The air hummed with anticipation as his voice boomed through the megaphone, his words echoing through the night, "Running will only kill you faster; the gates have been barricaded. Even if you do make it out, the storm will pin you down; there is nowhere to run. Call for help, but I doubt your phones would work. Nothing inside these grounds will help you reach the outside world. You're trapped in here with me. And I will bathe this campus in your blood!

"The Ripper is only out for those who abuse love; no more blood needs to be shed here today. Among you is the person who started this four years ago; rip her heart out as she did mine, and you all go free. However, the longer you take to do so, the number of people who will find death at the end of a knife will climb fast! You have until the rain begins; the moment the first drop touches the ground, my blade will start tasting the blood of the innocent…."

As the doppelgänger tapped the tablet, an earth-shattering explosion engulfed Grounded Coffee House. The force of the blast shattered glass, sent shards of concrete flying, and scattered debris across the parking lot. Helplessly, Dana and Galan watched as their beloved establishment, their labor of love and greatest achievement, crumbled in the inferno.

Amidst the confusion and destruction, a chatter of voices emerged from the crowd. Whispers of uncertainty mingled with the realization that a choice lay before them—to accept an offer and leave alive. The tension in the air grew palpable as people's conversations grew louder, each weighing the risks and possibilities that lay before them.

Dana looked around at the mumbling crowd. Galan's gaze scanned the surroundings, taking in the growing tension and the shifting dynamics of the people around them. His mind raced, evaluating the options and weighing the consequences of each decision.

"I say screw him! There are more of us than there are him! Let's wait for his sorry ass to get off the roof and end him!" shouted a man from the crowd.

As the doppelgänger remained perched atop the burning café, an air of determination settled over the gathered mob. United by a shared desire for justice, they formed a tight-knit circle around the structure, standing just outside the reach of the intense heat. Their eyes fixed upon the imposter, patiently waiting for him to descend from his vantage point.

The doppelgänger maintained an unnerving calmness, his stoic demeanor unfazed by the unity displayed by the surrounding crowd. He surveyed the assembled individuals from his elevated position, their collective strength pulsating through the air. The imposter's calculated gaze met the unwavering determination of the mob, a silent standoff of wills.

Amid the crackling flames and billowing smoke, time seemed to stand still. The heat from the fire mirrored the intensity of the moment, a palpable tension that hung in the air. Fueled by a deep sense of betrayal and the longing for resolution, the mob held their ground, unwavering in their resolve to confront the doppelgänger and end the torment that had befallen them.

"Why don't you come down here, you coward!" the man who rallied the crowd shouted.

"Is that what you want?" asked the doppelgänger.

As a single drop of rain splashed upon the rooftop, a precursor to the impending deluge, an air of anticipation enveloped the scene. Gradually, the drizzle transformed into a torrential downpour, the raindrops cascading to the ground with increasing intensity and frequency.

The doppelgänger, standing atop the roof, felt the rain soak through his clothes, matting his hair against his face. Each droplet served as a reminder of the changing tides, the shift in the atmosphere that mirrored the impending climax of the confrontation. Unfazed by the rain, he stood steadfast, his gaze fixed on the man who had taunted him.

I'M BROKEN TOO

In a decisive move, the imposter's eyes honed in on a rope intricately tied off to an anchor point. Without hesitation, he seized the rope and sprinted toward the edge of the roof. With a leap of calculated precision, he flung himself into the void, his body propelled forward by the momentum gained from the swing.

For a fleeting moment, the rope kept him suspended just above the ground, his feet inches away from touching the earth at full extension. In that intoxicating instant, he relinquished his grip on the rope, releasing himself into the exhilarating freedom of the descent. Seizing the opportunity presented by the swing's downward momentum, he charged forward.

The swift and brutal act unleashed by the doppelgänger left an eerie silence in its wake. As the knife found its mark, impaling the man through the throat, a gruesome scene unfolded before Galan, Dana, Avan, and Belle. The doppelgänger's agile movements carried him forward; swiftly seizing the knife's handle, he executed a whirlwind maneuver before landing on his feet. With a chilling display of detachment, he discarded the severed head, sending it crashing to the ground while the lifeless body slumped and mingled with the rain-soaked earth.

Galan instinctively shielded Dana, pulling her behind him as they bore witness to the gruesome murder. Avan and Belle sought refuge behind Galan, their trembling bodies huddled together, their cries stifled as they tried to contain their horror.

The screams of terror pierced through the rain and thunder, merging with the chaotic scene unfolding. Panic engulfed the crowd as they scattered in every direction, desperately running for their lives. The doppelgänger pursued—a merciless predator claiming one life after another, his actions painting a chilling portrait of cold-blooded brutality.

As the crowd fled towards the gates, their hopes for escape were dashed as they encountered a pileup of burning vehicles blocking their path. Their cries for help fell upon deaf ears, for no phone or wifi signal was available on the campus, leaving them trapped in a nightmarish landscape of death and chaos.

Amidst the turmoil, a group of students wearing shirts emblazoned with the words "Justice for Eder" emerged onto the streets. They surrounded the fleeing mob, their intentions unclear, but their presence evoked a sense of ominous anticipation.

"The Ripper doesn't want you! Take his offer and live through the storm!" one of the students wearing the shirt announced.

"And if we don't," asked a woman.

"Then may the blade of the Ripper relinquish you from this fragile existence!" the student responded.

Chapter Twenty-five

Galan, Dana, Avan, and Belle sprinted towards the campus, maneuvering through the frenzied crowd that scattered like a sea of ants in every direction. Amidst the chaos, Galan's gaze fixated on the doppelgänger towering over its latest victim as he turned and locked eyes with Galan.

"Please, I can't die; I have student loans to be paid off!" Avan screamed.

"We're trapped in here; we need to hide!" Dana remarked.

"This is a big campus," Belle stated as they neared the campus buildings.

"Fuck hiding; we need to kill that son of a bitch. Where can we find things we can use as weapons?" asked Galan.

"The Dorms! That building has a massive dining area that feeds every student on campus! We can raid the kitchen!" Avan informed him.

"The dorms are the safest place on campus; those doors don't open for anyone except the students who aren't locals. Plus, the inside is six floors of nothing but rooms. We can hide until we can call for help!" Belle exclaimed.

"Perfect!" Galan replied.

Guided by Avan's decisive lead, the group hurried towards the building, their steps pounding against the wet ground as rain poured down relentlessly. The haunting echoes of screams reverberated through the courtyard, heightening their sense of urgency and trepidation with each passing moment.

"There! The red brick building!" Belle pointed out.

A man abruptly lunged at Belle, forcefully bringing her to the ground with a bone-jarring tackle. The assailant's hands clenched tightly around her throat. "Sorry, but my life is worth more! If we kill the girl he loved, I will see my family again!"

Galan stopped, "Keep moving! We'll catch up!"

Avan and Dana paused momentarily but swiftly gathered their resolve, pushing forward with conviction. Galan, however, reacted swiftly, channeling his strength and agility. With a powerful kick, he struck the assailant's elbow, shattering it and forcing his grip to release on Belle's throat. Rolling over, Belle gasped for air, relieved to be free from the assailant's suffocating hold.

Not wasting a moment, the man's enraged sons rushed towards Galan, fueled by a desire to protect their fallen father. Galan's instincts kicked in, propelling him into action. Charging forward, he leaped into the air, his knees connecting forcefully with their chests. The impact sent the sons crashing to the ground, their bodies colliding with the rain-soaked pavement.

Swiftly regaining his balance, Galan landed gracefully on his feet. With an assertive stomp, he delivered a decisive blow to their faces, rendering them unconscious and neutralizing the immediate threat.

Galan hurried to Belle and helped her to her feet. "I'm ok," Belle reassured him, so they swiftly resumed their sprint once more. However, their momentum was abruptly halted as they spotted a group of students clad in "Justice for Eder" shirts blocking their intended route.

Without missing a beat, Belle called out, her voice filled with urgency, "This way!" The duo swiftly pivoted, veering in a different direction and dashing through a narrow alley nestled between towering buildings. Hope flickered within them as they presumed this detour would provide a clear path to safety.

However, their optimism quickly waned as they encountered yet another blockade, this time formed by the determined students. With each attempted route, they found themselves confronted by individuals clad in "Justice for Eder" shirts, staunchly blocking their passage. The situation grew increasingly tense, their options dwindling, as they desperately sought an escape from the relentless pursuit.

"What do we do?" asked Belle as she grabbed onto Galan's arm.

"Go through them!" Galan declared. "Stay close to me." Galan's resolve surged within him as he sprinted towards the group of four students standing firmly in their path. With determination etched across his face, he propelled himself forward, unleashing a powerful and swift kick aimed at the chest of one of the students. The unexpected impact caught them off guard, their expressions transforming into shock as their comrade was forcefully sent crashing to the ground, a resounding thud echoing through the air.

Driven by instinct and fortitude, Galan wasted no time as he followed up his initial strike with a swift and devastating uppercut, landing squarely on another student, leaving them momentarily stunned. Seizing the opportunity, Galan swiftly turned his attention to the remaining two who attempted to restrain him.

However, their efforts proved futile against Galan's sheer strength and skill. With an impressive display of power, he forcefully slammed them both onto the ground, their bodies crashing against the unforgiving surface. In a flurry of intense motion, Galan unleashed a rapid succession of punches, raining blows upon their faces, ensuring that any resistance was swiftly subdued.

"Let's go!" Galan yelled. With a renewed sense of urgency, Belle and Galan raced toward the safety of the dormitories. However, their momentary relief was shattered as the doppelgänger emerged from an alleyway, brandishing a menacing knife. The glint of danger reflected in their eyes as the doppelgänger unleashed a slashing attack towards Galan and Belle.

In a remarkable display of reflexes, Galan swiftly reacted, narrowly evading the deadly edge of the knife. Acting quickly, he pulled Belle out of harm's way, sparing her from the doppelgänger's assault. Harnessing his strength, Galan retaliated with a powerful and precise kick aimed at the doppelgänger's chest. The force of the impact sent the doppelgänger hurtling backward, crashing into a cacophony of trash cans that lined the alley, momentarily stunned and disoriented.

Seizing the opportunity, Galan and Belle wasted no time and resumed their desperate sprint, leaving the doppelgänger behind in the alley, their adrenaline-fueled escape propelling them further away from immediate danger.

As Dana and Avan neared the dorms, their hearts were pounding with a mixture of exhaustion and urgency as their hopes were quickly dashed when their attempts to open the doors proved futile. Frustration etched their faces; Avan reached for his student ID card, hoping it would grant them access to safety.

With a flicker of hope, Avan swiped his student ID card against the electronic reader, but the doors remained obstinately shut, refusing to yield to their desperate pleas for entry.

"Why won't it open!" Avan shrieked as he vigorously shook the doors, attempting to pry them open.

"Is there another way in?" asked Dana.

"I don't know," Avan exclaimed.

"There must be another entrance, an open window, something!" Dana remarked as she pulled Avan from the door.

"Ahhh, my shoulder!" Avan yelled.

"Sorry, I forgot you got stabbed!" Dana apologized.

"Time is running out. There are few left to be killed! Kill the girl who broke my heart while you still have your life!" commanded the doppelgänger through the megaphone.

Overwhelmed by the urgency of their situation, Dana and Avan frantically scanned their surroundings, their senses heightened in an attempt to locate the source of the commotion that surrounded them. The chaotic scene unfolded as several individuals, drenched by the pouring rain, suddenly emerged from various directions, their gaze fixed upon Dana and Avan.

"Go! Go! Find us a way in!" yelled Dana as she shoved Avan. With adrenaline coursing through their veins, Dana and Avan swiftly changed their course, running alongside the side of the building in a desperate quest to find a potential entry point. Their eyes scanned the tall structure, scouring its façade, hoping to discover an open window or door that would offer them refuge.

Relieved to have escaped the confined alleyway, Galan and Belle emerged into a more open space, their breaths heavy and their hearts still racing. With a sense of urgency, Belle pointed out the dorms ahead, their destination within reach.

Feeling a mix of relief and caution, Galan turned to glance behind, only to find that the doppelgänger was no longer in pursuit.

As Galan and Belle sprinted through the courtyard, a chilling proclamation cut through the chaotic air. The words, "Kill the girl!" pierced their ears, causing them to instinctively turn their heads to survey the tragic scene unfolding around them.

A scene of utter despair and violence greeted their eyes. The once bustling courtyard had devolved into a macabre theater of humanity turning against itself. People were locked in a savage frenzy, attacking one another with unbridled ferocity. The air was thick with cries of anguish and the sickening sound of violence.

"This is madness," Belle commented.

"There is another one!" shouted a man as a small group of three ran toward Belle and Galan.

"Fuck!" Galan exclaimed. Frustration and fear surged within Galan as he took in the grim reality unfolding around them. The once-familiar faces donning "Justice for Eder" shirts now acted as obstructive barriers, further impeding their path to safety. Meanwhile, within the chaos, terrified customers of Grounded Coffee House resorted to desperate acts of self-preservation, ruthlessly attacking innocent individuals to evade the Ripper's blade.

Galan's eyes swiftly darted around, searching for an alternative escape route. As an alleyway appeared on their left, he instinctively grabbed Belle's arm. He quickly pulled her into the refuge of the narrow passageway. The echoes of their pursuers' frantic screams filled the air, growing closer with every passing moment.

Navigating the labyrinthine alley, Galan and Belle hurriedly traversed to the other side, skillfully evading their pursuers. In an attempt to throw off their scent, the men decided to split up and search for them, unknowingly providing Galan and Belle with a much-needed opportunity to break free.

While the men stood confused and separated, above was Galan and Belle climbing a ladder affixed to the side of a nearby building. They wasted no time, swiftly climbing its rungs and pulling themselves onto the rooftop, seeking solace and respite from the relentless turmoil below.

Exhausted and drenched by the pouring rain, Galan and Belle found a momentary sanctuary as they sat down against the roof's ledge. Their chests heaved with labored breaths, their bodies drained from the adrenaline-fueled pursuit. The relentless rain showered down upon them, mixing with their gasps for air.

Dana and Avan's hearts pounded in their chests as they desperately evaded the relentless pursuit of the people chasing them. They had exhausted every potential opening or entry point they could find, circling the building in a desperate search for an escape route. However, hope seemed to fade with each passing moment as no signs of entry revealed themselves. "Fuck!" Dana shouted.

"If only my card—" Avan began. A chilling silence fell upon the scene as Avan abruptly came to a stop and let out a cry. Dana's heart sank as she spun around to witness the horrifying sight before her— the doppelgänger drove a merciless knife into Avan's back. Gasping in shock and horror, Dana instinctively stepped back, her mind reeling with disbelief at the sudden and brutal attack. Time seemed to stand still as the doppelgänger callously dropped Avan to the ground.

"Noo…." Dana gasped as she backed away.

In a moment of impending danger, a shadowy figure, Kaito, swiftly intervened, charging toward Dana and the doppelgänger. The doppelgänger's proclamation of "Justice for Eder" echoed through the air, serving as a chilling reminder of the chaotic circumstances.

With lightning speed, Kaito executed a powerful kick, propelling the doppelgänger forcefully into a nearby wall. Drawing a short katana from his waist, he skillfully impaled the doppelgänger through the chest, piercing the heart of the merciless assailant. The doppelgänger's futile struggle to remove the sword from his chest ceased as life abandoned his body, his hands dropping lifelessly to his side.

Kaito calmly retracted the blade from the doppelgänger's chest, a somber resolve etched on his face. With a gentle push, he toppled the lifeless body of the doppelgänger, causing it to collapse beside Avan as blood pooled around their fallen forms.

"Kaito…." Dana exclaimed.

As the echoes of the previous confrontation lingered in the air, the tense atmosphere was shattered once again as two additional men appeared, sprinting around the corner with intent directed towards Dana and Kaito.

"Head to the Admin building in the north wing; move!" Kaito instructed as he and Dana took off running.

While running, Dana questioned, "Why are we running? We just killed the Ripper; it's over!"

"It's not just him that's killing people. Shut up and run; ask questions later," Kaito retorted as he led her back to the Admin building.

As Dana and Kaito rushed towards the door, they were met with a welcome sight: Genji and a group of people anxiously awaited their arrival. Relief washed over Dana as they swiftly entered the building, and the doors were secured with chains and reinforced with filing cabinets to fortify their position.

Taking a moment to catch her breath, Dana surveyed her surroundings. The Admin building had become a sanctuary, a gathering point for those involved in their plan and other students seeking refuge from the chaos that engulfed the campus.

"Dana, are you ok?" asked Genji.

"I'm not hurt if that's what you're asking. But I am not ok," Dana replied.

"I was against this stupid fucking plan of endangering everyone, including my brother, to leave and go get you. Now everyone is going to be coming here. Someone must have seen us; there were men chasing us back there. Baka!" Kaito raged.

"That's enough! Look, we're all in this together, like it or not. But we can't stay here as my brother said. We need to find safety, and those doors aren't going to stop them from coming in no matter how much we barricade it," Genji exclaimed.

"If only we could get into the dorms. According to the students, no one can get into there," Dana informed them.

"That's right, that building is made to withstand anything, hurricane, flood, you name it. It's the muster point for any kind of danger; it would take an army to get through those doors once the building is locked down," another student confirmed.

"We tried scanning into the building, but the ID didn't work," Dana remarked.

"Same here," another student added.

"It's the power. They took everything down, the security protocols, everything, no cell service, no wifi… There is nothing here, and because of the mountains, we can't get a signal," another student stated.

"So we're trapped here, with a mob of scared people killing innocent girls in an attempt to save their own skin," Kaito surmised.

"Not to mention the Ripper," Genji reminded them.

"Not anymore; Kaito killed him," Dana stated.

The room erupted in cheers and smiles.

"Shut up! What does that do us now? Those people are scared, and there are dozens of bodies all over this school that stretch from here to where Grounded once stood. They won't listen to anyone right now, and you can't talk to them; the rain is falling so hard I needed to shout while I was a foot away from Dana. Not to mention the thunder that's drowning everything out," Kaito exclaimed.

"He's right; we're sitting ducks here, and it's only a matter of time before they come looking for us. It's not like any other building has chains on the doors and cabinets blocking it," said Dana.

"Hey, you said power was down, right? Couldn't we boot it up from here?" asked Genji.

"I guess; the Admin building is just floors of servers and shit. Everything on campus runs through here," a student confirmed.

"Then boot it back up; if we can get the power on, we can call for help," another student claimed.

"Help won't get here in time; the storm is maybe one of the worst one's I've ever seen; the streets would be flooded, and it could take a while for a response team to get here," Kaito pointed out.

"Then what's the point of getting it back online?" asked the student.

"The dorms… If we get it back online, the student IDs will open the doors. If we make it there and close the doors, we can wait this out indefinitely," Dana proclaimed.

"So you're not a complete idiot after all," Kaito smirked.

Dana looked over at him.

"The dorms are our best bet," Genji agreed.

A shiver of dread swept through the room as everyone's attention was abruptly drawn to a chilling sight. The doppelgänger, seemingly undeterred by his previous defeat, stood outside the glass door, his bloodied hands pressed against its surface. The eerie sound of the knife being dragged across the glass sent shivers down their spines, the disconcerting noise echoing through the room.

Chapter Twenty-Six

The group of people gasped in fear, their bodies instinctively retreating to a corner, seeking solace in the safety it provided. Yet amidst their apprehension, Kaito stood resolute and unaffected, boldly positioning himself at the forefront, emanating an unwavering sense of composure and strength.

"I thought you said you killed the Ripper!" one of the students stated.

"I did!" Kaito confirmed.

"Maybe you stabbed him in a non-vital area?" asked Dana.

"I've done this hundreds of times; I know I killed him when my kodachi pierced his chest," Kaito exclaimed.

The doppelgänger turned to the scattered mob with the megaphone, "Storm the Admin building; no more need for bloodshed. Open these doors, and you are free to seek refuge until the storm ends! Fail, and I'll slaughter you all first!"

As a crowd of anxious onlookers congregated outside the doors, the doppelgänger gracefully stepped aside, making way for the flurry of desperation that ensued. Frustration and anger propelled the crowd as they hurled rocks at the unyielding barrier, their collective efforts aimed at shattering the door that stood stubbornly in their path.

"Fuck!" Dana remarked.

"That door will hold against those rocks, but it's only a matter of time until they hit it with something that will break through. We need to find out how to get the power back on," Genji advised.

"Scatter! It's not going to be any ordinary room. Look for warning signs or anything that restricts the public. Move!" Kaito instructed as he sheathed his sword and walked to the stairs. "Genji, you stay with me; everyone else, fan out and look. Start at the bottom; we will start at the top. Work your way up till we meet in the middle."

"I'm coming with you," Dana claimed; her words were ignored as Kaito and Genji kept moving and headed to the stairs.

In pursuit of their shared objective, two determined students trailed behind Dana and the boys, commencing their ascent from the highest point of the structure. Meanwhile, the remaining seven individuals embarked on their mission from the ground floor, each step resonating with a mix of anticipation and determination.

Kaito and Genji swiftly scaled the floors, their legs propelling them to the fourth level, where they raced through the corridors, their senses acutely tuned to identify any signs of a control room. Simultaneously, Dana and the accompanying students ventured in the opposite direction, navigating the unfamiliar terrain with unwavering focus.

Within the dimly illuminated building, courtesy of the sporadically functioning emergency lights, their path was partially illuminated, yet it was the beams of their cell phone flashlights that served as their primary guide. The ambient glow offered a small measure of reassurance as they traversed the maze-like structure.

Galan and Belle cautiously treaded along the rooftop, their eyes transfixed on the pandemonium unfolding beneath them. The piercing cries of victims being attacked were swiftly muted by the relentless downpour, the heavy rains acting as a veil for the gruesome scene below. However, the fierce storm unleashed its fury, obscuring their view and rendering the chaotic commotion on the ground a blur of shadows and distorted shapes.

Seeking respite from the relentless assault of raindrops, Galan and Belle retraced their steps back to the edge of the rooftop wall. With the winds gusting in the opposite direction, it formed a temporary refuge where the rain's onslaught was slightly diminished. Weary and disheartened, Galan settled beside Belle, slumping in an attempt to find some semblance of comfort amidst the desolation.

They shared a glimmer of hope as they persistently attempted to establish a signal on their smartphones, desperately yearning to reach out for assistance. However, their efforts proved futile, the network weakened by the chaotic circumstances that engulfed them. After a prolonged period of fruitless attempts, they reluctantly conceded, stowing away their phones.

"Looks like we're stuck up here," said Galan.

"It could be worse... We could be stuck down there," Belle pointed out.

"You do have a point," Galan remarked.

"You think they're ok? Avan and Dana, you think they made it to the dorms?" asked Belle.

"If I know one thing, Dana is a survivor; even if they didn't get to the dorms, I am sure they're ok," Galan proclaimed.

"Speaking of, thanks for saving me," Belle stated.

"Well, you helped me when I needed it; I owed you one," Galan replied as he chuckled.

"I'm sure you would rather be stuck with Dana than me on this roof," Belle exclaimed.

"I wish all of them were here; we'd all be safe on the roof," Galan responded.

"I'm not," Belle stated as she turned to him. "It would be awkward when I did this." Belle leaned in and kissed Galan.

Galan's reflexes kicked in as her hands instinctively moved toward his chest, intercepting her touch before it could make contact. He recoiled, his lips parting from hers, a mixture of surprise and disbelief etched across his face. "Belle...." he managed to utter, his voice tinged with shock and uncertainty.

"Yes... Sir," Belle answered.

Galan felt a rush surge through his body as the words dripped off her lips. "You wanted to know what I would call you if I wasn't behind that desk?" Belle straddled Galan and looked into his eyes, "I would call you 'Sir,' and I would want to please Sir until he calls me his good girl."

Despite Galan's initial attempt to halt Belle's advance, she effortlessly slipped her hand from his grasp, determined to make her intentions known. Undeterred, she firmly placed both palms against his chest, closing the distance between them, and pressed her lips against his in a passionate embrace. "And now that I am not behind that desk, what does Sir want?" asked Belle with a smile.

Belle's words reverberated within Galan, triggering a flurry of memories from his past relationships. As her voice echoed in his mind, a montage of other women he had been involved with intertwined with her words. The cadence and timbre of their voices intertwined, blending together until they melded into one unified sound. And then, as if rewinding time, the memories took him back to the very beginning.

For the first time, Galan recalled Paige, his mind conjuring her image as vividly as if she stood before him. The way she called him 'Sir,' the tone she had used, mirrored Belle's in an uncanny manner. Their desires intertwined, their passion seemingly evenly matched.

Fuck it!

In the grip of their shared desire, Galan pulled Belle closer, their lips meeting once more in an ardent kiss. Urgency hung in the air as they hurriedly shed their garments, discarding the layers separating their heated bodies. In a rush of passion, Belle was gently guided to the ground, a splash of water from the rain pooling on the surface, mingling with the sensation of their entwined skin.

Galan leaned over Belle, his lips capturing hers once again, their kisses deepening with each fervent touch. The rain, relentless in its downpour, beat down upon his exposed back, its cascading droplets tracing a path down his neck and onto Belle's supple form. Despite the tempestuous weather, their connection remained unyielding as Galan held her gaze, their eyes locked in an electric exchange that intensified the fire burning between them.

"Hands together," Galan instructed, his voice laced with a firm yet reassuring tone. Belle obediently brought her wrists together, her fingertips brushing against each other, and a small, genuine smile graced her lips. With a swift, practiced motion, Galan retrieved his shirt and skillfully bound her wrists. Guiding Belle's hands back behind her head, he gently cradled her in his arms as if she were precious cargo. Carefully, he tucked the shirt under her back; taking the tail of the shirt, he deftly wrapped it around his palm. Leaning closer to Belle's ear, Galan's voice lowered to a hushed whisper, "Don't pull on this, and

I'll make you cum. Do as you're told, and I'll reward you. Do you understand?"

"Yes, Sir," Belle replied.

Galan's fingers inched down her now exposed legs, ever so delicately pulling off her panties. He lowered himself to her thighs, pressing his lips against her. Belle shivered in anticipation of the pleasure that was to come. His tongue moved ever so slowly against her pussy, dancing around it before finally delving into its depths before two fingers glided inside. Belle eagerly resisted the temptation to move her hands, the tension of her tugging on his shirt built as Galan skillfully tendered each nerve ending. Her back arched in sweet agony as he expertly coaxed desire from deep within her. His circling tongue adroitly toyed with her clit while his fingers masterfully flicked and teased her G-spot. Belle's breathing escalated until she released a wave of passionate bliss that enveloped Galan's lips, coating them in her hot nectar. Galan languidly rose up and leaned over her, Belle's warm essence dribbling from his chin.

The warm drops contrasted the cold rain on her skin as he made his way to her lips. He licked his fingers before he leaned down and hovered just before her lips. "Come find out what you taste like," Galan commanded. Belle lifted her head and kissed him, his lips still warm. He leaned to her ear, "Good girl—"

Galan pulled on the shirt and crossed one leg over her; with his back facing her, he slid his leg behind her bent knee. Galan turned quickly from his knees to a seated position, flipping Belle onto her stomach; he pulled on the shirt, lifting her to a seated position on his lap. Galan let go of the shirt and untied it as he kissed her neck. Tossing the shirt aside, Galan unbuttoned his jeans and slid them down past his hips. He got a firm grip on Belle's throat and pulled her body against his, the rain beating down on them as she felt a wave of pleasure wash over her as he guided himself inside her.

Dana ventured alone, determined to search the labyrinthine halls of the massive administrative building. Lightning crackled across the night sky, casting intermittent bursts of illumination as she hastened from one door to another. Time was slipping away, their urgency amplified by the growing clamor emanating from the front entrance. With a sense of urgency, the group of students vacated the upper floor, their hurried footsteps resonating down the staircase. Dana, however, couldn't resist exploring one last room at the far end of the hallway.

As she cautiously peered around the corner, her eyes fell upon yet another ordinary door. Without hesitation, she swiftly pivoted and sprinted back towards the staircase, her heart pounding with anticipation. Just as she approached the descent, two familiar figures, Genji and Kaito, materialized down the corridor. In a graceful display of agility, Genji effortlessly leaped over the railing, executing a flawless parkour maneuver, while Kaito caught a fleeting glimpse of Dana.

"Find anything?" asked Kaito.

"Nothing up here," Dana confirmed

"Go down two floors; Genji and I will search the next one; we're running out of time," instructed Kaito as he attempted to walk away.

"Thank you for saving me," Dana quickly exclaimed.

Kaito's step halted, "Thank me when we get to the dorms. We don't have time for me to accept your thanks right now; now go!"

The students on the second floor successfully located the control room and immediately called out to Kaito and the rest of the group. Hearing their cries, the remaining students hastened to the second floor, their footsteps echoing through the corridors. Suddenly, a loud crash reverberated from the ground floor, causing panic to ripple among them. Realization dawned upon them as they comprehended the front door had been forcefully breached.

I'M BROKEN TOO

Reacting swiftly, Kaito and Dana hurriedly descended to the second floor, curiosity compelling them to steal a glimpse of the chaos below. Peering over the railing, Kaito witnessed the intruders attempting to move the cabinets, obstructing their path. With a sense of urgency, everyone quickly assembled. Kaito took charge and motioned for silence as they hastily made their way toward the designated room, their footsteps muted and hearts racing.

As the group advanced, they reached the control room, marked with a sign stating, "Employees Only Beyond This Point." Undeterred by the warning, they entered the room, their determination overpowering any hesitations. Aware of the impending threat, they swiftly took action, barricading the door to fortify their position. A chair was hurriedly positioned beneath the door handle, effectively jamming it in place and creating an additional layer of security. With the barricade in place, they felt a momentary surge of relief, knowing they had bought themselves some precious time to strategize and regroup.

"Work fast; they are minutes from storming the building. They don't know exactly where we are, so once we get this power on, we'll make a break for it through the windows," Kaito advised.

As the group entered the control room, their eyes darted around, searching for any clues or indicators that could help them restore power. Amidst their rapid search, Genji's keen gaze fell upon a panel adorned with a conspicuous lever boldly labeled "Reboot." Recognizing the urgency of the situation, Genji wasted no time and decisively grasped the lever, swiftly pulling it down before pushing it back up again.

A resounding rumble reverberated through the empty corridors as the generators sprang to life, their steady hum resonating through the building. Within moments, the once dimly lit space was bathed in a renewed glow as the lights flickered back to life, dispelling the pervasive darkness that had shrouded the surroundings.

"Yes!" shouted a student.

"Hey, I hear them!" said someone outside the door.

"You idiot!" Dana hissed.

"Sorry," the guy apologized.

"Everyone out the window and head to the dorms now!" ordered Kaito.

Exiting through the window, the group found themselves perched on a protruding concrete ledge, a small foothold in their treacherous escape. Just a few steps away, a sturdy metal staircase clung to the building's exterior, its emergency exit doors clearly labeled on each floor. Braving the fierce winds and torrential rain, they hurriedly made their way toward the beckoning staircase.

The surrounding buildings offered a modicum of respite from the howling winds, providing a temporary shield as they carefully navigated the fire escape. Step by cautious step, they descended, their footsteps intermingling with the symphony of raindrops and gusts of wind. Each landing on the fire escape offered a brief pause, allowing them to catch their breath and steel their resolve before continuing their desperate descent.

With the storm raging around them, the group of twelve pressed onward, their determination propelling them through the darkened skies that mirrored the encroaching night. Battling against the elements, they raced toward the safety of the dorms.

Belle and Galan sat intimately, their connection palpable as they dressed. Straddling his lap, Belle maintained unbroken eye contact with Galan, their gaze a magnetic force drawing them closer. While Belle effortlessly slipped her top back on, she tenderly assisted Galan by deftly buttoning his shirt, their touch filled with both tenderness and a lingering desire.

Leaning against the roof's ledge, the world around them seemed to fade away as they indulged in a passionate make-out session, their lips and bodies entwined in a moment of pure bliss. However, their stolen moment of intimacy was abruptly interrupted by the jolting sound of the generators, startling their attention away from each other.

Reacting swiftly, Galan and Belle leaned over the edge, their eyes fixated on the campus below. A surge of relief washed over them as they witnessed the lights flickering to life across the expansive grounds, illuminating the previously shrouded darkness. Yet, amidst the newfound illumination, Belle's gaze was captivated by the sight of Dana, Kaito, and Genji leading a group toward the dorms, their conviction evident in their resolute stride.

"Galan, look!" Belle pointed.

"Come on, let's go!" Galan exclaimed, urgency tingeing his words as he and Belle swiftly finished dressing and descended the ladder attached to the side of the building. Emerging from the alley, their eyes widened in alarm as they caught sight of the doppelgänger hot on the heels of the group. Determined, they sprang into action, racing to intercept the impending danger.

As the pursued group reached the doors, one of the students swiftly scanned their IDs, causing the doors to unlock with a resolute click. Pushing the heavy doors open, the group streamed inside, guided by collective urgency. Kaito and Dana, positioned at the entrance, held the door open, urging their companions to seek refuge within the safety of the building.

Dana's gaze pierced through the storm, her sharp eyes detecting the doppelgänger's relentless pursuit. With a surge of adrenaline, she and Kaito rushed inside, the door slamming shut just as the malicious figure closed in. The students peered through the bulletproof windows, their hearts pounding as they observed an unexpected figure trailing behind. Dana's sharp recognition sparked hope as she spotted Galan amidst the chaotic scene, bravely engaging the doppelgänger, buying precious seconds for Belle to seek shelter.

Seizing the opportunity, Kaito dashed outside, his kodachi gleaming in the dim light. Galan and the doppelgänger grappled on their feet, their struggle intense, until Kaito swiftly approached from behind, expertly slitting the doppelgänger's throat. In a swift and coordinated move, Galan seized control, snapping the assailant's neck, neutralizing the threat.

Breathing heavily, Galan and Kaito swiftly retreated, making their way inside the building, their backs pressed against the closed door. The tension of the moment eased as they exchanged a silent, mutual understanding, their fists connecting in a victorious bump, their smiles reflecting the triumph over their formidable adversary.

Chapter Twenty-Seven

As the group took a moment to catch their breath and compose themselves, Belle's concerned gaze scanned the room, her eyes searching for any sign of Avan. Noticing his absence, she turned to Dana, her voice tinged with worry.

"Where is Avan?" Belle inquired, her tone filled with concern.

Galan and Kaito turned their attention towards Belle and Dana, their expressions mirroring her concern. Sensing the gravity of the situation, Dana's head bowed slightly, a somber acknowledgment of the troubling news to come. The silence in the room grew heavy, anticipation hanging in the air as they

awaited Dana's response, hoping for some clarity about Avan's whereabouts. "Avan didn't make it. The Ripper got to him before Kaito could save us," Dana answered morosely.

"No...," Galan mumbled.

Belle's knees gave way beneath her, and she crumpled to the ground, overwhelmed by a rush of emotions. Unable to contain her distress, she instinctively covered her mouth, attempting to stifle the wave of anguish that threatened to consume her. Sensing Belle's vulnerability and deep sorrow, Dana immediately knelt beside her, her arms enveloping Belle in a comforting embrace, "I'm so sorry," she said.

"Come on, let's get everyone inside. There is a fireplace in the common area; we can all stay warm until the storm passes," Genji spoke softly as he extended a helping hand to both Dana and Belle, aiding them in rising from the floor. With a gentle touch, he supported them, guiding them toward the center of the room, where the warmth of the fireplace beckoned.

As they gathered around the crackling flames, the sight before them was awe-inspiring. The massive common room stretched upwards, its high-rise ceiling extending across three floors. It was a space designed to accommodate the needs of the thousands of students residing there. Within the expansive area, a multitude of features unfolded—a variety of comfortable couches, table tennis setups, entertainment systems, a dining area, and even a well-stocked bar; the common area stood as a testament to the grandeur and scale of the student residence.

The common area sat at the end of a hallway that came from the main entrance. As the group gathered in the expansive common area, their attention was drawn to the towering curved staircases that led to the upper levels. Dana's face lit up with a sudden realization. A sense of urgency filled her as she swiftly reached into her pocket, retrieving her phone, "Guys, if the power is back, we should be getting signals. We can call for help!"

As Dana and the group frantically retrieved their phones, a sinking feeling settled in as they realized the extent of the damage caused by the water. The majority of their devices had succumbed to the deluge, leaving them with limited options. However, a glimmer of hope emerged as Galan, Dana, and Belle discovered their waterproof phones remained functional.

Their hands trembling with urgency, they dialed emergency numbers, desperate to reach out for help and connect with the authorities. But their efforts were met with frustration as the storm had taken its toll on the cell towers, rendering them inoperable. Each attempted call ended in disappointment, the sounds of failed connections and distant static mocking their plight.

"Guys use the internet, post it on social media; someone is bound to see it and send help," suggested a student.

"I don't have a large following; my profile is private," said Dana.

"Same here," Galan replied.

"I've got it; I can post about it here. I'll make a video; we can use the Ripper attack to get people's attention," Belle ran to the door with her phone and recorded out the window as she spoke, "Help us! We need help; SPU is under attack. The Blood Rain Ripper is killing everyone on the premises, and we have no way out! We killed him, but he still…." Belle turned the camera toward the deceased Ripper, only to find a pool of blood on the ground.

"Where's the Ripper?" Belle mumbled. "Guys!!! Where is the Ripper!!!" her urgent cry reverberated through the hallways, instantly jolting Galan, Kaito, and Dana into action. Sensing the gravity in her voice, they wasted no time and swiftly descended to the hall, trailed closely by two other students.

Peering through the window, their hearts sank as they noticed the body of the Ripper was nowhere to be found. A gasp escaped one of the students, drawing the attention of Belle and the rest. They turned their gaze to the hallway, their hearts pounding in their chests. There, standing ominously, was the doppelgänger, his neck visibly bleeding, crimson droplets falling onto the floor. In a chilling display of self-preservation, the doppelgänger produced a silk handkerchief, tightly wrapping it around his injured neck. The once-white fabric rapidly absorbed the blood, transforming into a deep red hue as he secured the makeshift bandage.

A bone-chilling crack echoed through the hallway as the doppelgänger twisted his neck, seemingly unbothered by the injury. His eyes darted from side to side, surveying the scene before locking onto the group. With a menacing air, he brandished his knife.

"What the fuck!" Dana exclaimed.

"I slit that fucker's throat…." Kaito claimed.

"I broke his neck... I felt it snap…" Galan stated.

As the sense of urgency surged through Kaito, he quickly scanned his surroundings, his gaze darting around the hallway in search of Genji. Panic gripped his heart as he couldn't immediately spot his brother amidst the chaos unfolding before them. "Where the hell is Genji?" he exclaimed, his voice laced with frantic concern.

Suddenly, Kaito's gaze locked onto a gathering of students further down the hallway, recognizing Genji among them.

"Justice for Eder…," shouted the doppelgänger as he turned on his heel and ran down the hall.

Galan and Kaito sprinted down the hallway, their determination propelling them forward, while the remaining students scattered in all directions, desperately seeking refuge in their respective dorms. The doppelgänger, relentless in its pursuit, entered the common area, eliciting screams of terror from the students, who frantically dispersed in a state of panic.

A brave group of students attempted to confront the doppelgänger together, their united efforts a testament to their courage. Two guys and two girls launched an attack simultaneously, hoping to overpower the menacing figure. However, their bravery proved futile as the doppelgänger swiftly retaliated, slashing open their necks before they could land a single blow. Shock and horror hung heavy in the air as the room was stained with the crimson evidence of their failed resistance.

With steely determination, Genji stepped forward, discarding his jacket and preparing himself for the impending confrontation. Just as the doppelgänger's gaze shifted towards him, Kaito emerged from the hallway, unsheathing his kodachi. He aimed for the doppelgänger's neck, but his strike was intercepted by the doppelgänger's swift counterattack, blocking his slash with the blade of his knife.

In the midst of the chaos, Galan leaped into action, unleashing a powerful double-legged jump kick that connected with the doppelgänger's body, sending him tumbling toward the edge of the room, leaving a trail of blood in its wake. The momentary advantage allowed Kaito to swiftly secure his brother before regrouping with Galan, determined to pursue the fleeing doppelgänger.

As they chased the doppelgänger, their pursuit intensified up the stairs. However, their target slipped away, disappearing from their sight. Galan and Kaito reached the top of the stairs, their breaths heavy, only to realize that the doppelgänger could be on any floor, his location now uncertain.

"Genji's room is on the top floor, rally everyone and get them inside. We can stand guard outside if he comes back," Kaito advised.

"Or… we lure that fucker out. The common area is huge; he can't sneak up on us if we wait him out down there. He could be hiding anywhere between these floors; I say we let him come to us," Galan suggested.

"Alright, but if that doesn't work, I'm going after the Ripper myself," Kaito stated.

"I've got your back; come on, let's gather everyone," said Galan.

As Kaito and Galan swiftly descended the stairs, their footsteps echoing through the tumultuous atmosphere, the panic among the students intensified. Fear and confusion enveloped the air, manifesting as screams and frantic movements as students desperately sought the safety of their rooms.

Meanwhile, Genji, Dana, and Belle remained grounded in the common area, standing steadfast amidst the chaos. Their resolve and unity served as a beacon of strength amid the dwindling group of students, who dispersed in smaller clusters, seeking alternative refuge.

"Everyone ok?" asked Galan as they rushed toward them.

"We're fine for now," Dana claimed.

"What are we going to do?" Belle inquired.

"Don't worry, Belle, the video you posted must alert someone. Authorities will be here to save us," Genji replied.

"Oh crap, the video!" Belle exclaimed. With her phone in hand, she realized she hadn't stopped recording. Belle ended the video and typed the caption, "Help us SPU!" The post began to upload.

"Listen, the common area is huge, right? And we outnumber the Ripper. If we stay here, he has to come back if he wants to kill us. When he shows, we kill him first," Kaito declared as he raised his kodachi.

A slow, mocking clap echoed through the common area, drawing the attention of Genji, Dana, Belle, and the remaining students. Their eyes shifted upward, focusing on the balcony above where the doppelgänger perched, his presence oozing with sinister confidence. A chilling silence settled over the room as all eyes locked onto the figure, uncertainty mingling with trepidation.

Perched on the railing, the doppelgänger seemed almost at ease, his knife lodged securely in the wooden top of the railings. His posture exuded a malevolent aura.

"That's not a bad plan; how about I tell you mine? This building has unique features like bulletproof glass, biometric locks, and even the dorm rooms are coded so no one can get in or out unless they are supposed to be there. Now let's say there is an emergency, say, a lockdown because the power went out or there is a killer on campus. Students are safe inside because nothing can make it through those doors. But for the people inside, well, their rooms have a special feature in the event of this unfortunate fate.

"To prevent them from being locked in their rooms and starving when the power goes out, those biometric locks release every single door so that there is no chance of a student being trapped inside," the doppelgänger explained.

"Fuck…." Galan muttered.

"Now, you're all trapped in here with me, nowhere to run, nowhere to hide," the doppelgänger snapped his fingers, and the lights went off, the sound of every biometric scanner on the doors simultaneously unlocking. "There goes your wifi signal; I think I gave you enough time to get your little SOS out into the world," the doppelgänger exclaimed.

Belle's eyes flickered with a glimmer of hope as she witnessed her video had successfully uploaded, the loading bar finally reaching one hundred percent. A sigh of relief escaped her lips, mingling with the collective exhale from the group. They understood the significance of her accomplishment—their message had been shared with the outside world, an act that might bring them the much-needed help and support they desperately sought.

With a renewed sense of purpose, their attention shifted back to the doppelgänger.

"Salt Pine Acres you couldn't enter. But here, there is no escaping. You're trapped in here with me," as the doppelgänger's chilling words echoed through the air, the group felt a shiver run down their spines. Their gazes followed his fleeting form as he turned and disappeared into the darkness, leaving them in an eerie stillness. The storm outside raged on, its fierce winds and pounding rain a stark contrast to the deafening silence that enveloped the room.

Minutes stretched out in silence, the group remaining frozen, their senses heightened, attuned to any sign of the doppelgänger's return. The weight of anticipation hung heavy in the air, each breath held in apprehension, mingling with the storm's howls.

Suddenly, the suffocating silence was shattered by a sickening thud as a body hit the floor, ejected from the balcony above. Panic and terror seized the group as their screams pierced the air, blending with the cacophony of the storm. Wide-eyed and trembling, they witnessed the grey eyes of the doppelgänger piercing through the darkness.

Chapter Twenty-eight

Galan and Kaito's gaze fixated on the fading image of the doppelgänger, its once-piercing grey eyes now dissipating into nothingness. The air grew heavy with an overwhelming sense of dread as panic took hold of the students gathered in the common area. Trembling with fear, they huddled together, seeking solace in each other's presence, their hearts pounding in their chests.

"Are we really going to just leave these people to die while we wait here?" asked Dana.

"That's exactly what we're going to do. Fuck those students; this is about life or death. It's everyone for themselves," Kaito exclaimed.

"How could you say that, Aniki!" Genji remarked.

"Yamero! Otouto," Kaito snapped.

"These people live with me; they have been kind to me since I started here, and we are like a family in the dorms. If you don't help them, I will," Genji retorted.

Kaito grabbed Genji and pulled him off his feet, "My job is to protect you; it's what I swore the day we lost our parents. I couldn't care less about what happens to these students; they are not my responsibility!"

"Ease off your brother; he just doesn't want any more bloodshed," Galan stated.

"You don't speak for my brother, so why don't you mind your own business, baka!" Kaito barked.

Feeling the tug on his arm, Kaito paused as Dana's hand firmly clasped his, her voice piercing through his intense focus. "Stop!" she pleaded, her eyes filled with concern and urgency. Kaito's muscles relaxed, and he released his grip on Genji, allowing him to regain his footing.

"He's not going to stop; he's going to kill what's left of those students if we don't do something," Galan surmised.

"And what do you think we should do? We killed the Ripper twice, and it didn't take; in fact, how the fuck did it get into the dorms?" questioned Kaito.

"Maybe you didn't kill it? Maybe the wound wasn't deep enough," Dana proposed.

"I stabbed that guy through the heart; I felt my kodachi go through his breastbone," Kaito declared.

"Kaito's right, I felt his neck snap in my arms, plus his throat was slit open," Galan added.

"What the fuck are we being hunted by here!" Kaito wondered.

As chaos consumed the dormitories, the horrifying scene unfolded with relentless intensity. Two more bodies crashed onto the cold floor, their impact mingling with the terrified screams that resonated through the halls. The doppelgänger, fueled by an insidious purpose, continued its relentless pursuit, methodically invading room after room, each encounter sparking fresh waves of panic among the students.

Within the confines of the dorms, the atmosphere grew suffocating, heavy with a palpable sense of despair. Frantic footsteps echoed against the walls as desperate students sought refuge, their cries of fear merging into an agonizing chorus.

"We have to fucking do something!" Dana remarked.

"I agree! Aniki, are you in?" asked Genji.

"Listen, that guy bleeds; he sealed the wound on his neck, but his chest is still bleeding. Maybe Dana is right, and we just haven't fatally wounded him. So let's make sure he's dead this time," Galan proclaimed.

"It's not unheard of for a slit throat to not be fatal, and you said you stabbed him in the chest, right? There are cavities in the chest, but even if you were shot point-blank, there would be no fatal damage; maybe you're just missing the mark. There are lots of things to consider, like the rain impeding your vision and the adrenaline of the moment," a student suggested.

Galan looked to the girl, "Med student?"

"Final year," she replied.

"What about the rest of you?" asked Galan.

"Culinary arts, med, pharmacy, lit," the group answered.

"Culinary arts... Guys, Avan said the dorms have a massive kitchen. We can raid the kitchen and all hunt the Ripper. Turn the predator into the prey," Dana beamed.

"I like that," Belle replied.

"That's right, the kitchen!" Galan recalled.

"If we armed the students, we become the ones in charge," said Genji.

"We don't become anything; you stay your ass right here and stick to the plan, baka," Kaito stated.

"Fine, the rest of us will go raid the kitchen; we've got the numbers here anyway," Galan declared.

"Alright, follow me to the kitchen!" Belle urgently exclaimed, her voice laced with resolve. Galan, Dana, and a group of terrified students quickly rallied behind her.

In the midst of the frantic escape, Genji and Kaito made a difficult decision to stay behind. As the others hurriedly moved forward, Genji turned to face his brother, "You don't have to be like that, you know. They're scared; the least you can do is not be a dick about it."

"That's not my concern; I'm not going to let anything happen to my little brother," Kaito's demeanor softened, and a warm smile crossed his face as he playfully ruffled Genji's hair.

"Do it for me; we're a team. I have your back just as much as you have mine. You know either one of us can tear that Ripper apart. But these are just students; they are not Ex-Yakuza like you. Whose blade do you think has seen more blood? The Ripper's or your kodachi?" asked Genji.

"I left the Yakuza behind so I could be there for my little brother while he chased his dreams here. I'm not here to meddle in a love affair gone wrong with some wanna-be copycat killer. My only goal is to see my little brother be happy and live the life our parents wanted for him," Kaito expressed.

"And we may not get that chance unless we help them stop this madness," Genji pointed out.

"You're stubborn, just like I was. Baka! Alright, but you don't leave my sight, hear me?" asked Kaito.

"Done!" Genji agreed.

"Come on, we can do this without them," Kaito claimed.

With a sense of urgency, Galan and the others reached the kitchen, their eyes scanning the surroundings for any available means of defense. Spotting a basket nearby, they wasted no time, swiftly grabbing large knives and filling the container. Each blade represented a flickering hope, a slender lifeline amidst the encroaching darkness.

With the basket brimming with weaponry, they wasted no time in retracing their steps, their hearts pounding in synchrony with the panicked screams echoing through the dormitories. The sound of heavy footsteps reverberated from the floors above, a haunting reminder of the desperate scramble for survival happening throughout the building.

"Go! Start distributing knives to anyone you can find! I'm gonna go find the Ripper," Galan instructed.

"I'm coming with you," Dana stated.

Galan and Dana stopped. "No, go back with Kaito; stay safe. This is my mess; let me do this. I'm sorry I couldn't be the man you deserved, so at the very least, I won't stand between you and him. Now go," said Galan as he broke away from the group and sprinted upstairs.

As Kaito and Genji pressed forward, their ears attuned to the terrified screams that pierced through the building, they meticulously searched each floor, their conviction etched on their faces. The deafening thud from above resonated through the stairwell, serving as a haunting signal that drew their attention.

In unspoken synchronization, Kaito and Genji exchanged a knowing glance, their shared bond fueling their resolve. Without uttering a word, they shifted their focus upward, ascending the stairs with a mix of trepidation and steely determination.

With each step, the atmosphere grew heavier, the air thick with an indescribable darkness. As they reached the upper level, their worst fears materialized before them. The hallways were adorned with macabre paintings of crimson, a gruesome testament to the havoc that had unfolded. The doppelgänger stood at the center, a sinister figure, his malevolence palpable.

Their breath hitched as they beheld the grisly scene. The doppelgänger's attention was momentarily diverted from his gruesome work. With his bloodied knife in hand, he turned to face the brothers.

"Let me get to enjoy this!" Genji's voice cut through the tension, his words resonating with quiet confidence. Stepping forward, he squared his shoulders and flexed his muscles, a display of readiness for the impending confrontation. With deliberate movements, he tilted his head to the side, eliciting a satisfying pop from his neck, further steeling himself for the battle that lay ahead.

The doppelgänger, aware of Genji's approach, turned his head slightly, his gaze fixated on the resolute young man. A brief moment of recognition passed between them, an unspoken acknowledgment of the clash that awaited them.

In that charged silence, intense energy enveloped the hallway as if time itself held its breath. Genji's eyes locked with those of the doppelgänger, their gazes reflecting determination and an unwavering will to protect.

The stage was set, the battle lines drawn. Genji took another step forward, his fists clenched tightly at his sides. The air crackled with anticipation as he moved closer to the doppelgänger.

"Shine!" Genji shouted as he rushed forward.

The intense clash between Genji and the doppelgänger unfolded with lightning speed and lethal precision. Genji's instincts kicked in as the doppelgänger executed a horizontal slash, swiftly ducking beneath the attack and narrowly evading the deadly blade. But the doppelgänger was unrelenting. Seamlessly flipping the knife in his fingers to change its direction, he aimed a swift downward thrust at Genji.

Reacting with agility, Genji leaped back, but the confined space forced him against the wall, and his escape abruptly halted. The doppelgänger's blade impaled the floor, and with a swift motion, he retrieved it, hurling it towards Genji, who had his back against the wall.

Genji's head tilted to the side in a split second, allowing the blade to narrowly miss him, burying itself into the wall instead. A strand of his hair fell from the knife's blade, a chilling reminder of how close the confrontation had come to claiming his life. Undeterred, Genji's focus remained unwavering.

As the doppelgänger rushed toward him once again, Genji met the attack head-on. With a swift and well-executed double-legged kick, he sent his opponent hurtling backward, crashing into the opposing wall. The impact reverberated through the hallway, momentarily disorienting the doppelgänger.

Taking advantage of the opportunity, Genji swiftly regained his footing, his hand firmly gripping the knife embedded in the wall. He yanked the blade free with a fluid motion, his eyes never leaving the doppelgänger. Leaning against the wall, Kaito watched with a smirk, a silent acknowledgment of his brother's tenacity and skill.

"Is that all the Ripper has? What a fucking disappointment!" Genji exclaimed loudly.

Genji seized the opportunity as the doppelgänger pushed off the wall, swiftly hurling the knife back at his opponent. Reacting with uncanny agility, the doppelgänger managed to evade the deadly projectile, narrowly escaping its lethal trajectory. Undeterred by the missed strike, Genji unleashed a relentless barrage of punches, his fists becoming a blur of motion.

Each punch landed with precision and force, driving the doppelgänger back, testing his defenses and endurance. The rhythmic sound of the impact echoed through the hallway as Genji's strikes found their mark. The doppelgänger fought back, but with each retaliatory blow, his strength faltered, and his attacks grew feeble and ineffective.

Genji's determination surged within him, fueled by a mix of adrenaline and resolve. He pressed forward, his assault unyielding, determined to incapacitate his foe and end the reign of terror that had plagued the dormitories.

Amidst the relentless exchange of blows, the doppelgänger's resistance waned, his guard slipping. Fatigue and pain clouded his movements, his once formidable presence reduced to a fading shadow of its former self. Genji sensed the advantage and was driven by a surge of confidence.

However, unbeknownst to Genji, the doppelgänger's weakened state was a calculated ruse, a deceptive ploy to exploit his opponent's ego and vulnerability. As Genji's guard momentarily dropped in the heat of the battle, the doppelgänger seized the opening, his hidden strength emerging.

Kaito's keen eyes caught the glimmer of a hidden knife concealed beneath the doppelgänger's sleeve in a split second. Reacting with lightning speed, he sprang into action, propelled by a surge of protective instinct for his brother.

Meanwhile, Genji's unabated assault forced the doppelgänger into a corner, his final blow poised to strike. But as the doppelgänger saw his opportunity slipping away, he cunningly revealed the concealed knife, slashing viciously at Genji's exposed throat.

The air crackled with tension as time seemed to stand still. In a moment of tragic realization, Genji's eyes widened as the blade neared its deadly mark.

"Genji!" Kaito yelled.

Genji's lips curved into a resolute smile amidst the chaos. In a moment of swift reflexes, he reached out and caught the doppelgänger's arm, halting the impending strike. Genji's grip tightened around the doppelgänger's arm, "Like I said, what a disappointment!" Genji executed a swift and decisive move, breaking the doppelgänger's wrist, causing the knife to slip from his grasp. Seizing the advantage, Genji forcefully pulled the doppelgänger towards him, delivering a powerful headbutt that disoriented his opponent. Utilizing the momentary confusion, Genji swung the doppelgänger towards Kaito, who had unsheathed his kodachi with deadly intent.

As Kaito lunged forward, aiming to sever the doppelgänger's head from his body, the elusive adversary displayed surprising agility, quickly ducking under the slashing attack. With a burst of speed, the doppelgänger made a desperate dash towards the stairs, his only chance at escape. Kaito and Genji, undeterred, pursued the doppelgänger without hesitation, their determination propelling them forward. Genji's eyes caught sight of the fallen knife left behind in the chaos.

Galan emerged onto the scene just as the doppelgänger reached the balcony, desperate to escape. Seizing the moment, Galan swiftly thrust his knife into the doppelgänger's head, piercing his skull with precision.

The doppelgänger convulsed, his body writhing in a desperate struggle. His eyes filled with malice as he reached out, attempting to grasp Galan steadfastly, despite his futile attempts. Galan decisively withdrew the knife from his head, redirecting his strike toward the doppelgänger's chest. He swiftly and forcefully tore through the doppelgänger's flesh, revealing a gaping wound and exposing the dark, dying heart within.

The doppelgänger's movements grew weaker, his malevolent energy fading, but his final intentions remained evident. Unfazed by his dying struggles, Galan firmly grasped his heart, ripping it from the doppelgänger's chest with an indomitable ferocity. "Justice for Eder, bitch. Now die like he did," Galan's voice carried a whispered breath of finality as he let out his words, the weight of their accomplishment palpable. With a resolute yet solemn expression, he released his grip on the lifeless body, allowing it to plummet over the balcony's railing. The doppelgänger met the hard surface below with a sickening thud, blood pooling around his motionless form.

Turning his gaze towards the group of students gathered below, Galan tossed the heart to the floor, a symbolic gesture of their triumph over the darkness that had plagued them. Kaito and Genji stood beside him, their presence a testament to the strength and unity that had led them to this moment. The three of them looked down at the fallen doppelgänger, the embodiment of their struggles and fears, now lying defeated beneath them.

I'M BROKEN TOO

A wave of jubilation swept through the students as they witnessed the demise of their tormentor. Cheers and applause erupted, echoing throughout the dormitory. Belle and Dana looked up with smiles at their triumph.

Chapter
Twenty-nine

Cheers erupted in a crescendo of ecstasy, reverberating through the dorm and shaking the very foundation of the building. Kaito, Galan, and Genji descended the stairs, their triumphant strides magnetizing curious gazes. Doors swung open, and students emerged from their rooms cautiously, drawn by the thunderous celebration that resonated through the corridors.

With a mixture of trepidation and anticipation, the students leaned over the ornate balconies on their respective floors. Their eyes widened as they beheld the scene unfolding below. Lifeless bodies lay scattered on the ground, a chilling testament to the

GENJI SHINODA

AGE: 21

SIGN: LEO

FUN FACT: "I DON'T SPEAK ANY JAPANESE SO MY BROTHER USES SOME WORDS SO I LEARN GRADUALLY."

Ripper's reign of terror. And amidst the haunting tableau of victims stood the three valiant heroes, having vanquished the malevolent Ripper.

Moved by a surge of relief and gratitude, students hurriedly converged behind the bar, their nimble hands grasping bottles of intoxicating elixirs. Booze flowed freely, a tangible symbol of their collective liberation. Thankful screams and embraces intertwined as they celebrated the heroes, their courageous saviors.

Amid the jubilant chaos, Dana raced toward them, her eyes radiant with admiration. Galan's heart danced with anticipation as her captivating figure drew nearer. Like a blossoming flower, a smile graced his face, but its growth halted abruptly as he observed Kaito enveloping Dana in his protective embrace. Galan's smile froze, his eyes silently betraying a mix of longing and sorrow as he witnessed Kaito holding Dana in his strong arms.

Is this the cost of true love? Seeing them happy even without me. Why couldn't it be me? Why couldn't you choose me? What is wrong with me that you couldn't love me?

Belle's perceptive gaze locked onto Galan, keenly aware of the anguish that plagued his heart. Without hesitation, she glided toward his side, her touch delicate yet resolute as she clasped his trembling hand. Looking up at him, her eyes brimming with compassion, she conveyed a silent message—an unspoken invitation to depart from the scene of bittersweet torment.

Galan's gaze lingered momentarily on Dana and Kaito, his heart heavy with unspoken desires and unfulfilled longing. Reluctantly, he tore his gaze away, yielding to Belle's guiding presence. With a final, wistful glance, Galan bid farewell to the sight of Dana nestled in Kaito's embrace, letting Belle steer him away from the jubilant throng.

As they traversed the winding hallways, their steps synchronized in a delicate dance of solace and companionship. Meanwhile, unbeknownst to Galan, Dana's eyes fluttered open, and her vision momentarily blurred. Yet, amidst the haze, a fleeting glimpse caught her attention—an image of Galan and Belle ascending the staircase, heading away from the clamor and into the seclusion of the upper floors. Curiosity tugged at Dana's heart, a question whispered on the edge of her consciousness as she tried to decipher the significance of their departure.

"What the fuck is he doing with Belle?! That snake!" Dana's gaze drifted down to her hand, where a glimmering ring adorned her finger—a symbol of commitment and tangled emotions. She twirled it absentmindedly, the weight of its significance causing her heart to flutter and ache simultaneously.

Meanwhile, Galan and Belle reached the pinnacle of the staircase, their footsteps a whispered echo in the hushed corridor. Guiding him toward her sanctuary, Belle led Galan to the far end of the fifth floor, where her dorm room stood in silent anticipation. Stepping inside, they closed the door with the utmost care, ensuring it remained shut by wedging a door jam under its weight, a fortress of privacy shielding them from the outside world.

Galan, enveloped by the shadows cast by the tempestuous storm brewing outside, stood by the window, his gaze fixated on the torrents of rain cascading down the glass pane. He stood there, a solitary figure in the dimly lit room, his soul mirroring the melancholic tears that trailed down his face, mimicking the descent of the raindrops.

Belle, drawn to him like a force of nature, approached Galan with measured steps. Her reflection neared his in the window as his tears matched the droplets of rain streaming down the glass. "Did you really love her?" asked Belle.

"I don't even know anymore. I've given love everything I had, played by every rule, fought every battle, and sacrificed everything I could. And in the end, they never choose me. I'm a fool for believing I deserve love. I'm too broken for love; how can I give all of myself to someone when most of me died so long ago," Galan remarked.

"You know, broken people tend to fill the void in others that are broken too; they complete each other," Belle expressed. "What does Sir want?" she said as she looked up at him. "Love?" she asked as she tiptoed closer to his lips.

"Fuck love, I want you," Galan huskily replied.

Belle smiled and reached for his lips; Galan moved away and said, "Kneel," commandingly.

Belle gracefully descended to her knees, maintaining unwavering eye contact with Galan. Her smile persisted as she surrendered to him.

"Good girl," Galan stated, removing his blazer and draping it over a chair. "Do you know why Sir wants you on your knees?" he asked as he rolled up his sleeves.

"So I can please Sir with my mouth?" Belle answered.

"Tempting, but I don't want you on your knees for that. If I wanted you to please me like that, I would lay you on the bed, lean over you with your head at the edge of the bed, and fuck your throat until you had cum dripping down the back of it," Galan informed her as he walked beside her and lifted her chin with his hands. "You're on your knees because good girls do as they are told, and that's what I want."

Belle held eye contact with Galan.

"And if I don't do as Sir asks?" questioned Belle.

"You'll be punished," Galan responded.

"Maybe I like a little punishment, Sir," Belle replied as she bit her lips.

"You would defy me?" Galan's initial hesitation dissolved into a gentle smile, his eyes mirroring the affection and admiration that welled within him. With a tender gesture, he extended his hand, bridging the gap between them and effortlessly lifting Belle to her feet.

"No, Sir," Belle answered with a mischievous smile.

Galan swept her up against the wall, his lips savagely pressing against hers. His tongue explored her mouth as Belle clung to him, her fingers desperate to keep him close. He ripped away her clothing and threw her onto the bed.

Galan released a soft moan of pleasure before he strode to the mini fridge for an ice cube. Galan stalked towards her, the cube of ice clinking against his teeth. He dropped to his knees between her parted thighs, and she wrapped her legs around him, drawing him closer. A hunger grew in his eyes as Belle's breaths quickened. His hands moved quickly, tearing off her blouse and bra, unveiling her soft skin beneath. With the cube still lodged between his lips,

Galan leaned in close and tenderly passed it to Belle's mouth.

"Don't swallow," Galan reverently undid Belle's jeans, his fingers dancing on her skin as the fabric loosened and glided down her legs. She tilted her hips, pushing her feet towards the ceiling as he guided them off. Her legs floated back down and found a spot on his shoulders. Galan lunged forward; Belle's body quivered beneath him as he grabbed the sliver of ice and pressed it against her lips. He slid the melting ice down her neck, feeling each shiver from its cold grasp as he slid down her spine. Rivulets of water trickled across her flushed skin like a raging river. Galan moved back, allowing her legs to fall back with him. His tongue circled the ice cube around her nipple and trailed down her body; Belle gasped with each movement. He slowly continued downwards until reaching her waistline. Galan raised up, taking the ice cube with his fingers and tracing trails of frigid slivers, starting at her ankle and dancing down. The cube melted in his fingers, dripping cold droplets down her leg.

As the water trail neared her inner thighs, Galan kissed the droplet and stopped its course. Galan leaned over her, "You would defy me? Let me show you what happens when you don't do as Sir says. Be quiet," he whispered as he kissed her.

Galan's freezing fingers commanded her body, invasively pulling her panties aside and plundering inside her. Belle gasped at the sudden pleasure flowing through her veins, her hips writhing against his cold touch as spasms of pleasure coursed through her. Galan didn't stop there; he pushed harder and deeper until Belle screamed out in exquisite agony, consumed by emotions she never knew existed. He held her gaze with a smirk of satisfaction as she trembled beneath him as he stopped and pulled away from her. "I said to be quiet. Do as you are told," he smiled.

His cold fingertips grazed her clit, and Belle's breathing became labored as she fought to contain her pleasure. As Galan listened to her body's responses, he explored the places that drove her wild, his fingers dancing across her skin in an intoxicating rhythm. His grip tightened, and he suddenly unleashed a sharp, delightful slap against her aroused flesh. Gutteral moans escaped her lips as she quickly apologized for breaking his rules. Galan's action ceased.

"Don't stop," Belle pleaded.

Teasing her as he continued, he whispered in her ear, "Do you like defying me?"

"No... Sir," Belle replied through shallow breaths.

"Then why aren't you doing as you're told," Galan's smile grew.

"It feels so good," Belle gasped.

"Then cum for me," said Galan as he continued. Galan's lips moved against hers in a passionate embrace. His fingers explored her body, and he could feel the heat radiating off of her. Reading every signal, he felt her tighten around him as she neared her peak. Just as she was about to fall over the edge, he pulled away, letting out a primal growl.

"Your punishment is knowing I decide when you cum or not. Disobey me, and I will decide when next you cum, maybe in a couple of minutes or maybe a couple of days. But I will keep you at the edge of your release until I decide you've earned the right to cum for me. Understand?" asked Galan.

"Yes... Sir," Belle responded, her breathing erratic.

"Do you wish to defy me now?" asked Galan.

"No, Sir," Belle immediately replied.

Galan took her off the bed and into his arms, "Then say you're mine."

"I'm all yours, Sir," Belle repeated his words.

"Good girl," Galan exclaimed.

Belle wrapped her arms around him as he slowly lowered her back to the bed.

Dana stood silently outside the door, unwittingly overhearing every word that was being said inside. Curiosity got the better of her, and she couldn't resist the urge to peek through the crack in the door. What she saw was heartbreaking—they passionately kissed on Belle's bed, his hands caressing her body. It felt like Dana's world shattered into pieces at that moment.

In an emotional outburst, Dana impulsively took off the ring he had given her and flung it against the wall, severing their shared connection. Feeling a mixture of anger, hurt, and humiliation, she hurriedly stormed off, trying to escape the painful scene before her.

As Dana stomped down the stairs, she joined the other students in the vicinity. Seeking solace in a drink, she poured herself one and gulped it down, trying to numb the overwhelming emotions that were consuming her.

Genji, noticing her visible frustration, approached her with a compassionate expression. "Hey, are you okay?" asked Genji.

"I'm not in the mood," Dana responded as she walked past Genji. Her actions spoke louder than words. She impulsively grabbed Kaito off the sofa and led him upstairs, unknowingly leaving Genji with a heart-wrenching realization. The girl he had feelings for was now seemingly taken from him by his own brother.

I'M BROKEN TOO

Feeling a mixture of hurt, disappointment, and anger, Genji couldn't bear to witness the scene unfolding before him. He walked over to the nearby bar and poured himself a drink, seeking some semblance of solace in the numbing effect of alcohol. Sitting by the comforting warmth of the fireplace, he took a big gulp, trying to drown the emotions that threatened to overwhelm him.

The intense rush of emotions inside him eventually gave way to a fit of rage. In a moment of frustration, Genji hurled the glass he was holding into the fireplace, the shattering sound punctuating the air. As the glass met the flames, they momentarily blazed brighter, mirroring the turmoil that consumed him.

As Dana walked down the hallway, her heart pounded loudly in her chest. The emotions swirling inside her were overwhelming, and she couldn't resist the pull she felt toward Kaito. Without a second thought, she approached him, and the air between them crackled with unspoken desire.

In a moment of raw passion, Dana pressed Kaito against the wall, her hands trembling as she tugged at his shirt. The chemistry between them was undeniable, and their lips met in a fervent kiss filled with longing and uncertainty.

In the heat of the moment, they found themselves lost in each other's arms, a trail of discarded clothes left behind as they sought a brief escape from the chaos outside.

Outside, the storm raged, mirroring the turmoil within their hearts. The darkened skies seemed to reflect the intensity of their emotions as they grappled with the consequences of their actions and the tangled web of feelings that entwined them.

Chapter Thirty!

As the day continued, students trapped inside the dorms sought ways to pass the time, and many resorted to engaging in conversation, games, and drinking.

Meanwhile, Belle and Galan stood in her room, the aftermath of their intense encounter evident in the disarray surrounding them. They exchanged glances filled with satisfaction and affection as they both started getting dressed.

What is this feeling? I feel happy, but not the kind you feel when you're in love. I feel fulfilled and satisfied. Is it the sex? No, even when I had sex with

Aria, Dana, and the rest of them... It never felt like this. The last time it felt like this was with... Paige.

"What are you thinking about? You seem so far away?" asked Belle.

"Just reflecting," said Galan.

"And what is Sir reflecting on?" Belle inquired.

A chill ran down Galan's spine, and a smile graced his lips.

That's it... She actually does what I want. Her submission is what makes this feel so different. Have I been searching for the wrong thing all this time? Have I been spending my life trying to find love when what I needed was someone who submits to me? I don't believe that; I love 'love.' I wouldn't be me if I wasn't driven by it. Nikki and Dana were right; I tried replacing the love I was denied. Aria, Lillie, and all the girls in between were all just replacements for the love I have been longing for. Paige was only a reminder of the love I'd lost when I lost Lillie, just like Dana is a reminder of Aria. Dana made her choice, and if I truly love her, I have to let her be happy.

Galan turned to Belle, his eyes softening as he gently placed his hand on her cheek, his touch tender and affectionate, "I just found the closure I needed. Now let's go downstairs and wait out this storm."

"Could we stay in here? I don't want to share your presence with anyone right now," Belle remarked.

Galan smiled. "Of course we can," Galan whispered softly, his voice carrying the weight of his emotions, and he kissed Belle once more, savoring the sweetness of their connection. With a sense of ease, they settled into bed, facing each other, their eyes locked in an intimate gaze.

As they lay side by side, they continued to talk, their words flowing freely, baring their souls to one another. Galan's fingers gently traced the delicate strands of Belle's hair, his touch a gentle caress that spoke of his fondness for her.

Kaito and Dana quietly got dressed, the atmosphere between them tinged with a hint of tension and uncertainty. No words were exchanged as they buttoned shirts and smoothed out creases, the silence speaking volumes about the complexity of their emotions.

Aware that Belle's room was nearby, Dana couldn't help but feel a mix of curiosity and apprehension. She stood still for a moment, her ears keenly attuned to any sound emanating from the direction of Belle's room. Hoping to catch even a faint whisper of what might be transpiring between Belle and Galan, she listened attentively.

"I'm going to find my brother; I'll be back soon," Kaito called out softly as he got up from the bed and left the room. As he walked down the hall, his bare chest exposed, he quickly slipped on his t-shirt.

Descending the stairs, he couldn't help but notice Genji standing behind the bar, attempting to find solace in the numbing effects of alcohol. Seeing Genji knocking back another large drink, he rushed to his brother's side, snatching it out of his brother's hand.

"Baka! What are you doing? I think you've had enough for one day. Come on, let's get you to your room so you can get some rest," Kaito suggested.

"Leave me alone!" Genji said harshly.

"What's the matter?" asked Kaito in a soft, concerned voice.

"You hooked up with Dana. You knew I had a crush on her," Genji stated.

"Is that what this is about?" questioned Kaito.

"You knew I liked her; how could you do this to me, Aniki?" questioned Genji.

"She wasn't right for you, Otouto," answered Kaito.

"But she was good enough for you?!" Genji's frustration and emotions boiled over, and he couldn't contain it any longer. With a mix of anger and sadness, he threw his glass into the fireplace, the shattering sound echoing through the common area of the dorms.

The sudden outburst drew the attention of the other students who were gathered in the common area. Their conversations were hushed, and all eyes turned toward Genji, curious and concerned about what had led to this commotion.

"Take it easy, Genji; come on, let's get you to your room, and we can talk," Kaito calmly repeated.

"No! Let's talk here! Tell me why my big brother would go after the girl I liked from day one," Genji exclaimed.

"I didn't go after her. She came on to me," Kaito corrected.

"I didn't see you reject her; you went upstairs with her in a hurry," Genji pointed out.

"Genji, this isn't the first time. I found her at a club, drunk out of her mind, and I had to take her and her friends to a hotel which ruined my night. She fucked me then and every other chance she got. She's nothing special; she's just a girl. Trust me, you dodged a bullet 'cause she had a ring on her finger when I fucked her the first time. How would you feel if you were the one who gave her your hand in marriage? She's not good enough for you. She's not worth anything to me, but I can't do a personal life, wife, and kids. This is the world I chose to live in when I abandoned my life back home to come watch over my little brother. And you will always be worth every sacrifice I make to be there for you, but that girl will never be worth anything more to me than what she is right now. A way to pass the time," Kaito explained.

"Is that all I am to you?" asked Dana as she stood behind Kaito with her arms folded.

"You're not anything to me," Kaito confirmed.

"Wow…," Dana exclaimed.

"Have I led you on somehow? We don't even talk. We fuck, and then leave the other to continue their day. I never expressed an interest in you; tell me I am lying right now!" Kaito remarked.

"What about when you cared enough to take me to a hotel because I was too drunk to find my way home," questioned Dana.

"It's called decency. I would have taken you home, but you were out cold, and excuse me if I didn't feel like wasting my night waiting for you to get over your drunken state and then take you home. Or maybe I should have left you at the club where the bartender was feeding you and your friends' drinks so that you couldn't think straight!" Kaito stated.

"And when you looked at me and said I was yours now and you didn't care whose ring was on my finger… I guess I imagined that, huh?" Dana retorted.

"You had a ring on your finger, but you were out getting drunk with your friends and winded up fucking a stranger in a hotel; how did your fiancé feel about that when he picked you up?" asked Kaito.

"He was dead! My fiancé was dead, and I was hurting, and I couldn't deal with it. I went out there to clear my head and run from the shit storm that was hitting my life. And then you came along and acted like you cared about me, and all I wanted was for the pain to stop," Dana expressed as she broke down in tears. "I just wanted it to stop… How foolish of me to think I meant something to someone!"

"That doesn't sound like my problem," Kaito replied.

"You heartless piece of shit…," Dana hissed.

"Funny… That you would call him heartless," the room fell silent as the doppelgänger's words hung in the air. His voice carried an eerie calmness that sent shivers down everyone's spine. The unexpected turn of events shifted the focus from the emotional turmoil between Kaito, Genji, and Dana to the mysterious figure before them.

With wide-eyed astonishment, the students turned their attention to the pile of bodies where the doppelgänger lay, fighting to rise despite the grievous wound he had sustained. Blood flowed from his chest as he clutched his heart in his hand, examining it with an almost detached curiosity.

"What the fuck…." Dana gasped.

Kaito's protective instincts kicked in, and he swiftly positioned himself between the doppelgänger and Genji. Sensing the impending danger, he took a cautious step back, his eyes locked on the mysterious figure before them.

The room fell into an eerie silence, the students holding their breath as they watched the tense confrontation unfold. The doppelgänger's unsettling presence seemed to cast a shadow over everything, and their hearts pounded in anticipation of what might come next.

With a twisted smirk, the doppelgänger tossed his heart over to Dana's feet, "My heart was ripped out years ago; there is nothing you can do to hurt me anymore."

The room erupted into screams as students broke out into a panic once more. "Time is almost up; listen up! If you want to live, bring me Dana Scarlet's heart, and those of you who remain will be allowed to live. Or the next person I kill will be Genji Shinoda!" the doppelgänger instructed. Genji's heart skipped a beat at the mention of his name, and he felt a chill run down his spine. The doppelgänger's words hung heavily in the air, singling him out with unsettling precision.

Galan snuck up from behind and stabbed the doppelgänger through his spine. The doppelgänger fell to his knees, and Kaito rushed in without hesitation and drew his kodachi. Letting out a rage-filled scream as he severed the head of the doppelgänger, his body hit the floor, and his head rolled a few feet away.

Chapter Thirty-one

"What the hell is going on!" Dana's scream pierced through the tension-filled air, her voice echoing with fear and alarm. Kaito and Galan exchanged quick glances, their eyes scanning the room, taking in the panicked expressions of their fellow students.

"Did the Ripper get off the ground and toss his fucking heart across the room? Or am I losing my fucking mind!?" Kaito asked.

"I could believe maybe we didn't finish the job before, but I stabbed the Ripper through his head, tore his heart from his body, and dropped him from the highest balcony. The ground is covered in his blood; what the hell is happening here...." Galan exclaimed.

"This isn't going to stop; he's just going to keep coming back," Kaito stated.

"Not without a head, he's not," Galan claimed.

"But he was fine without a heart?!" Kaito retorted.

"Take it easy; he's dead!" said Galan.

"He should have been dead the first time! People keep saying maybe I wasn't sure, but I know the feel of a man's life leaving his body! The Ripper should have died the first time I crossed paths with him!" Kaito remarked.

"We're all gonna die in here!" Genji proclaimed.

"Shut up, Baka! We're not going to die! We need to get the hell out of this place!" Kaito voiced.

"Kaito! Calm down!" Galan bellowed, his muscles tensing as Kaito forcefully pushed him away. The intensity of their confrontation filled the room with palpable tension. "Hey, watch it!" Galan shouted.

Kaito raised his kodachi to Galan's neck, "Not another step! I'm taking my brother and getting out of here!"

"We don't have to run… If we kill her, then the Ripper will stop!" said a student as she pointed at Dana.

"Are you insane!?" Dana exclaimed.

In a swift display of determination, the students scrambled towards the basket of knives, their eagerness evident in their eyes. "This is life or death, and I am not choosing your fucking life over ours!" another student claimed.

"No!!! Don't... We're all in here together! The Ripper can't kill us all," Galan tried to appease the crowd.

"No! My brother is next on the chopping board. And I'll be damned if I let some bitch's life come before his!" Kaito declared.

"You don't want to do this...," Galan retorted, his eyes blazing with unwavering intensity.

"There is nothing I wouldn't do for my brother; her life isn't worth more than his. So you're wrong; you have no idea how badly I want to do this," Kaito replied as he touched the blade's tip to Galan's neck. "So, are you ready to die for her?"

"Die for who? The girl who left me for you?" Galan's chuckle echoed with a chilling touch, sending shivers down Dana's spine. In that fleeting moment, she sensed a darkness lurking beneath the facade of amusement. His laughter held a sinister edge, causing her heart to sink as if an invisible weight had been placed upon it.

As Galan's words spilled from his lips, Dana couldn't help but feel a sense of impending doom.

"Your only problem would be getting to her before I do," Galan stated

Galan's piercing gaze locked onto Dana, and in that haunting moment, her cries fell on deaf ears. The room seemed to hold its breath, transfixed by the unfolding scene. The atmosphere turned heavy and suffocating, charged with malevolence. As if in unison, the other occupants of the room turned their attention to her, their eyes filled with a cold, predatory gleam.

Dana felt an overwhelming sense of vulnerability as if she were defenseless prey surrounded by relentless predators. The killer intent emanating from every corner of the room was palpable and suffocating, and her instincts screamed at her to escape the trap closing in around her.

"You're her fiancé...?" asked Kaito.

"Was... She ripped my heart out," Galan corrected. With a calculated and deliberate motion, Galan lowered the blade from his neck, his eyes never leaving Dana's. The atmosphere thickened with tension as he started to close the distance between them. Each step he took felt like an ominous drumbeat, heralding an impending confrontation that could determine their fates. "Now I'll do the same to her!" Galan vowed.

In the midst of Dana's rising panic and tears, a sudden glimmer of hope flickered when she noticed an enigmatic smile on Galan's face. His wink was unexpected, and for a brief moment, uncertainty clouded her mind. He spun with remarkable speed in a blur of motion, and a forceful crossbody kick found its mark on Kaito's chest. The impact sent Kaito sprawling backward, caught off guard by the unexpected attack. "Run!!!" Galan shouted as Kaito fell to the ground, still holding his kodachi.

The room erupted into chaos as Galan swiftly retrieved the knife from the doppelgänger's back. Meanwhile, Dana sprinted towards the staircase, her heart pounding in her chest as the students pursued her, brandishing their knives menacingly.

Dana's adrenaline-fueled legs propelled her forward with each step, her mind racing for a way to escape the relentless pursuit. The staircase offered a potential means of getting away, and she clung to that hope like a lifeline.

Kaito, recovering from the earlier attack, regained his footing with determination burning in his eyes. As Galan squared off for battle, he made a surprising move, ignoring the confrontation entirely. With incredible agility, Kaito ran up the wall, using it as a launchpad, and grabbed hold of the staircase railing, putting him in Dana's path.

"Shine…," Kaito whispered. Belle, appearing around the corner, swung a laptop with surprising force, connecting it harshly against the side of Kaito's head.

The impact stunned Kaito, momentarily disorienting him and creating an opening for Dana to escape. Sensing the chance to break free, Dana wasted no time and darted past the dazed Kaito, following Belle's fleeing figure. Shaking off the disorientation, Kaito quickly regained his senses and realized Dana was getting away. Determination blazed in his eyes as he mustered his strength to give chase. However, his path was abruptly blocked by Galan, who had finally made his way upstairs, determined to halt Kaito's pursuit.

"Move! Or the next time you do so will be when your dead corpse hits the floor!" Kaito ordered.

"You make a move on her, and I will send your brother to you in pieces!" Galan retorted.

"What did you just say?!" Kaito growled as he stepped closer.

"There are people that look out for Dana who will bring a world of problems to your door, including your brother. You kill Dana, and those people will come for you; trust me, I know!" Galan explained.

"You mean that old bitch whose house I burnt to the ground for threatening my brother? She doesn't scare me, and neither do you," Kaito exclaimed.

"You burnt down that woman's house?! I was inside that place when you attacked. And I got blamed for it; Dana thinks I died because of that fire! And my whole relationship died with it! Listen to me; I'm not saying we do nothing; I don't want anything to happen to your brother either. We need level heads, or we are no better off than those students running scared down there!" Galan voiced as Genji came up the stairs, followed by the hoard of students.

"I don't care; I will not let anything happen to my brother," Kaito repeated.

"Aniki!" Genji called out.

"Listen to yourselves; you're following the words of a madman. The Blood Rain Ripper has sent people insane. We outnumber him, dozens to one, help is probably on the way, and this storm will pass. We just need to wait this out! Do you really believe the killing would stop? Dana rallied all of us to put an end to the Ripper killings, and here we are, going against what she stood for. If I had to guess, I'd say someone found out about this plan and tried to stop her. Someone is benefitting from the Ripper killings, so let's not play into their hand," Galan explained.

"And how do you explain the Ripper who died four times tonight alone and won't stop," a student inquired.

"I don't know! But I know killing her isn't the answer. We killed the Ripper four times already. I say we keep him dead—throw his ass into the fire and let him burn. We just need to wait till help comes. Please, don't turn on each other now," Galan pleaded.

Feeling the weight of Galan's words, the students exchanged meaningful glances, their resolve strengthened by the gravity of the situation. They nodded in unanimous agreement, understanding that they needed to regroup and face the challenges ahead as a united front. In a synchronized motion, they turned away from the stand-off, marching back downstairs, their steps filled with purpose.

Kaito remained tense; Genji stepped beside him, "Aniki, don't."

"Alright, I'll do this your way, but if that Ripper comes back, I will go through anyone to save my brother," Kaito remarked.

"Fair enough, now let's go do the honors," said Galan as he extended his fist. Kaito hesitated for a moment but then reciprocated the gesture, bumping fists with his adversary. The students, witnessing this surprising display of camaraderie, erupted into cheers. With the doppelgänger's lifeless body now lying on the floor, Galan and Kaito worked together in a synchronized motion, dragging it across the room. Together, they tossed the lifeless form into the fiery abyss. As the body hit the blazing firewood, the flames erupted, their intensity growing as if fueled by the malevolence that once inhabited the doppelgänger.

As Dana and Belle looked over the balcony, the surreal scene below unfolded before their eyes. Galan and Kaito took care of the doppelgänger's body, utilizing alcohol to accelerate the cremation process in the fireplace. The flames roared with intensity, consuming all traces of the dark entity that had threatened their lives.

As the storm began to ease, the sound of the rain gradually diminished, settling into a gentle drizzle. The tempestuous weather mirrored the tumultuous events that had transpired, but with the threat neutralized, the atmosphere seemed to shift toward a newfound calmness.

Their attention was grasped at the sound of sirens piercing through the air. Law enforcement was on its way, responding to the chaos that had unfolded at SPU. The students hurriedly rushed to the doors, their faces filled with relief as they peered outside at the approaching fleet of emergency rescue vehicles.

Relief washed over the students as they chanted the words, "We're saved!" Their cheers echoed through the building, a collective expression of gratitude and hope as the sound of the approaching sirens grew louder.

Kaito and Galan, feeling the weight of the night's events lifting off their shoulders, exchanged glances of understanding. The tension that had held them on edge for so long now began to ease, knowing that help was finally at hand.

Dana and Belle, still standing by the window on the balcony, peered outside to witness the arrival of the law enforcement vehicles. As the sirens blared, they knew that their encounter with this darkness had not gone unnoticed by the authorities.

"Thank God…," Dana and Belle mumbled.

As the convoy of vehicles came to a halt on the campus, a sense of urgency filled the air. Swarms of police officers and medics quickly poured out of the vehicles, responding to the call for help and intervention. The gravity of the situation was evident in their expressions as they prepared to attend to the grim scene that had unfurled at SPU.

Dana and Belle waved their arms from the window, signaling for the authorities' attention. The group of officers and medics immediately noticed them and rushed toward the dorms, guided by their gestures.

As they approached the dormitory, they knocked on the door. "SPPD, we're here to help; standby as we get the doors open," said an officer.

"The doors won't open by force; it's built to be a safe bunker in case of emergencies. Restoring power to the building will enable you to open the locks," a student informed them.

"Understood; we already have a team trying to get that underway. Stay calm, and you all will be out in no time," the officer replied.

The horror on Dana and Belle's faces was mirrored in the eyes of the group downstairs as they rushed to the common area. The sight that greeted them was chilling beyond words—the doppelgänger, seemingly undeterred by the flames that had consumed its body, stood just outside the fireplace. His clothes were burnt, and his body was smoking, yet he held his decapitated head in place with a makeshift cloth tied around his neck.

The air was thick with terror as the students' screams pierced the air, sending shivers down the spines of everyone present. The room filled with panic, and a collective sense of dread consumed them. Realizing that the malevolent entity had not been fully defeated brought a new wave of terror and confusion.

In a desperate bid to escape, they pounded on the doors, praying for them to open. The doppelgänger's slow approach added to their terror, and a sense of helplessness engulfed them as they struggled to find a way out.

With the chaos unfolding inside, the officers outside peered through the windows, witnessing the grim scene transpiring before them. Their expressions turned grave as they realized the severity of the situation, and they quickly sprung into action, attempting to find a way to intervene and provide aid.

Scattering in all directions, the students screamed for help, their voices trembling with fear. Panic drove them to seek safety as they ran from the malicious presence that continued to haunt them. The once-united group was now scattered, each trying to find a way to escape the relentless pursuit of the doppelgänger.

The officer's quick thinking led him to draw his gun and fire at the windows, hoping to create a way of escape for the students. But to their shock and dismay, the bullets had no effect on the windows.

Amidst the rising panic, the officer's eyes darted around outside the building, searching for any other means of escape. It was then that they noticed the dorm windows overhead. The officer took another shot, aiming at the window with resolve. This time, the bullet shattered the glass, providing a glimmer of hope for their desperate situation.

With adrenaline pumping through their veins, they realized that the dorm windows could be their only chance of escape. The officer motioned for the students to climb up and follow him, seeking refuge on the higher floors of the building. "It's not bulletproof up there. Get the firetruck to hoist the ladder up there; we need to get those students out!" instructed an officer.

Chapter Thirty-two

Amidst the chaotic dispersal of the remaining students throughout the echoing halls, a defiant few, armed with knives, stood firm. Kaito and Galan watched with both dread and fascination as a determined group of twelve students charged recklessly at the smoldering form of the enigmatic doppelgänger. The figure moved with uncanny swiftness. Quickly disarming one of the students, his movements were almost a blur before turning his attention to the rest who dared to challenge him. The rhythmic thud of blood hitting the floor reverberated through the tense air as they fell, one by one, under the relentless assault

Kaito and Galan stood there, frozen in shock, their eyes locked on the ominous figure before them. The encounter had taken a sinister turn, and they were now faced with an entity that seemed nigh unstoppable. Fear and uncertainty gripped their hearts as the menacing figure slowly turned to fix his gaze upon them, the chilling intensity of his stare sending shivers down their spines.

"Justice for Eder!" the doppelgänger shouted. In a reckless frenzy, the doppelgänger sprinted towards the bar, seizing bottles of alcohol and wildly dousing the common area with the flammable liquid. With an unsettling calmness, he then grabbed a blazing piece of firewood from the hearth and hurled it over to the bar, igniting the alcohol-soaked surfaces. The room erupted into a raging inferno, flames licking hungrily at the walls, sending sparks and embers dancing through the air.

Galan found himself paralyzed, his feet rooted to the spot as if time had suspended its usual flow. The macabre scene before him was all too familiar, resembling a haunting replay of his past. The fire's relentless advance, the acrid smoke that stung his nostrils, and the overpowering smell of alcohol engulfed him in a visceral flashback, transporting him back to a traumatic moment from his history.

Amidst the chaos of the present, Galan's mind was consumed by haunting memories, threatening to engulf him just as the flames roared around him. His heart raced, each beat echoing the turbulent emotions within him. The burning room mirrored the turmoil in his soul, leaving him grappling with a torrent of emotions as he confronted the haunting echoes of his past.

As Galan stood there, gripped by the overwhelming inferno surrounding him, the flickering flames seemed to transform into haunting visions from the depths of his memory. Amid the fiery chaos, his mind involuntarily conjured vivid and painful images of a tragic event he had long tried to bury.

In the harrowing vision, Galan found himself standing amidst the charred remains of a home—a place that once belonged to his first love, Lillie. The memory was a reawakening of the nightmarish scene he had witnessed before, one that had left an indelible scar on his soul.

With a heavy heart full of grief and guilt, Galan saw himself standing over the lifeless bodies of Lillie's family. *This isn't happening; how did it come to this? This isn't me; this can't be me! No! I'm just a kid. I didn't kill all these people!*

As Galan's gaze locked onto his doppelgänger, the boundaries between his haunting memories and the foreboding events yet to unfold became increasingly indistinguishable. The figure before him seemed to morph, blurring the lines of reality, shifting between the innocent young boy he once was and the remorseless Ripper, whose actions had left a haunting trail of lifeless bodies in his wake.

Amid this turmoil, Kaito's urgent call shattered the haze of Galan's thoughts. With newfound resolve, he snapped back to the present. Kaito rushed upstairs in a desperate search for his brother, his heart pounding as he feared for his brother's safety. The doppelgänger showed no mercy, relentless in his pursuit of the fleeing students. With cold precision, he slit their throats, leaving them to gasp for air as they desperately tried to escape the clutches of death, crimson trails marking their path.

With a sense of urgency and determination, Kaito's voice echoed through the halls, calling out for his brother, Genji. The fear in his heart drove him to sprint forward, searching desperately for any sign of his sibling amongst the chaos that had engulfed the dorm. Galan, mirroring Kaito's fervor, moved agilely along the opposite walls. Kicking open doors one by one, their eyes scanned each room for any trace of Genji, Dana, and Belle.

As the chaos unfolded on the school campus, the police raced across the grounds, fervently signaling the firetruck to follow suit. Smoke billowed from the dormitory, darkening the sky and carrying the scent of destruction with it. The fire's relentless advance had created a shroud of haze, making visibility increasingly difficult for those trying to navigate the area.

Galan's heart pounded in his chest as he rushed through the halls, attempting to locate them. The seriousness of the situation pressed upon him, but as he burst into a room, his breath caught in his throat, and he came to an abrupt halt. A chilling sight greeted him, one that froze him in place.

In the dimly lit room, the flickering flames cast a haunting glow upon Lillie, whose once radiant appearance was now marred by the macabre scene surrounding her. Her figure was covered in blood, the crimson staining her clothes and hands, painting a horrifying picture of the chaos that had occurred.

Relief washed over Galan as Belle, Dana, and Genji appeared amidst the confusion, reaching out and grabbing onto him. As Kaito arrived, rushing down the hall at the sound of his brother's voice, the bond between the siblings shone brightly, reinforcing their decision to stay together and protect each other in this nightmarish situation. The group's collective coughing from the thickening smoke served as a harsh reminder of the peril they were all in, urging them to find a way to safety as quickly as possible.

Galan turned back to the room he had just entered, but it was now empty, to his bewilderment. The sight of Lillie, covered in blood and standing there, had vanished into thin air. It was as if the haunting vision he had witnessed was merely a fleeting echo, a manifestation of the turmoil within his mind.

"We have to move!" Belle instructed.

"I don't think so! Time's up, kill Dana or Genji dies," the doppelgänger announced.

"You're outnumbered! Let's go!" Galan shouted.

"I don't think so," the doppelgänger replied as a group of students marched down the hall. "Let's see what happens first; you try to kill me again, or these students gain some extra credit and kill Genji!" Tensions grew as the smoke thickened; the doppelgänger ran out of patience. "Kill the boy!" he commanded.

In a sudden turn of events, Kaito's emotions seemed to overwhelm him, and without warning, he turned and swung at Dana. Galan's instincts kicked in, and he reacted swiftly, lunging forward to tackle Kaito to the ground. "Run!" Galan urgently shouted to Dana.

The air crackled with tension as Kaito sprang to his feet and charged at Galan. Galan gripped his knife tightly, his eyes locked onto Kaito as he continued his relentless assault. Their blades clashed, each strike carrying the weight of their animosity toward each other.

Genji, Dana, and Belle ran through the halls as the chaos unfolded around them, desperately trying to escape the relentless pursuit of the doppelgänger and the students under his influence. The harrowing scene had left them breathless and on edge, their hearts pounding in their chests.

Genji, however, struggled to keep up. The effects of the alcohol he had consumed earlier were taking their toll, blurring his vision and dulling his motor skills. He stumbled, his steps becoming unsteady, as he tried to maintain his balance and keep running alongside his friends.

Dana and Belle recognized the seriousness of the situation and knew they couldn't afford to slow down. They rushed to support Genji, each taking an arm to keep him steady and prevent him from falling behind. Their grip was firm but gentle, a display of unwavering camaraderie even in the face of danger.

Genji stopped, "They want me! Go on and find a way out. I'll hold them off."

"Genji, no!" Dana exclaimed.

"Ja ne!" Genji turned to Dana and smiled. As the small mob of students charged at them, Belle pulled Dana away, urging her to keep running for their safety.

Genji knew that he had to act quickly and decisively. With a few resolute slaps to his cheeks and several deep breaths, he tried to shake off the effects of the alcohol and regain control of his faculties. His heart raced, but he refused to let fear or inebriation cloud his focus.

Genji braced himself as the students closed in on him and rushed into the fray. His movements were surprisingly swift and calculated, a testament to his natural athleticism and fighting skills. Despite the odds stacked against him, he held his own, deflecting their strikes, countering their attacks, and using their momentum against them.

The battle was fierce; the clash of bodies and the echo of blows filled the air.

The tension between Kaito and Galan reached its breaking point as they continued their intense struggle. Each of them was determined to overpower the other, their rivalry fueling the ferocity of their clash.

Locked in a heated hold, they grappled with all their might, trying to gain the upper hand. Their steps led them to the balcony, where the stakes grew even higher as they teetered dangerously close to the edge.

Galan, in a desperate attempt to break free, headbutted Kaito repeatedly. The impact disoriented them both, causing momentary dizziness, but they fought through the pain, their resolve unwavering.

With a quick and decisive move, Galan threw the knife he held at Kaito's head, but his opponent's reflexes were equally sharp. Kaito reacted with practiced ease, slashing the oncoming projectile from the air, preventing any harm.

Unarmed but undeterred, Galan refused to back down. He swiftly grabbed onto Kaito's arm, trying to restrain him from using his kodachi. In a fluid motion, Kaito dropped the sword from one hand to the other, catching it out of the air and thrusting it toward Galan's gut; Galan felt the cold steel pierce his abdomen.

"Shine!" Kaito's heart raced as he locked eyes with Galan, his determination shining through. Without a second thought, he swiftly drew the kodachi from Galan's gut, a glint of steel reflecting the fiery chaos around them. With a resolute kick, he sent Galan hurtling over the balcony's edge.

As Galan's figure disappeared from sight, the unsettling thud of bodies on the ground softened his descent, yet, the engulfing flames encroached; the blazing inferno crept closer, crackling with a menacing intensity.

As Dana and Belle frantically ascended to the top floor, their breaths came in ragged gasps, and their hearts pounded in their chests. The relentless pursuit had left them with no other choice but to seek refuge in the building's uppermost reaches. With desperation etched on their faces, they exchanged a fleeting glance, silently vowing to protect each other at all costs.

Suddenly, the echo of hurried footsteps reverberated through the dimly lit corridor, signaling the relentless approach of yet another danger. Turning towards the sound, their eyes widened as they spotted one of their fellow students quickly approaching. Fear tightened its grip on Dana and Belle's hearts, but they were not alone in this perilous encounter.

In an unexpected twist of fate, the doppelgänger, driven by a sinister intent, shifted its attention to the oncoming assailant, catching them off guard. With ruthless precision, he struck, the blade flashing like a deadly streak in the dim light. The unfortunate pursuer barely had time to comprehend the impending doom before their throat was mercilessly slit.

"Noo... She dies by my hand!" the doppelgänger claimed.

"Split up!" Belle shouted. As Dana and Belle's desperate escape led them down different corridors, the menacing doppelgänger relentlessly pursued Dana with chilling resolution. Darting down the steps to the lower floor, Dana's heart pounded in her chest as she found herself cut off by the relentless entity. Panic surged through her veins, but her survival instincts kicked in, scanning her surroundings for any advantage.

Amidst the chaos, her eyes fell upon a glimmering knife lying among the lifeless bodies scattered on the floor. Without missing a beat, she seized the opportunity, pretending to stumble while deftly grabbing the weapon, concealing her actions from the doppelgänger's watchful gaze. With the knife in hand, she darted away, each step echoing with a mix of fear and perseverance.

As Dana weaved through the dimly lit halls, she took a sharp turn, effectively concealing herself from the doppelgänger's line of sight. The doppelgänger followed into a narrow corridor, leading him to an unexpected dead end. Dana took a leap of faith to perform a daring maneuver, diving from a room adjacent to where the doppelgänger stood. With precision and courage, she thrust the knife into the doppelgänger's side, causing him to crash into another room across the hallway.

Seizing the moment, Dana positioned herself on top of the wounded doppelgänger, her grip tightening around the knife, ready to deliver the final blow. Her hand was abruptly grabbed from behind, and a sudden searing pain tore through her back as she was stabbed. As she tried to look, she caught a glimpse in a mirror; standing behind her was another doppelgänger.

The shocking revelation left her weakened, her strength waning as she clung to consciousness. Belle rushed into the room, bravely attempting to protect Dana, but her efforts were in vain. The doppelgänger effortlessly overpowered Belle, violently throwing her against the wall before getting another knife and mercilessly stabbing her in the gut.

As Belle slumped down the wall, her blood staining the floor, the sound of approaching sirens and police echoed through the building. The long-awaited reinforcements had finally arrived, their presence an ominous reminder that time was running out; both doppelgängers turned to Dana and Belle and chanted, "Justice for Eder" before escaping the room.

In the midst of this deadly encounter, Kaito, searching for his brother, emerged from the chaos, finding him bleeding against a wall.

The once-hostile students now lay lifeless on the floor as Genji stood victorious but at a cost. Kaito, acting swiftly, lifted his wounded brother onto his back, determined to carry him to safety. As the police team rapidly closed in, Kaito and his brother were found and guided toward a nearby window where a ladder awaited their escape. With adrenaline coursing through his veins, Kaito descended the ladder, his brother clinging to his back.

"Aniki… Save Dana," Genji whispered.

"She's not my concern," Kaito replied as he hurried down the ladder.

"Please, I don't want you giving up your life to take care of me; I want my brother to be happy too. And I know she made you happy; you don't fool me," Genji responded.

"Yamero! Otouto," Kaito remarked.

"I was wrong to feel the way that I did; rather than be happy for my brother, I felt jealous that the girl I liked was interested in my brother. When all along, I should have been happy that you found something special. Please, Aniki, promise me you'll go back for her," Genji pleaded.

"Baka…," Kaito muttered, his voice tinged with both frustration and concern as he glanced back at the blazing building.

The authorities searched the dorms, ensuring the safety of the few remaining students. The survivors were carefully escorted to the window, where a ladder awaited to carry them down to safety into the hands of the waiting medical team.

As the chaos intensified, Dana's consciousness began to slip away. Her vision blurred, and the world around her became a hazy blur. The last image she could discern was the flurry of footsteps approaching, and at the helm, she saw Kaito leading the team of officers to rescue them. Kaito took her in his arms as she struggled to stay awake. Dana and Belle were gently guided out the window and placed into an ambulance, accompanied by the two officers who discovered them. The vehicle raced through the campus, the sirens wailing, their destination set for the nearest hospital.

Galan was discovered amongst the chaos, lying wounded on the floor. The medical team carried him outside and swiftly attended to him, skillfully working to stop the bleeding and stabilize his condition. As he lay there, his eyes fixated on the dorms consumed by flames, a sense of horror and helplessness washed over him. The firefighters bravely battled the relentless blaze, their valiant efforts aided by the descending rain, which seemed to offer a helping hand in the fight against the fire's fury. The sound of crackling flames and the scent of smoke filled the air, adding to the surreal atmosphere surrounding Galan.

Amid the crisis, Galan's mind played tricks on him, as if time itself folded, blending the past with the present. In the chaos, he saw her once more—Lillie, standing among the pandemonium, her form smeared with blood. The haunting image of her disappearing into the crowd haunted him, obstructed from his view by the encircling officers and medics.

Arriving at the hospital, the atmosphere was charged with tension and anguish as Dana's loved ones, her father, and Mama B rushed into the emergency room. Their hearts pounded with fear as they witnessed her struggle to hold onto life. Time seemed to slow to a crawl as the medical team urgently worked to seal her wounds, the monitors echoing the gravity of the situation with every passing second. Mama B and Mr. Scarlet stood helplessly, their souls heavy with worry and sorrow, as they watched the doctors fight to save her.

The heart rate monitor's static beep overcame them. Their cries of pain and desperation seemed to go unheard, drowned out by the sounds of life-saving efforts. With every ounce of determination, the doctors raced against time; their expertise and dedication focused on stabilizing Dana before it was too late. Miraculously the static hold of the beep returned to a steady rhythm.

In the room a few doors down, Kaito sat vigilantly at Genji's side, bearing the physical and emotional weight of the ordeal they had both endured. Genji, who was severely beaten but had miraculously avoided fatal wounds, lay unconscious as he began the slow process of recovery. Kaito refused to leave his brother's side, staying there day and night, providing the unwavering support that only a devoted sibling could offer.

Chapter Thirty-Three

*I*n the blink of an eye, weeks hurried past, leaving Galan grappling to reclaim his life. Once discharged from the hospital, he mustered the strength to return to Grounded Coffee House, determined to keep his business afloat. Yet, the haunting memory of the harrowing event persisted, and the specters of his past relentlessly tormented his mind. Even as he stepped back onto the grounds of Salt Pine University, he couldn't escape the vivid apparition of Lillie at every corner he turned.

With each passing day, Galan's struggle to push through the anguish intensified. His visions grew more intricate and unsettling as he saw not only Lillie but Aria covered in blood around the campus, intertwining their presence in his very perception. It was as if the lines between reality and memory had blurred beyond recognition.

Meanwhile, the chilling tale of the Ripper attack at SPU reverberated worldwide, capturing the attention of millions. The survivors, grappling with their trauma, found themselves thrust into the spotlight, with their heart-wrenching experiences now destined for the silver screen. A major motion pictures studio in Hollywood seized upon this dark chapter of history, offering them a movie deal to bring the story of the infamous "Blood Rain Ripper of Salt Pine Acres" to life on the big screen.

In the face of relentless media coverage and the persistent pursuit of closure, Galan found himself caught in a storm of emotions, haunted by the past and uncertain of the future. The journey to healing and reclaiming his life seemed fraught with uncertainty as he grappled with the dual struggle of preserving the legacy of his beloved coffee house and seeking solace in the wake of unimaginable loss.

Late at night, Galan's phone rang; his gaze fixed on the screen, revealing Dana's name. "We need to have that talk now," she stated.

Galan's heart pounded in his chest as he rushed over to Dana's place, unable to shake the urgency of the situation. The elevator seemed to take an eternity, and with every passing second, his apprehension grew. When the doors finally opened, he was met with a surprising sight—Kaito and Dana sitting side by side on her sofa. The tension in the room was palpable, and Galan couldn't help but wonder what had transpired in his absence.

Kaito's eyes flickered briefly to Galan as he stepped off the elevator, a mix of emotions dancing in their depths. But then, his gaze returned to Dana, "I'll be upstairs; give you two some privacy."

Dana's gesture invited Galan to sit beside her on the sofa, and he obliged, taking a seat as his curiosity got the better of him. However, his attention couldn't help but be drawn to Kaito, who was heading upstairs to Dana's room.

"Thanks for coming, Galan," said Dana.

"What is he doing here?" asked Galan.

"We found each other, Galan, and I really am sorry for the pain I put you through," Dana replied.

"Do you love him?" Galan inquired.

"Yes," answered Dana.

"Dana, he tried to kill you. He burnt down Mama B's home and was willing to let you die in the dorms—" Galan protested.

"To save his brother, to protect the one he loved. Have you never done horrible things for the people you love?" questioned Dana with a smile.

"Dana, he doesn't love you like I do," Galan stated.

"Maybe he doesn't, but he was there for me when you weren't," Dana pointed out.

"Dana—" Galan tried to interject.

"Let me finish; I know that wasn't your fault. The timing was just bad, and you couldn't be there for me like he was. Does that sound familiar?" asked Dana.

"Dana, please...." Galan's voice trembled with emotion, and tears welled up in his eyes as he looked at Dana.

"Galan, you were only around for a little over a week. We have known each other for four years, but I have only spent a week with you; Kaito has been there every day since you were gone, and I thought you had died. I lost everything when I lost you; a part of me died back then, and I couldn't go on without you. Then Kaito came along, and he stepped in and filled a gaping hole that you left in my life, and the only way I could have kept on going was latching on to him. I'm sorry, Galan, but the timing just wasn't right," Dana explained.

"You're punishing me for not loving you sooner?" Galan remarked.

"No, this isn't punishment. Galan, I care about you, and I will always treasure what we had, but moving on from you broke me," Dana professed.

"Please don't leave me," Galan begged.

"Galan, stop," said Dana.

"Let me," Galan whispered.

"Please, Galan, don't," Dana repeated.

"Let me love you; let me show you there is still hope," Galan replied.

"There is nothing left to love, Galan. You don't deserve the part of me that was shattered," Dana whispered. Galan held her face in his hands and leaned in close.

"Maybe I like broken toys…," Galan whispered. He leaned in to kiss her, but Dana placed her hand on his cheek and stopped him. Tilting his head down, she kissed his forehead and held him in her arms.

"You deserve someone who wouldn't do that to you," Dana murmured in his ear.

Galan left SPU, the memories of his past behind him, and embarked on a journey back to his home in the serene Salt Pine Acres. However, upon reaching his familiar abode, the once comforting sight of the locked room now served as a painful reminder of Paige's absence, engulfing him with an overwhelming sense of loneliness. The weight of solitude led Galan down a dark path, and he found solace in the comfort of alcohol, falling back into his old habits.

Yet, his thirst for adventure took him on a whirlwind expedition around the globe in the following months, seeking out vibrant parties and lively gatherings. It was in a grand house in Dubai that we found Galan transformed by his travels, his hair grown out, and his beard rugged and untamed. He grabbed a drink off a tray as a waiter walked past him and turned to walk out onto the balcony. As he stood on the balcony, clutching a drink tightly, he attempted to drown his sorrows in the intoxicating allure of the moment.

Amid the bustling party, amidst the laughter and the music, a voice from the past, gentle and familiar, seemed to whisper softly into his ear.

"Galan?..." someone called out to him.

As he turned, her presence caught Galan off guard, and for a moment, he was at a loss for words. His eyes met the worried gaze of Lillie.

What?...

LILLIE PAIGE

AGE: 29
SIGN: VIRGO

Chapter Thirty-Four

"Lillie…." Galan remarked in shock.

"Sweetie, what happened to you?" asked Lillie.

"You're alive?" Galan exclaimed.

"Why do you keep acting like I died every time you see me?" Lillie inquired.

"They found you dead in the hotel," Galan stated.

"I highly doubt that, sweetheart. I am here, and I feel quite alive," Lillie chuckled. "Did you really think I died?"

"Of course I did," Galan answered.

"After you told me that my sister and I could go to hell, I left right after you walked out that door," Lillie informed him.

"I didn't mean to say that. I thought Paige was manipulating me, and I said what I said," Galan explained.

"I figured as much. Do you know when we were kids, she would always pull stuff like that? I knew something was up when I ran into you. I looked for you for years before giving up that search. Then suddenly, you popped up on a boat in the ocean with me and mentioned her name. That could have only meant trouble. She had booked me at that hotel and told me she had a surprise for me. At first, I thought it was the champagne, but when I saw you, I figured she wanted to make up for the stuff she'd done when we were kids," Lillie began.

"You knew?" asked Galan.

"Of course I did; she wasn't allowed to date, so she made sure everyone was miserable too. Always threatening me to tell Mom and Dad I liked you if I didn't do her chores and stuff," Lillie explained.

She doesn't know…

"I was so pissed, I left immediately, figured she just wanted to get back at me for getting her in trouble back then," Lillie continued.

"In trouble?" Galan probed.

"I got tired of her bossing me around, and I told my parents what she had been doing; she got in a lot of trouble for it," Lillie clarified.

"But wait a minute; someone died in the hotel; they found someone. Paige thought it was you; she even cried. She told me she wanted to make amends for the past," Galan stated, confused.

"Like my sister has any capacity for good in her wretched body," Lillie rolled her eyes.

"I believed her," said Galan.

"Why?" asked Lillie.

"I mean, based on what you said, it sounds like your sister is the last person you would want to talk to. So putting us in the same place without your knowledge seemed like the only way you would even agree to it," Galan mused.

"True, I would have hung up the moment I heard her voice," Lillie agreed.

"I blew it; I let my paranoia run wild and destroyed a chance at something I always wanted," Galan remarked.

"I'm here now…." Lillie pointed out with a smile.

"After the things I've said to you?" asked Galan.

"Everyone makes mistakes. Maybe the time wasn't right back then, but it is now. Galan, I haven't stopped thinking about how you made me feel; I spent my whole life trying to replace the love you showed me over twenty years ago. We couldn't be together back then, but we're not kids anymore," Lillie expressed as she took his hand.

"Lillie…," Galan whispered.

"Come on, let's get you home and cleaned up; you look like you survived a werewolf bite," Lillie chuckled.

In the comfort of Lillie's Dubai apartment, Galan found solace and support as she lovingly took care of him, cutting his hair and helping him overcome his drinking habits. Their bond grew stronger with each passing day, and they built a life together filled with love and adventure. Traveling alongside Lillie as she hosted events, Galan discovered new places and rediscovered the joy of living.

Their intimacy deepened as they explored the world together, and their love blossomed in the vibrant cities they visited. Galan felt like he was falling in love all over again, captivated by Lillie's spirit and the happiness they found in each other's arms.

However, as they embraced this newfound happiness, Galan's past traumas resurfaced, haunting him like restless ghosts. The memories of Salt Pine Acres and SPU lingered, their shadows casting doubt on his ability to fully embrace the present. The vivid sightings of Aria, a bloody face amidst the crowds, were a persistent reminder of the darkness he had endured.

Yet, Lillie remained steadfast in her love and unwavering support. She stood by Galan's side through the tumultuous times, offering a guiding light in the darkness. With her care and understanding, the sightings of Aria began to diminish, slowly retreating to the depths of Galan's mind until months passed without her haunting presence.

As Galan woke up next to Lillie one morning, a sense of peace washed over him. He gazed at her lovingly, realizing that he had found everything he ever wanted in Lillie.

As Lillie's eyes slowly fluttered open, she found Galan's gaze fixed on her with a tender smile on his face. His next words took her by surprise, yet they felt like the most natural and heartfelt thing she had ever heard.

"Marry me," Galan whispered, his voice filled with love and vulnerability.

"Yes…," Lillie agreed.

"Really?" asked Galan.

"Yes, really," Lillie replied. With a tender smile lingering on her lips, she leaned in and kissed Galan softly, sealing their unspoken agreement with the warmth of her affection. The kiss conveyed all the love, joy, and excitement that words alone could never express.

"Anything you want, love, I'll make it happen," Galan declared.

"I don't care about a big wedding; I just want you. But there is something I would like," Lillie stated.

"Name it," Galan replied.

"I want us to start a family where it should have begun. Let's buy my old home. I know it wasn't easy for you there, but it's where we fell in love, and I think it's a representation of our love standing the test of time," Lillie remarked.

"I figured you might have said that," Galan answered with a smile.

"What?" Lillie exclaimed.

"I spoke with the owners; our wedding ceremony is going to be there. And when we are husband and wife, the first thing you sign as Lillie Rain will be the deed to that house," Galan informed her. In that tender moment, he kissed Lillie lovingly.

"Oh, Galan…," Lillie whispered.

"Come tomorrow; it will be our new beginning. I will meet you at the altar tomorrow. I have flights and hotels booked already; I don't want to spend another day without having you as my wife," Galan declared.

"Then get out of here; it's bad luck to see the bride before her wedding," Lillie smiled.

"I think I can stay a bit longer; I'll just close my eyes," Galan replied. Sharing a passionate kiss, Galan poured all of his emotions into that moment. He held her close, cherishing the taste of her lips and the way her touch made him feel alive. Their bodies pressed against each other, and the world seemed to fade into oblivion, leaving only the two of them in their own universe of love.

Chapter Thirty-five

As the vibrant sun heralded the dawn of a new day, Galan found himself adorned in a finely tailored suit, exuding an air of elegance and confidence. He stood before the glistening mirror, a perfect reflection of his determination, meticulously adjusting his tie to achieve that impeccable touch.

Just then, a soft chime signaled the arrival of a message, and Galan's phone lit up with the name "Lillie" gracing the screen. A sense of anticipation flickered in his eyes as he unlocked the device to read her words. "I can't wait to hear you say those two words."

Galan smiled and replied, "You mean, 'Good girl?'"

Lillie replied, "Maybe… But I need to hear two more before that. My driver is here; I'll see you soon, future husband."

Galan's smile grew even brighter as he read Lillie's message, filling him with a sense of contentment that he couldn't contain. With a heart full of joy, he responded to her, "I'm on my way to the house now; I'll see you soon, future wife."

Galan's car glided smoothly through the familiar streets of the neighborhood he once called home. With each passing block, memories of his childhood and youth resurfaced, weaving a tapestry of nostalgia that intertwined with the present moment. As he approached the house where he would celebrate a new chapter in his life, the flood of emotions intensified.

The memories were bittersweet, but there was something poetic about returning to the place where it all began. The echoes of laughter, the innocent adventures, and the tender moments with loved ones played like a cherished film in Galan's mind, reminding him of the journey that had brought him to this momentous day.

Stepping out of the car, Galan felt a sense of awe wash over him. The sight that greeted him was nothing short of enchanting. The elegantly decorated tent, adorned with thousands of lights, transformed the property into a mesmerizing wonderland reminiscent of a starry night sky. It was as if the universe itself had conspired to create a magical backdrop for their wedding day.

Galan's heart swelled with love and admiration as he took in the immaculate lawn and glamorous surroundings. Every detail seemed to be curated with care, symbolizing the beauty and significance of the occasion. The journey through the past had brought him to this very moment, where the wounds of yesterday were being healed by the embrace of a rekindled flame.

Walking with purpose, Galan made his way to the back of the property, where the altar stood as a symbol of commitment and devotion. As he stood there, a mixture of emotions welled up inside him. Tears of joy and gratitude glistened in his eyes, signifying the depth of his love for Lillie and the overwhelming happiness of sharing this day with her, rose petals falling gracefully from the ceiling.

"What a beautiful ceremony this could have been; I'm almost sad I won't get to see it," Paige greeted holding a black rose.

The warm glow that once adorned Galan's face now gave way to a flicker of surprise and discomfort. He turned toward the source he recognized all too well—the voice of someone from his past, someone whose memory he had hoped to leave behind. As Galan turned, his expression shifted from one of joy to an unexpected display of disgust. The sound of her voice seemed to strike a chord within him.

"Hello, my sweet boy," Paige giggled, clad in a black dress, holding a drink in her hand.

"Paige…," Galan groaned.

As Galan watched Paige take a big gulp of her drink and set down the glass, he couldn't help but notice the confidence in her stride as she made her way toward the altar. "Sir looks fine in that suit; too bad your fiancé won't get to see you in it," she remarked.

"Is that so?" asked Galan.

"Well, that all depends on her, don't you agree? She needs to show up for there to be a wedding," Paige chuckled.

"What the hell did you do…?" Galan clenched his fists.

"Easy there, 'Ripper,' we wouldn't want you shedding blood at your 'wedding,' now would we?" Paige teased.

"You wouldn't stoop so low; you wouldn't dare touch your sister, especially not today," Galan hissed.

"And why not?" Paige smiled.

"Paige, I swear to God…," Galan fumed.

"You'll what? Hurt me? You could never hurt me more than you have; there is nothing in this life you could do to me that hurts more than what was already done to me," Paige stated, her playful tone gone.

"I'll kill you—" Galan promised.

"I'm already dead! After what you did to me, I don't want to feel anything anymore," Paige responded.

"What did I do to you?!" asked Galan, "You ruined me! You were the reason I lost everything!"

"No… I wasn't, but I am about to be…," said Paige, her smile creeping back on her lips.

"What the fuck does that mean, Paige?" questioned Galan.

"You took everything from me, and now, I have taken everything from you," Paige answered.

"You better not have touched Lillie; I will kill right now.…" Galan claimed. "Where is she?"

"She's dead; she's buried right here," Paige replied.

"What…?" Galan exclaimed as he approached her.

"You're going to want to hear what I have to say before you kill me," Paige claimed.

"Tell me you're lying because I will not hesitate to break that fucking neck of yours!" Galan growled as he stepped closer to her.

"Aren't you curious about who died at Écarlate that day?" Paige smiled.

Galan stopped.

As Paige's giggles filled the air, Galan couldn't help but be curious about what she was up to. He watched intently as she reached into her pocket, her playful demeanor adding a layer of intrigue to the moment. With a mischievous smile, Paige pressed play on her phone, and to Galan's surprise, a projector beamed an image onto the far wall of the tent. As he looked closer, he couldn't believe what he saw—it was Nikki, lying on the floor in her hotel room.

"Nikki…." Galan gasped.

"Nice try, getting a bottle of champagne from the outside and switching it at the door, pretty sneaky. I took a page from your book. When you left, I switched the bottles in the room, and when you delivered that bottle to Nikki at her store, it was easy swapping them there. So the bottle intended for me, well, you killed Nikki with it, that poor girl. She was supposed to be married soon after that; how devastating it must have been to have the bride die before the wedding," Paige exclaimed.

"You didn't—" Galan hissed.

"That's not all I did. See, Galan, for what you did to me, I needed to make sure I broke every part of you so you felt but a fraction of the pain I felt," Paige began.

"What the hell did I do to you!?" asked Galan in tears.

"You robbed me of love!" answered Paige.

"WHAT!!!" Galan shouted. "How did I rob you of love?! How? I was a kid, and you forced me to do unspeakable things to you when I was just a child. You leveraged my love for Lillie to force me into doing those things to you. Is this about me killing your family and burning down your home?" Galan inquired.

"Sweetie, you didn't kill my family; I did," Paige finally confirmed for him.

"I knew it! I may not remember what happened back then, but I know I wouldn't have killed the people that took me in," Galan remarked.

"That's part of it, but that's not what you did to me," Paige stated.

"What then? Lock you away for years? You killed eight girls, all the girls that I loved!" Galan countered.

"They hurt you, and when you turned up on my door broken and hopeless, I felt protective of the person I had fallen for. You weren't a kid anymore. You were grown, and I could have finally had you, and the things you told me about them made me crazy that anyone would hurt you. I know you were a sweet kid, and you didn't deserve the things they did to you.

So yeah, I killed them, but what you did to me was unforgivable," Paige declared.

"Then tell me what I did that was so bad that you had to kill Lillie," said Galan.

"Why don't you call 'Lillie' and see how far away she is right now?" asked Paige.

As Galan's confusion mounted, he instinctively reached for his phone, his fingers rapidly dialing Lillie's number. His heart pounded with anticipation as he waited for her to pick up, unsure of what was unfolding before him.

"Lillie, what did you do?" Galan inquired.

"My name is not Lillie, we never grew up together, and I'm sorry, you seem like a really nice person, but I am not the person you think I am," Lillie replied before she hung up.

"What is going on…?" questioned Galan as he watched the call end.

"Back in Salt Pine Acres, when I was free, I wanted to take everything you loved away from you: Dana, Aria, Grounded. I wanted to take it all from you. But I was short-sighted then. With time and resources, I came up with something that would ensure you lost everything," Paige began.

Paige's thoughts drifted back to when she and Mr. Scarlet first met on his private jet. The day Galan went to see Dana on her yacht.

I went to Mr. Scarlet; I figured he and I had something in common. So I pitched him my plan: I would help him find the Blood Rain Ripper, and he would give me access to anything I needed. Now that I had spent four years putting this together on my own, all I needed was the resources to make it happen.

Then with access to an unlimited pool of money, I found the things I needed. I found "Lillie," her job was simple, distract you. So when you found the post I'd made to bait you to go back to Dana, you would run into her.

But that was only a setup for what was to come. See, while everyone was having the time of their lives on that boat, I had two accomplices carrying out my tasks.

While Dana was partying on her yacht, a guy bumped into her just before she met Galan.

"Dude, watch where the fuck you're going!" Dana said without looking up.

"Sorry," the guy replied.

Dana shook her head and mumbled, "Asshole." The water beaded off her top, so she was able to wipe it off easily.

"So, you just happen to walk around in a suit that is water resistant?" asked Galan standing beside her.

Quickly looking back with a phone in his hand was Avan, the moment he'd bumped into her, he'd switched her phone with a clone.

Meanwhile, Belle charmed a group of guys to go back to a hotel on the shore with her, leaving them dead on the floor. Later Paige stepped over their bodies as she walked out onto the balcony and gazed at Dana's yacht on the Caribbean Sea after returning from her meeting with Mr. Scarlet.

Now that I had Dana's phone, I controlled everything that came from her: all her texts and whether or not she made or received calls from you. It's amazing what you can do when you remove the affectionate parts of someone's text messages. Makes them question whether or not you really love them.

Galan backed away, "You didn't...."

Paige smiled, "Lillie served one purpose, make sure you question Dana's love for you. Her showing up and the phone I sent to Dana was nothing more than distractions to send your mind into paranoia. Then my little waterworks show had you fooled into thinking Lillie died, stirring all those thoughts in your head about what could have been. But you're stronger than that, so I had some insurance."

See, I had someone handpicked for you; I know exactly what you like. I know you better than anyone, and I gave this girl every single trick in the book to win you over.

Belle was sitting at the front desk as Galan approached her for Paige's room information.

Through Mr. Scarlet, I planted both of them in your path and sent them off to SPU, where we made an unlikely alliance. See, your actions affected not just me but others as well. And I'd found out a diabolical little film student was dating Eder Barlow on the side when you killed him.

In my attempt to blackmail Mr. Scarlet into doing what I wanted, I had all the dirty files on the events of Salt Pine saved to a private post on Eder's profile that only Mr. Scarlet could see. This person also had Eder's password and had logged in to shut down his account when they stumbled onto what I'd posted, and we had a little back and forth on his profile. I opened it one day and saw another private post saying, "What is this?" and when I reached out to her, things got interesting.

She had it out for Dana; my only criterion was that she couldn't touch you. So when Avan told me you guys went for the champagne and stopped at Grounded at SPU, I sent Sydney to introduce herself.

I'M BROKEN TOO

Her plan was diabolical, and even for me, it was dark, so I gave her whatever she needed to make it happen. While Avan, Belle, and Sydney riled Dana up about the killings on campus, they made her play into Sydney's game. First, it was destroying the trust between you two and creating a look-alike to leave a body outside of your Coffee House. A well-put-together wig, grey contacts, and a little face mask; would fool even you.

Simple enough, but that wasn't a coincidence; even if that failed, the other part of my plan was insurance. I kept my eyes on you, knowing you were searching for someone to replace Aria. I sent one to you and another and another over the course of four years. I just needed one to show up and time the first killing with your presence outside.

As Galan's breathing grew heavier, Paige's smile seemed to hold a hint of mischief, deepening the mystery of what was unfolding before him.

Now, my plan wasn't perfect; I almost lost you when Dana's overprotective guardian stepped in. Mama B was a pain in the ass; she was this close to robbing me of my victory. Then another unplanned event happened, Kaito; my word is that man is sexy. Dana thought so, too, and he stole her away in no time. At that point, I was grateful for Mama B; that miscalculation turned into a happy accident.

Now rather than me alone trying to tear you apart from Dana, there was Kaito pulling her away too, which made it so much easier. That left room for you to seek the arms of another, Belle. Everything I taught her was put to good use as she ticked every one of your boxes.

As Galan stood under the tent, surrounded by a swirling mix of emotions and intrigue, memories of Belle unexpectedly surged forward. It was as if a floodgate had been opened, releasing a wave of recollections from the depths of his mind. "You did all this to break up Dana and me?!"

Paige laughed, "Please, like I care about that petty relationship. No, my endgame was something else."

Paige's mind, too, ventured into the past, back to the beginning of the SPU attack.

Sydney's plan was put into play; she died first and was forced to be left inside the building. She ensured they found her upstairs so that when the doppelgänger crashed through the doors, she would be out of harm's way. So, while everyone was busy running from the building, Sydney got up and stepped into character as the Blood Rain Ripper.

Galan thought back. "I don't understand; if it was Sydney in disguise, how did she keep coming back to life? We killed her multiple times," Galan exclaimed.

As Galan looked back, memories of confronting the fake Ripper surged through his mind like an unrelenting storm. Each recollection weighed heavily on his conscience, a haunting echo of the battles he had fought. The vivid images of him decisively breaking the doppelgänger's neck, tearing out their heart that harbored deceit, and severing the head to ensure it was truly vanquished all played like a haunting reel in his memory. Even the final act of disposing of the lifeless body into a roaring fire was etched indelibly in his mind.

This is why I love Sydney; that was her plan from the jump. She let you kill the Ripper over and over. See, when you met her, she was with a group of people, a group of six. They each took a turn embodying the Ripper. All were willing to die in the name of love to gain her favor, doing it willingly for her as she sought justice.

Sydney, Avan, and Belle were in on it together. They used a prop knife to "Kill" Avan and Belle. A fake knife with a retractable blade that injected fake blood once fully retracted was pretty convincing when you have two of the best actors. Those three

designed the costumes and set up this entire gig.
Three skilled film students put on this entire show for
the world. Avan and Belle were left to tell the story of
the Ripper and destroy your image when their movie
deal took off. I mean, what studio would turn down A-
Class film students who survived the Blade of the
Ripper with authentic accounts of the incident and
video of the incident?

As Dana and Belle were finally discovered amidst the chaos, Kaito swiftly guided two determined police officers through the perilous labyrinth of the burning building. With calculated precision, they managed to navigate the treacherous surroundings, ensuring the safety of the two women. As the rest of the officers diligently scoured the compound, their search yielded a surprising discovery—two meticulously crafted Ripper costumes lay discarded on the floor.

Dana and Belle were placed gently inside an awaiting ambulance, accompanied by the officers who had bravely come to their rescue. The ambulance's siren pierced the air as it sped away, its urgency matching the gravity of the situation they had narrowly escaped.

Once the chaos subsided and the adrenaline began to fade, the officers removed their tactical helmets, revealing their true identities—Sydney and

Moons. Belle, who had been lying on the stretcher beside Dana, opened her eyes and let out heartfelt laughter. Rising from the stretcher unharmed, she playfully lifted her shirt, revealing the absence of any knife wounds. "How long till we make it to the hospital, driver?" Belle shouted. Peeking through the window was Avan, driving the ambulance.

They dropped her off and disappeared. Don't bother looking for them; you will never find them. I made sure you never would.

Galan stood in disbelief, "You monster…."

"No, sweetie, that was just for fun. That was just 'Justice for Eder.' My plan wasn't done yet," Paige remarked.

Back in Dubai, Galan found himself standing in a luxurious house, the opulence of the surroundings contrasting with the gravity of his thoughts. As he gazed pensively from the balcony, taking in the breathtaking view of the city's skyline, Lillie joined him. Meanwhile, tucked away in a quiet corner of the room, Paige observed the scene.

Let's talk about my "sister" after you flew off the handle and started drinking because you started seeing Aria and Lillie covered in blood everywhere you went!

Galan gasped, "How could you possibly know that!?"

"Because I put them there!" Paige declared with a sinister smile.

"What the hell are you talking about?!" Galan replied.

"You know what Aria and Lillie have in common? They are both dead, and I was the one who killed them. Aria is Salt Pine Acres four years ago, and Lillie, right here, fifteen years ago," Paige stated.

"But I saw her…." Galan claimed.

"No, see, I learned a lot from Sydney. So just like how she used doppelgängers of you to mess with you, I found an Aria and a Lillie look-alike," Paige laughed.

"No…," Galan backed away.

"That girl you were going to marry today… She really is an event planner who just happens to bare a striking resemblance to my sister. I fed her your childhood, your memories, how she felt about you, and how you felt about her. That fairy tale love story you lived for the past few months was all my creation. In fact, every girl you felt anything for in the last four years was all my doing except Dana. The only person who truly loved you chose someone else over you in the end," Paige explained.

"Why would you do that to me…?" Galan fell to his knees.

"Because you took away my last love," Paige growled.

"You did this because I didn't love you back?!" questioned Galan.

"You think you were my last love? No, sweetie, you could never be that important to anyone. No one would love you, not even as a child. The first woman a man loves is his mother, and that was a love you were denied. But a woman's last love is her son…," Paige expressed.

Galan looked up at her, "What are you talking about?"

"I killed my family back then, and I did it for love, but it wasn't for you. They found out I was pregnant with your child, and they were going to force me to have an abortion. I would never let that happen, so I killed them and left everything behind. And when you came to my doorstep all those years ago, I understood the pain you felt because I gave birth to a son. Every bone in my body was screaming at what I did to you, so I tried to repent by killing those girls who had hurt you. Because I felt guilty, and I couldn't bare the thought of my own son bearing the pain you did. But you took me away from my four-year-old son, our son. I had no one left, Galan… There was no one to take care of him, and I hoped to

God someone heard his little cries, but I knew it would never be so.

After the harrowing events at Salt Pine Acres, Paige had returned to her house, her mind still reeling from the intensity of the ordeal she had just experienced. As she stepped through the familiar threshold, a mix of emotions washed over her, the weight of the recent events weighing heavily on her heart.

The apartment didn't allow kids, so I soundproofed his room. The owners lived above us but couldn't hear him screaming. It wasn't a particularly good place to live; it was never close to anything, that's why the rent was so cheap. I had hoped they found him, but they never did. At least, not in time to save him. He died there alone; they found him months later when they came looking for me because they didn't get their rent money. You took everything from me, so I swore I would have taken everything from you. And for my son, I swore that you would die alone too. Nobody to love you.

Paige's trembling legs could barely support her as she staggered, tears flowing freely from her eyes, "No matter where you turn to, for the rest of your life, you will never know if that person was put there by me. The only person left who could have loved you is with someone else, someone they chose above you. The one was forced to love you is dying in your arms. And the only person who could have ever loved you unconditionally, your son, is dead because of you. The only thing you wanted was love, and now you will never taste it again, nor will you taste revenge, 'cause I stole that from you too." In a sudden and alarming turn of events, Paige stumbled and collapsed to the ground, her body wracked with convulsions. Her distress escalated as she began to vomit and froth at the mouth.

Reacting swiftly, Galan rushed to Paige's side. A peculiar aroma caught his attention as he got closer—the distinct and overwhelming smell of nutmeg.

"I saved some from that bottle because now, they are going to tie all of this to you. Every single file has been leaked to the media, all your pictures, your recordings, your texts, everything. You were the last person to see me and Nikki before we died of the same thing. You were on the boat when those people went missing and were found dead in the hotel on the beach; you were there when the Ripper attacked SPU. Good luck starting a new life now," Paige whispered as she smiled and died in his arms, the rose falling from the her hands onto the altar.

MORRIGAN PAIGE

AGE: 38
SIGN: SCORPIO

Chapter Thirty-Six

In the midst of the heart-wrenching scene, Galan knelt, cradling Paige's lifeless form in his trembling arms. Tears streamed down his cheeks, falling upon her delicate skin as his voice quivered with sorrow and grief. His voice was laced with pain, "All of this because I didn't love you…."

Is this love? This has done nothing but hurt me. Why did I sacrifice for this? Why did I put this above all else? This cannot be the thing I chased my entire life; this isn't how it ends…

I have had my heart broken and my happiness torn from my grasp every single time; what have I done to deserve this fate? These people casually toss your heart aside without knowing the pain it took to give it to them. Maybe that's the problem; they just don't know what that pain feels like.

Galan stood tall, his eyes lifeless as he gazed up at the house where his heartaches had begun. With a resolute expression, he gently scooped Paige into his arms, holding her close to his chest. He entered the house and dropped Paige on the floor. He turned the knobs on the stove's burners, opened the gas release valves, and lit a candle in the next room after dousing Paige's body in alcohol.

Galan stepped out of the house, reaching the end of the property just as the flames ignited behind him. The tent burned intensely, its roaring flames soaring high as the fire reflected in his cold grey eyes.

Galan reached up and pulled his tie off, a gesture of letting go of the constraints of love that had bound him for so long. He looked down at the ring on his finger, a reminder of how fragile love could be.

With a deep breath, Galan turned away from the engulfing flames. He moved towards his car, parked nearby, got in, and drove away without looking back. The sound of sirens in the distance approached as he drove off.

The leaked files on Eder Barlow's social media sent shockwaves across the globe, prompting emergency broadcasts and widespread panic. Days later, the world learned the chilling truth: the enigmatic serial killer responsible for the gruesome murders known as the "Blood Rain Ripper" had been unveiled as Galan Rain. The revelation left communities in disbelief, grappling with the realization that someone they once knew could commit such heinous acts.

As the news unfolded, the pieces of the puzzle began to fit together. The mysterious deaths of Nikki at the hotel and the murdered men from Dana's yacht were now connected back to Galan, painting a grim picture of a disturbed individual lurking in the shadows.

Authorities swiftly launched investigations into Grounded Coffee House, the place where Nikki and Paige's lives intersected with Galan's. Traces of the lethal substance used to kill them were discovered in the glasses they had left behind, turning the quaint coffee shop into a haunting crime scene.

But the most damning evidence came from Paige's files, which provided the crucial link to Galan's past. The files revealed that the eight previous girls who had tragically lost their lives were all connected to him. Paige's cunning trap had finally brought justice to the victims and unveiled the true face of evil that had eluded capture for so long. Plastered was an enhanced picture from the Salt Pine Acres Massacre, a blood-soaked Galan, wearing an unstained suit and a sinister smile, clearly revealing his face.

———◆———

Sitting in their homes in different cities, Dana, Mr. Scarlet, Mama B, and Kaito all saw the breaking news about Galan. Dana's phone vibrated next to her; the light from the screen and the sound of the vibration was overshadowed by the rain outside and the television's raised volume as the news unfolded.

———◆———

Mr. Scarlet's concern grew as he repeatedly failed to reach Dana on her phone. Worried about her safety and well-being, he knew he had to act swiftly. Without a moment's hesitation, he jumped into his car and sped towards the nearest private airport, where his personal jet was waiting.

As he raced down the rain-soaked streets, he dialed the local police department, his voice filled with urgency as he reported the situation and requested their assistance in locating Dana, "I want every single officer you have heading over to my daughter's place right now. I want you to escort her safely to Écarlate. Lock down that hotel; nobody in or out. Am I clear!?"

———◆———

Mama B wasted no time when it came to the safety of her loved ones. As soon as she learned that Dana wasn't answering her phone and saw the escalating situation, she immediately mobilized her trusted security detail. The rain continued to pour relentlessly as the convoy made its way through the city streets, sirens wailing, cutting through the cacophony of the storm and the busy urban sounds. Mama B's mind was filled with concern for Dana. During the tense ride, Mama B attempted to reach Dana through various channels, including phone calls and messages. However, the calls went unanswered, adding to the growing sense of urgency and worry. "Come on, sweetie, pick up!" she shouted while in the front seat of an SUV.

Genji's heart raced as he sat in his dorm room when the news suddenly broke, sending shockwaves through him and the entire campus. His phone began to ring insistently, and upon seeing the name "Kaito" on the caller ID, he knew he needed to answer immediately. "Aniki?" he answered.

"Pack up; I'm coming to get you," Kaito instructed him before he hung up.

Kaito arrived at the dorms; he hurriedly made his way to Genji's room. Each step felt imperative, fueled by a sense of protectiveness over his younger brother. Kaito raised his hand and gently knocked on the door.

As Genji hastily gathered his belongings, the knock on the door diverted his attention. He paused momentarily, setting aside his belongings, and quickly went to the door. He unguardedly swung it open.

Meanwhile, Dana had been preoccupied with the unfolding news on the television, the sound of which had overwhelmed the earlier vibrations and notifications on her phone.

Finally, as she turned off the news to gather her thoughts, she noticed the faint glow of her phone's screen, indicating an incoming call. Quickly realizing that it was Kaito, she picked up the phone, her voice tinged with curiosity and concern.

"Hello?" Dana answered, waiting for Kaito's response on the other end of the line.

"Genji's gone!" Kaito remarked.

"What…?" Dana shook.

"I came for him at the dorms, and he wasn't there. I found a card from Grounded Coffee House; its address is in Salt Pine Acres," Kaito exclaimed.

"Galan…." Dana muttered.

"There is a note at the back: no police are allowed inside Salt Pine Acres; come alone to get the one you love. Your entrance fee has been paid," Kaito read.

"I'm coming with you," Dana declared.

"No time!" Kaito responded.

Dana's heart pounded in her chest as she rushed back to her room and opened the drawer on her nightstand. Her hands trembled slightly as she retrieved the gun Mama B had given her from the drawer and tucked it discreetly into her pant waist.

Feeling a little safer now, Dana hurriedly made her way to the elevators, still aware of the sense of urgency. As the elevator doors opened, she was startled to find Galan stepping out, dressed sharply in a suit. Her fear momentarily froze her in place, and she hesitated to proceed.

"Please don't be afraid of me; I didn't kill those people. Paige did; you have to believe me!" Galan professed with teary eyes.

"What are you doing here, Galan...?" Dana shook.

"You're the one who knows me better than anyone. You know I'm innocent; I was there with you when they found Nikki in that room. I was also with you when they found the bodies of those men in the hotel. You know it wasn't me; please don't look at me like I am a monster," Galan pleaded.

"Please don't hurt me... Please, Galan," Dana whimpered.

"I never wanted to hurt you; I love you. Please love, don't let them do this to me," Galan begged.

As Galan stepped closer to Dana, she felt her heart racing, her fear increasing with every step he took. She slowly backed away, her mind racing with thoughts of what might happen and why he was there.

"They found ingredients we use at Grounded. How did Paige get that?" asked Dana.

"She didn't, that was me, but it wasn't meant for her. It was supposed to kill Paige, not Nikki. Please, Paige is behind all of this; she stopped us from communicating. She cloned your phone and replaced it when we were on the yacht; she set up that whole Ripper thing at SPU, this was all her, and she's making me take the fall for it. Please believe me," Galan expressed, his voice quivering with emotion as tears streamed down his cheeks.

"Paige did this?" Dana's retreat came to a halt.

"She did! Love, I swear she did. All I ever wanted was to love you and support you. I would never have done those things to jeopardize our love. It's because of her I couldn't reach out to you to tell you I didn't die when Mama B's house burnt down," Galan explained.

"That moment changed everything… The day I lost you, my life felt like it was over," Dana told him.

"It broke me when the first thing I heard after seeing you was you calling out another guy's name. I just wanted you to be happy even if it excluded me from your life. But that pain is too much; I don't want to break what you have now, but I just want you to know I love you. And I am willing to surrender myself if it proves to you that I would give all this up for you," Galan declared.

"If you love me that much, why did you move on so quickly with Belle? Why did you try to turn me into Paige? Why did you try to replace my sister?" asked Dana.

"I'm not perfect; I know I am Broken, but I am trying to be better for you. The day you said you would marry me, I let it all go," Galan replied.

"Except Belle, I heard what you said to her, the obedience she gave to you; it's what you want, not me," Dana remarked.

"That was all Paige; she sent Belle, Lillie, the Aria replacements; it was all her just so she could show me that I will never find love. But the only one she had no power over was you; what we had was real, not what you and Kaito have. She played a part in that too; that is as real as Belle and I," Galan continued.

"What are you saying?" Dana walked closer to him.

"I'm asking you to not give up on me. Love comes with its challenges, and if it was easy, it would not be worth it in the end. Please, love, if letting myself be taken into custody and taking the fall for all the pain that happened because of me will appease you, then I will do it. I will do it in the name of love and prove myself to you that my heart is pure, and I only ask that you don't abandon me. Please don't look at me like I am a monster. I am the same person you fell for in Salt Pine Acres, and I want the same thing then as I do now. I just want you to be with someone who deserves your heart," Galan replied.

"Galan…," Dana walked closer and touched his chest. Galan closed his eyes, and his breathing changed. "I don't know if I can be the person you need me to be because I said this before, I do care about you. And, like you, I want you to be with someone you deserve. But I am not that person now…" Dana claimed.

"Please, Dana…," Galan pleaded.

"Shh…," Dana whispered as she touched his lips and looked into his eyes. "I may not be what you need now, but I can try. Baby steps," she murmured.

"Baby steps?" asked Galan.

"Yes, Sir," Dana smiled.

Galan felt an exhilarating rush course through his body as her words cascaded from her lips. A radiant smile adorned Galan's face. Dana gently reached up, and they shared a tender, passionate kiss. Four shots were fired as Dana held the gun to his gut. Galan stumbled backward, anguish etching lines across his face before he collapsed to the floor in pain. Dana's body began to tremble uncontrollably, and she instinctively covered her mouth, letting out a piercing scream. The fear of death loomed when Galan entered her apartment, forcing her to betray him for her own safety; she tried to compose herself as Galan lay motionless on the floor.

Kaito's car pulled up to the entrance of Salt Pine Acres. With a sense of urgency, he hurried towards Grounded Coffee House. As he approached the building, its disheveled state from the previous incident was evident. Ignoring the wreckage, he parked the car and stepped inside the structure. "Genji!!!" he called out.

Mama B's unit arrived first, rushing up the stairs and the elevator. As they made it onto Dana's floor, they saw her body on the ground, blood pooling at their feet.

"Kaito Shinoda—" Galan called out as he entered the main floor of what was once Grounded Coffee House.

"Where is my brother!?" questioned Kaito.

"You know, Dana was all I had, and you took her from me. Going after the person someone loves the most in this world is something that would break you into pieces. Love makes you weak; someone as weak as you will never survive in this cruel world. You wanted to win Dana's heart so bad?"

As Galan lay on the floor, Dana ran to the elevator and pressed the button to go down. Just as the door dinged open, the tip of a knife came protruding through her forehead.

"I learn from my past heartbreaks. And I learned from your sister that people will use your love for them to make you drop your guard, only to stab you in the back. But you ensured that I would never let someone use a gun on me again."

Galan's mind instantly flashed back to when they were meticulously preparing for Dana's plan to end the dreaded Ripper killings. With determination in his eyes, he had entrusted his suit to a skilled tailor. This masterful artisan had ingeniously sewn a layer of bulletproof fabric, far thinner and more efficient than Kevlar, between the garment's layers.

Galan ripped the knife from her head, "Kaito wants your heart so badly?" He stabbed her in her throat, pulled the knife down, and cut her chest open. He reached in and pulled her dying heart from her chest.

I'M BROKEN TOO

"You can have it," Galan replied, tossing Dana's heart to Kaito. "Is that Dana's? Or Genji's? I can't tell; maybe you should go see which of their bodies is scattered in pieces across her apartment," he taunted.

Kaito's anguish erupted into a primal scream, and in a swift motion, he unsheathed his kodachi, cunningly concealed in his pant leg. Galan, undaunted, drew a knife and effortlessly flipped it through his fingers as Kaito approached with reckless abandon. The clash of their blades filled the air, and Kaito's screams of pain echoed, a haunting reminder of the loss of his brother.

Yet, instead of fear or remorse, a wicked smile adorned Galan's face, turning into a joyous, unsettling laugh as he relished Kaito's suffering. With careless swings, Kaito left himself vulnerable, and Galan seized the opportunity. A powerful kick sent Kaito hurtling backward, slamming into his own car.

Without relenting, Galan swiftly followed up with another forceful kick aimed at Kaito's head, the impact crashing through the car door's window.

Galan pulled him from the car and threw him on the street. "This is what love does to you. Look at Grounded; it's broken and empty, just like everyone who falls into the allure of love," he exclaimed.

In a swift motion, Kaito sprang back to his feet and hurled his kodachi at Galan, seeking to catch his opponent off guard. However, with almost casual ease, Galan intercepted the flying blade, snatching it between his fingers before tossing it aside, showing little effort. "You took my love from me, so I did the same to you. And now you'll live out the rest of your lonely, miserable life with no one to love you," Galan declared as he smiled.

"I'm gonna kill you!" Kaito growled.

"I'm already dead—" Galan smiled. "You want to kill the Ripper? This isn't going to be like SPU; I'm not some copycat running about in a sealed building. It's gonna be the Ripper unleashed on a whole world. Every cop in the world will be coming for me, each of them with the potential to rob you of revenge. Do you think you can get to me first? Come get it!" Galan taunted as he dropped his knife.

As Kaito charged forward, determination etched across his face, Galan swiftly pivoted on his heel and fled in the opposite direction, heading up the rugged mountain trail. A sly smile played on Galan's lips, knowing his familiarity with the terrain would give him the upper hand.

As Kaito pursued, the distance between them gradually widened, and before long, Galan disappeared from sight, leaving Kaito frustrated and unable to keep up. Galan's wicked laugh echoed through the mountains as he vanished from Kaito's line of sight.

"FUCK!!!!" Kaito screamed.

Later that day, Kaito's car screeched to a halt outside Dana's opulent penthouse. Determined to find answers, he pressed on, navigating past the tight security measures, and swiftly made his way up to her floor. However, what awaited him was beyond his worst nightmares—a chilling tableau of horror left behind by Galan.

There on the floor lay Dana, lifeless and heartbreakingly, her heart torn out and discarded. The once luxurious living room was now a gruesome scene, awash with blood and strewn with severed body parts. The sheer brutality of it all overwhelmed Kaito, and he couldn't hold back the tears that streamed down his face.

Amidst the carnage, his eyes were drawn to a haunting sight—the trail of blood leading to the living room. And there, in a nightmarish display, lay Genji's head on the floor.

Galan perched on the mountain's peak, overlooking the majestic waterfall of Salt Pine Acres as it cascaded down the rocks. The sun began its descent, painting the horizon with hues of red, creating a breathtaking view of the city below.

Amidst this serene setting, Galan held a phone to his face.

"As entertaining as this has been, I do not want the name of the Ripper to be tainted by these cheap copies. The Ripper's clothes will never be stained by the blood of those who are incapable of love. These stories and these killings end now. There can only be one...."

Mama B and Mr. Scarlet cautiously entered Dana's apartment, their expressions a mix of shock and dread as they were met with the horrifying scene that lay before them. The once elegant and inviting space was now a grim tableau of carnage and devastation, bearing witness to the unimaginable horror Galan had wrought.

I have read many names, 'The Blood Rain Ripper,' 'The Butcher Barista,' and 'The Salt Pines Slayer.' It's all very entertaining, but it's not me.

Amidst the cries and the overwhelming grief that filled the room, Kaito approached Mama B with a heavy heart.

One even called me the 'Scarlet Rain Ripper;' honestly, I quite like the sound of that. Came from the original, a play on the 'Blood Rain Ripper;' it's cute. But it goes against what I stand for. Love is a fool's game, it's a form of suicide that you survive physically, but the rest of you die.

I'M BROKEN TOO

Kaito and Mama B returned to her new mansion.

I liked 'Scarlet Rain Ripper' because it took both our names; it's quite romantic in a sense. But in my journey to find love, she rejected my last name, so now, I have to reject hers. From this day, I haunt those of you who tarnish the name of love. I will come for you and show you what it's like to have your heart ripped from your chest. Eder Barlow was a waste of life, and I took pleasure in killing him. He bowed to my will before he died, so instead of chanting "Justice for Eder," you will call my name.

Sydney's game was quite entertaining. Paige's game truly broke me. But I have been distracted by the temptation of love...no more. Now that I am free from that burden, I will teach this world a fear so profound. I'm coming for all of you, and the last words you speak will be the true name of Ripper. Learn these words now and I will show you the mercy of a quick death...

Kaito and Mama B stood face to face, "You were the one who burnt down my home. And now you are at my doorstep asking for help, Yakuza. You're not in Japan anymore; I run these streets," Mama B declared, holding a gun to Kaito's head. In a room filled with henchmen, nobody saw his movements as he pressed the blade of his kodachi to her neck.

"He killed Dana, and he murdered my brother. I want you to help me kill him. And this time, we make sure he stays dead," Kaito remarked.

Chapter Thirty-Seven

'Rain the Ripper!'

END